Six blue-shelled creatures emerged from the darkness, clawed fingers spread wide, mouth parts clacking softly, compound eyes unreadable.

"Jason, you take the ones in back. Lazara, Sal, we'll deal with the ones in front. Don't–"

The creatures emitted a high-pitched screech, the cries amplified by the cavern walls. Aisha raised her machine gun, set the selector switch to full auto, and started firing. The gunfire was loud as thunder in the cavern, and it countered the creatures' screams to a degree. Their rounds tore chunks out of the aliens' carapaces and broke off a number of spines, but they didn't penetrate further, and they certainly didn't slow the creatures down. If anything, the things sped up, clawed feet flying across the rubble of the cavern ceiling's collapse, the uneven terrain no impediment to their advance.

ALSO AVAILABLE

PLANET HAVOC

TIM WAGGONER

ACONYTE

First published by Aconyte Books in 2022

ISBN 978 1 83908 124 8

Ebook ISBN 978 1 83908 125 5

Cover art by Rafael Teruel

Distributed in North America by Simon & Schuster Inc, New York, USA

Printed in the United States of America

9 8 7 6 5 4 3 2 1

ACONYTE BOOKS

An imprint of Asmodee Entertainment Ltd

Mercury House, Shipstones Business Centre

North Gate, Nottingham NG7 7FN, UK

aconytebooks.com // twitter.com/aconytebooks

This one's for Robert Bloch, who, in his Star Trek episodes "Wolf in the Fold", "Catspaw", and "What Are Little Girls Made Of?" created perfect fusions of science fiction and horror.

ONE

"Long-range sensors have picked up a ship."

These were *not* the words Luis Gonzalez had wanted to hear, but they hadn't been unexpected.

"How far?" Luis asked.

"A little over half a million kilometers."

"That's the outer range of the sensors, isn't it?" Luis' hands tightened on the arms of the command chair. He might have been commander of the *Kestrel* for this mission, but it was his first time flying this ship – hell, it was the first time for any of them – and he wasn't as familiar with its systems as he'd like.

"That's right."

"Can you tell what it is?"

Junior McManus was a big British man of African descent, and he had to hunch over to work the computer screen in front of him. His large hands looked ill-suited for anything other than breaking things, but they flew deftly over the controls. "Readings aren't clear, but my guess is that it's a light frigate. Out here, that probably means a Coalition ship."

A large wall screen that looked like a forward-facing

window dominated the room, but which was actually a computer recreation of the view outside the ship. It *felt* like a window, though, and that's how Luis tended to think of it. He grimaced as he stared at a hazy blip, nestled among a field of stars displayed on screen, representing the other ship. The *Kestrel* was a caravel, a small craft, less heavily armed than a frigate, but faster and more maneuverable. Plus, it was fresh out of the shipyard. The Galactic Coalition encompassed a great deal of territory – hence the word *galactic* – and its forces were spread thin. The best crafts were reserved for admirals, Coalition Council members, and Guild leaders. Soldiers had to make do with whatever craft they were assigned, and those ships were rarely top of the line. As old as the frigate was likely to be, its sensor range would be less than theirs, which meant that at this distance, the *Kestrel* was for all purposes invisible to them.

"Is this going to be an issue, commander?"

Jena Woodruff – blonde, with the merest trace of a Swedish accent – stood next to Luis' command station, her hands clasped behind her back, face utterly devoid of expression. She wore a gray jacket and pants, with Leviathan's logo of a serpent coiled into a circle on her shoulder. She was the Guild's representative on this mission, which meant that despite Luis' title, she was ultimately the one in charge.

A woman of African descent with a shaved head stood on Luis' left, and she answered for him. "Whatever happens, we can handle it. We're the best – that's why you hired us, isn't it?"

Sirena Hancock was second in command on this mission, and Luis had worked with her for a number of years. He was used to her shooting off at the mouth, but Jena wasn't.

Jena glared at the other woman. "I wasn't asking *you*."

Sirena glared right back. Luis stepped in before the two could start arguing. He disliked Jena as much as Sirena did, but the woman represented the Guild that was paying them, and that meant she had to be kept happy – to a certain degree.

"You've given us a good ship. It's fast and has sensor deflectors." *Prototype deflectors*, he thought, but didn't say this aloud. "With any luck, we'll be able to make planetfall without being detected." *Luck being the operative word.*

"I have full confidence in the ship," Jena said. "As for its crew…" She gave Sirena a last look before facing forward.

Luis glanced at Sirena. She was clenching her teeth so tightly he thought they might shatter under the pressure, but she didn't immediately lunge for Jena and wrap her hands around the woman's throat, and he considered that a win. Leviathan was paying Luis' team extremely well for their services, and he was certain that helped Sirena restrain herself. Killing an employer's representative wasn't the best way to ensure you received your pay.

Tensions were running high on the *Kestrel*, and it was a wonder they weren't all at each other's throats. The PK-L system was off limits to anyone but Coalition military, and the penalty for unauthorized travel here was a lifetime prison sentence – no trial, no appeal – assuming your ship wasn't simply destroyed by a missile or mass-driver projectile. No one Luis had ever spoken with knew why this system was forbidden, although he'd heard plenty of rumors. He was certain the Coalition Council knew, and he figured Leviathan did too, or at least they suspected, otherwise they'd have never risked sending in a team.

They were headed for planet PK-L10, nicknamed Penumbra, and their mission was to land, get something, and take it to a Leviathan research outpost several light years distant. What this something was, Luis didn't know. Jena did, but she refused to tell the team until they landed on Penumbra. When he'd asked her why she wouldn't give them all the details of their mission ahead of time, she'd said, "In case we have to abort for some reason. Leviathan doesn't want you to be able to sell the information about why Penumbra is important. And some of you would sell it. You're mercenaries, aren't you?"

He had to admit she had a point.

But whatever they were supposed to get on Penumbra, the almost obscene amount of money Leviathan was paying them made the risk worth it. A score this size, if Luis and his team pulled off the job, meant that they could retire if they wished – or, in his case, pay off a longstanding debt. It had hung on him like a crushing weight for so long, he couldn't imagine being free of it, but he was looking forward to finding out what it would be like.

The *Kestrel*'s bridge was small. Space was at a premium on any starship, but more so on a caravel, and the bridge was crowded to the point of being claustrophobia-inducing. There were nine people present, four more than Luis would've liked, but who had asked him? He was just the goddamned commander. The command station – a computer console in front of an unnecessarily uncomfortable chair – had been placed in the center of the bridge, and a quartet of workstations sat in front of the viewscreen. One was for communications and sensors, which was where Junior currently sat. Another was for weapons, and if the need arose, Sirena would take that one. The third was for life support, including control of the ship's artificial gravity, where Aussie Dwain Lange sat, and the fourth was for navigation, tended to by Bajan Lashell Brower. Three others stood off to the side – two men and one woman. Aside from whispering to one another occasionally, they remained quiet and kept to themselves. The man in the middle was a cyborg, and while he looked human, he remained eerily still when he wasn't performing a specific action.

Cyborgs had that in common with androids, Luis thought. It was an easy way to tell them apart from humans, but it creeped him out a little... not that he'd ever admit it to anyone. These three composed the documentary crew that Leviathan had insisted on sending to make a record of the "expedition", as they liked to call it.

The rationale for the trio's inclusion wasn't completely clear to Luis. Leviathan was a new Guild, one that had grown swiftly and amassed a great deal of power in a short time. Maybe they wanted this mission recorded for propaganda purposes, the footage to be used both inside and outside the Guild – assuming the mission was a success, that is. Luis' suspicion was the Guild wanted the record in case their "expedition" went tits up, so they could better prepare the next batch of poor bastards they sent. Not exactly the greatest show of confidence.

The cyborg, Oren, served as the crew's camera. When he was recording, his left eye lit green, and it was *always* green. When Jena had first told him the trio would be coming along, she assured him that they'd remain in the background, quiet and unobtrusive, and everyone would soon forget about them. So far, that hadn't been the case for Luis. He always felt their eyes upon him, especially the cyborg's. He told himself not to worry about it. Maybe the holo-footage would be a good advertisement for him and his team and lead to more Leviathan Guild work. Assuming they survived, of course.

Six more personnel were currently in the ship's galley, which doubled as a lounge, and tripled as a meeting room. It was just as cramped as the bridge, if not more so, but at least you could get a cup of khavi there. Luis wondered what the chances were of someone getting him a cup if he asked. Damn close to nil, he figured.

Their course through the system had been plotted before their departure, using the latest intel on Coalition patrol routes to ensure they wouldn't encounter any ships on the way to their destination. Based on the sensor readings showing their proximity to a Coalition ship, it looked like that intel wasn't worth the money that Leviathan had paid for it.

Luis felt a vibration beneath his feet then, accompanied by a queasiness in his gut. He recognized the sensation as a fluctuation in the ship's artificial gravity. Dwain quickly worked the controls at his station, but several seconds passed before gravity was restored to normal. The crew members exchanged uneasy glances, and he knew what they were all thinking. Getting to fly a brand-new, state-of-the-art ship was great, but they would've been a lot more comfortable if the craft had been given a proper shakedown cruise first before they'd been dispatched on their mission. Luis wasn't superstitious as a rule, but he couldn't help thinking of the gravity fluctuation as a bad omen. If any of the ship's systems were less than one hundred percent, if he was forced to put any strain on them – say by having to avoid a Coalition Frigate – they might crap out when he and his people needed them most.

He turned to Sirena. She was the most intuitive person he knew, and he trusted her sense of how a job was going to go down, a sense that became sharper the closer they came to their objective. He didn't know if she was psychic, but her instincts were good, and they'd saved the team's ass on more than one occasion.

"What's it looking like to you?" he asked.

Her eyes narrowed in concentration. After a few moments, she said, "I think I should go to my station."

Without another word, she walked over to sit at the weapons console.

"What did she mean by that?" Jena asked.

"It means you and your camera crew had better find something to hold onto. Junior, can you switch the front screen to a view of the frigate's location?"

Junior sighed. "Don't tell me. Sirena got one of her feelings again."

"Bite me," Sirena said, but Junior did as Luis asked.

There was nothing to be seen other than a starfield, one that looked similar to the thousand others Luis had seen in the course of his career, both as a soldier and as a mercenary.

"Computer enhancement," Luis said.

Junior's fingers worked the station's controls. The view zoomed in on a Coalition Frigate. Luis knew he was studying a simulation based on sensor data rather than the actual thing, but he got a cold feeling in his gut nevertheless. He debated the wisdom of increasing the *Kestrel*'s speed. A sudden burst of acceleration could alert the frigate to their presence, but it could also put them farther outside their sensor range, so…

"They've trained their sensors in our direction," Junior reported.

"On purpose or as part of a routine sweep?" Luis asked.

"Unknown."

"There's no cause for alarm," Jena said. "The *Kestrel*'s sensor deflectors will conceal our presence."

She sounded less confident than Luis would have liked. The deflectors were, after all, only prototypes.

"We'll find out soon enough," he said.

But he already knew what would happen. Sirena's instincts had told him.

TWO

Aisha Barakat sat in the command chair on the bridge of the *Stalwart*, bored out of her goddamned mind.

She was a tall, lean woman of Middle Eastern descent in her late twenties, young for a starship captain. The *Stalwart* was her first command, and she'd initially been honored and excited to obtain the post, especially after the mess on Janus 3 that she'd been involved in. She'd expected to be court martialed for that, at the very least, and as far as she'd been concerned, she'd deserved it. Instead, Coalition Command had made her captain of the *Stalwart* for "bravery in the face of overwhelming odds". That had been eighteen months ago. Now she was ready to eject herself out of an airlock.

It hadn't taken her long to realize that patrolling the PK-L system was a shit detail, and she'd been placed here as a punishment. Nothing ever happened in this system, absolutely *nothing*, and she and her crew of three were bored out of their minds. Although she wasn't sure about Jason. Who knew what androids felt?

Originally, Aisha and her crew were supposed to be rotated out of this post, but after the twelfth month, Coalition

Command had informed them they were required to stay on "for the duration". When she asked why, Command had said only that the Coalition Council was debating what to do about the PK-L situation, whatever that meant. She knew it had something to do with one of the system's planets, PK-L7, which she'd heard some soldiers refer to as Hellworld in hushed tones, though none of them had been able to tell her the name's origin. The Coalition had erected a network of satellites around the planet, both for defense and surveillance, although defending or surveilling what, Aisha didn't know. She wasn't even allowed to access the satellites' data. That was transmitted directly to Coalition Command. She'd tried to hack into the satellites' network once, but she'd been unsuccessful, and she'd received a scolding from Command along with a warning to never attempt that again unless she wanted to spend the rest of her life in military prison. She figured if Command could've found someone stupid enough to replace her, they'd have done so. Still, she didn't try to hack the satellite network again.

The *Stalwart* was the only vessel patrolling the system – something else which struck Aisha as more than a little odd. If PK-L7 was so damn important, why would the Coalition have only a single ship in the area? After her first two months on the job, she'd contacted her superiors and asked. The response she'd received was short and blunt.

Mind your own damn business, captain.

Her best guess was that Command believed the more ships stationed in the system, the greater the chance they'd draw unwanted attention to PK-L7. Too bad. If there had been more crews working this system, at least they could get together, drink synthetic alcohol, play cards, and watch holos. If nothing else, at least there'd be somebody different to talk to, now and then. The only outside contact her crew had was when they rendezvoused with a supply vessel every three months, and those crews didn't linger. They always had another supply run scheduled that they had to get to.

In reality, most of what she and her crew did on the *Stalwart* was maintenance. Not only was it an older ship, but most of its systems were automated, which was why only a few personnel were needed aboard. But automated systems could be finicky, and they tended to shit the bed at the least convenient times, so Aisha and her people spent most of their time putting out metaphorical – and sometimes literal – fires on the vessel. The *Stalwart* did have maintenance bots, but the machines could only do so much.

The bridge was typical for a military craft, all function without a hint of décor. Plain, unpainted plasteel made up the walls, and the workstations were simple computer consoles with thinly padded chairs bolted to the floor. The main viewscreen was a large rectangular section of wall, and while it worked well enough, there was a weird blue area on the bottom right corner, which bugged the shit out of Aisha. They'd tried fixing it, but they'd only made the blue area larger. Although it was against regulations, music played from speakers in all the consoles. Soldiers were supposed to always remain on high alert, and music was considered a distraction, but it kept them all from going crazy. Jason had chosen the current selection, crystal-synth music created by the Lomai, a race whose hearing was a hundred times sharper than a human's. Jason's android ears allowed him to appreciate the music. "Almost to the extent that a Lomai can," he'd once said. To Aisha, it sounded like broken glass being shaken in a metal cannister, but after eighteen months, she'd started to develop an appreciation of it.

Along with Jason, who, like most androids, didn't have a last name, Aisha's crew consisted of Italian Lazara Fiore and South African Sal Hendrick. All three of them rotated between the stations to minimize the monotony, and sometimes Aisha would take a turn as well. By this point, they could all perform just about any task required aboard the *Stalwart* – except cooking. Jason was their chef, and a damn fine one, which was more than a little ironic since he didn't eat.

"Aisha, I'm getting some weird sensor readings," Lazara said from her station at comm/sensors.

"Weird how?" Aisha asked. Lazara was better at interpreting sensor data than anyone else on the ship, Jason included. So if she thought readings were strange, something was up.

Lazara turned back to her console screen. "Sensors have detected an object that *might* be a ship, but according to the readings, it's there one moment and gone the next, like it's phasing in and out of existence."

"Impossible," Sal said.

"Not necessarily." Jason sat at the navigation station, and he turned around in his chair to face Aisha. "There are any number of naturally occurring space phenomena that could account for such readings. Quantum flux, hyperspatial distortion, etheric refraction…"

"All of which are extremely rare," Aisha said.

"Yes," Jason admitted. "But rare means unlikely, not impossible. And it could be something no one's encountered before. We should move closer and collect more data."

Androids had a drive to accumulate knowledge, and Aisha wasn't surprised by Jason's suggestion.

"Too risky," Sal said. "If we get too close and whatever it is damages our ship, it'll take help days to reach us. We could die before anyone gets here." He glanced at Lazara. "Assuming your readings aren't a glitch of some kind."

Lazara's face reddened with anger. "I ran a diagnostic on the system before saying anything. Everything's in working order."

"Run another diagnostic," Aisha said. "Just to be sure."

Lazara didn't look happy about it, but she did as Aisha asked.

"Jason, let's get closer, but not *too* much closer. Not yet."

Jason nodded. A moment later, the *Stalwart*'s ion engines came to life, and Aisha felt a slight vibration move through her chair. Spend enough time on a starship, and you know its strengths and quirks as well as those of your own body. The stars on the viewscreen began moving as the ship accelerated. Sometimes when this happened, Aisha imagined that she flew through space under her own power, the way she'd pretended when she was a child riding on her parents' cargo ship. She was a magical being who could traverse the galaxy through sheer willpower alone. A silly daydream, but it amused her.

"Second diagnostic came back as clean as the first," Lazara said. "Whatever's going on, it's not a problem with the sensors."

"Is the object still there?" Aisha asked.

"Yes. It's still flickering in and out of existence. It kind of reminds me of…" Lazara trailed off.

"Yes?"

"Do you guys read the tech updates Command sends?"

"Of course," Sal said. He sounded offended by the implication that he hadn't done so.

"Naturally," Jason said.

Aisha shrugged. She'd never been big into tech. All she cared about was knowing how to operate a piece of equipment. As long as it functioned properly, she was good. Weapons were her only exception. She could use, maintain, and repair any gun Command issued to its soldiers, and she always read the weapons updates Command sent out. But tech updates? Not so much.

Lazara continued. "For decades, pirates, smugglers, and traffickers have sought ways to evade Coalition ships' sensors, but the tech has never been reliable. They're getting close to perfecting it, though, and the current generation of sensor deflectors work decently enough, if only at a distance. They tend to cut in and out, resulting in readings like what we're getting now."

Aisha leaned forward in her command chair. Finally, something was happening.

"Cut the music," she told Jason, and he did so. "Lazara, keep a constant scan going. If the object *is* a ship with sensor deflectors, the closer we get, the less effective they'll be. We should be able to get a decent read on them then."

"On it." Lazara turned her attention back to her console.

"Jason, switch to weapons. Sal, take over navigation."

The men complied, and Aisha felt the crew's excitement

building. She was right there with them. A year and a half without a hint of action, and now they might be preparing to confront a ship equipped with stealth tech and a crew breaking the Coalition's ban on non-authorized travel within this system.

"Stay frosty," she said. "The last thing we want to do is make any mistakes because we're too gung-ho."

Her crew exchanged glances. They knew what had happened on Janus 3, and they knew of Aisha's role in it. They'd never treated her poorly because of it, but they understood why she'd given the warning. Aisha's face reddened with shame, but she continued, nonetheless. "Lazara, can you get the ship to render some kind of sensor image on the main screen?"

"I'll do my best."

A moment later, a hazy object appeared in the center. Gray with fuzzy edges, it fluctuated in size, sometimes growing small enough to almost vanish.

"Doesn't look much like a ship to me," Sal said. He sounded disappointed.

"It's too soon to tell for certain," Jason said. "But I know of no natural phenomenon that produces an image like that, even when rendered from incomplete sensor data. I'd say the odds of it being a starship of some sort just went up dramatically."

Aisha's pulse sped up. She had never commanded a ship in battle before, but she'd served as bridge crew on other vessels as a junior officer. She hoped she'd learned enough from her captains to get her and her own crew safely through the next few minutes, whatever they might hold.

"The object's sped up," Lazara reported. "Not a lot, but it's definitely going faster."

"They wish to stay outside our sensor range without making it seem as if they're fleeing," Jason said.

"My thoughts exactly," Aisha said. "Sal, burn the ion engines at max for a few seconds. I want to halve the distance between us."

"Are you sure that's a good idea?" Sal said.

Aisha couldn't believe what she was hearing. "Are you questioning my order?"

"No. It's just…" Sal looked at her for a moment. She thought he would say something, but instead, he shook his head. "Nothing," he said, and turned back to his station.

There it was again. Janus 3. The *Stalwart* was her first command, and she'd been given it, not as a reward, but to keep her isolated in a post where she couldn't make any more trouble for the military. Even though the Coalition had additional ships in adjacent systems to ensure no one breached the PK system, the planet PK-L7 was surrounded by a powerful satellite defense that would repel any ships attempting to land on its surface. The patrolling *Stalwart* and its crew were little more than an extra precaution, and they all knew it. Aisha might technically be in command, but since being stationed on this ship, this was the first time that anything had actually happened. And now that they were finally seeing some action, Sal revealed that he didn't trust her judgment, no doubt because of Janus 3. Despite herself, she couldn't help but wonder if he was right to do so.

Don't think like that. You have a job to do, so quit throwing a pity party for yourself and get to it.

"Jason, can the engines handle the strain?" she asked.

The android paused before answering, which for him was a long time. "Theoretically," he said.

"Good enough. Do it, Sal."

"Yes, captain."

The vibrations running through Aisha's chair and the floor tripled in intensity. At the edge of her hearing, she thought she could detect the whine of the engines as they were pushed to their limit. The artificial grav generators also functioned as inertial dampeners, so other than experiencing a slight pressure that pushed her back into her seat, she felt nothing from the *Stalwart*'s sudden acceleration. Sal cut the burn after three seconds. The ion engines weren't designed to perform at that capacity for long, and even a short burn was risky.

"How are the engines?"

Sal glanced at a readout on his console screen. "They're going to need a tune-up after this is all over, but they're good for now."

Aisha let out a soft sigh of relief. She hoped no one else heard it. "Lazara?"

"Re-rendering image."

The fuzzy gray blob sharpened into focus. It was indeed a ship, a small one.

"It's a caravel," Sal said. "I've never seen one quite like it, though."

"That's because there isn't one like it," Jason said. "At least, not one recorded in the Coalition network."

As an android, Jason was capable of interfacing with any computer, and he always connected to the ship's main systems while working at one of the bridge stations. He'd no doubt searched the ship's entire memory for a match to the unknown craft in the time it had taken Sal to speak.

"Could it be of nonhuman origin?" Lazara asked. "From a race unknown to the Coalition?"

"Highly doubtful," Jason said. "It's not an exact match for any Coalition-made caravel, but it shares too many features with basic Coalition design."

"Hail them," Aisha ordered Lazara. Then to Sal she said, "Push the ion engines as hard as you can without tearing them to pieces. Caravels are fast little bastards, and if they get too much of a lead on us, we won't be able to catch them."

"No response to our hail," Lazara said.

"Keep trying. Let me know if sensors pick up any indication that they're charging weapons."

Caravels were built for speed, not combat, so the craft wouldn't be heavily armed. They'd be carrying a small complement of low-yield missiles and *maybe* a mini mass driver, but that would be it.

"Sal, have the nav computer project the ship's route," Aisha said. "I bet a week's pay they're headed to Hellworld. What else is there in this system for them to be interested in?"

A moment later, Sal said, "You lose, captain. The computer says they're headed for PK-L10."

Aisha frowned. "Really? Jason, anything about that location in the ship's memory?"

"There's data from the initial survey of the system, but that's nearly a century old. The planet's mostly barren, with little water and few signs of life. Some primitive plants and insects survive there, but nothing sophisticated. Its atmosphere is primarily composed of carbon dioxide, and its gravity is around thirty-eight percent Earth standard. It's prone to sandstorms, some of them kilometers wide and quite intense." He paused and then continued. "There are several current mentions of the planet in military databases which refer to it as Penumbra, but I can find no additional details."

"Could be that anything else is classified," Lazara said.

Aisha thought the same thing. "What's the other ship doing?"

"Still moving away from us at the same speed," Lazara said. "If they were bothered by us leaping forward with an ion burst, they haven't shown it."

"Weapons?"

"Still offline as far as I can tell."

"Jason, do you think there's any significance to the planet's name?" Aisha asked.

"In astronomy, the penumbra refers to a shadow cast by a planet or moon during a partial eclipse. It also refers to the lighter area around the dark core of a sunspot."

Aisha thought for a moment. "You put the two definitions together, and you get a shadow of something."

"But a lighter shadow," Lazara said.

Sal frowned. "What would it be a shadow of?"

"PK-L7 perhaps," Jason said. 'It's the only known object of note in the system."

"So, Penumbra is the not-quite-so-dark shadow of Hellworld," Aisha said. "That doesn't sound particularly inviting, does it? Does it have any planetary defenses?"

"I can find no reference to any," Jason said.

"Then if there *is* anything there, it's evidently not worth protecting," Lazara said.

"Which begs the question why our new friends in the caravel would risk so much to go there," Aisha said. "I think we should pay them a visit and ask in person. Sal, squeeze out as much speed from the ion engines as you safely can. Let's catch up."

Sal looked worried, and Aisha thought he might protest her order, but he said, "Yes, captain," and did as commanded.

"Jason, bring our weapons online. I want them to know we aren't playing games."

"That might cause them to flee. Their ship *is* faster than ours."

"We've cut the distance between us in half already, and our weapons have a greater range than theirs. I'm willing to take the chance."

"As you wish." Jason began tapping commands on his console.

Aisha watched the image of the caravel on the viewscreen become larger.

Who are you? she thought. And what the hell are you doing here?

THREE

"They've spotted us," Junior said.

Lousy goddamned Leviathan tech! Luis thought. Aloud, he said, "Maintain current course and speed. Let's see what they do."

Jena motioned to the camera crew, and the cyborg began moving his head back and forth, recording everything happening on the bridge. Luis ignored the man. He couldn't afford to be distracted. He swiped a finger over a control on the arm of his command chair to open a shipwide channel. He wanted to make sure the crew in the galley knew what was happening, and that they were prepared in case they were needed.

"We've been located by a Coalition Frigate. They're still half a million klicks from our position, and if necessary, we can outrun—"

"Quarter of a million," Junior interrupted.

The Coalition ship had cut the distance between them in half.

"Did they do an in-system jump?" Sirena asked.

"No way," Lashell said. "Not even Coalition soldiers are that crazy."

Jump drive worked best when traveling outside star systems. Navigating a jump safely was always tricky, and even when everything worked right, you didn't always re-emerge in normal space exactly where you hoped. It was even more difficult to perform a jump *within* a system. The star's gravity, the planets' orbits, and any asteroids or comets all affected the outcome of a jump. You were as likely to reappear within a planet as you were anywhere else in the system. During his time in the service, he'd never known anyone to risk an inner-system jump, even if it meant a ship and its crew would be destroyed in battle. There was only one thing they could've done.

"They did a burn."

"What's that?" Jena asked.

"They fired their ion engines full blast," Luis said. "Doing so allowed them to reach near light speed for several seconds."

Jena didn't look worried, exactly. She looked she was trying *not* to look worried. "Why didn't they keep coming until they reached us?"

Sirena answered for him. "If they hadn't throttled back, they'd have burned out one or more of their engines. It's a smart move – when it works. But they can't do it again. If they try, they'll lose the engines for sure."

"And probably the ship with them," Junior said.

Despite himself, Luis was impressed. It was a bold gambit, and one he wouldn't have expected from someone babysitting a system so far from the Coalition's center.

Whoever the captain was, they'd been in the shit before. Only a veteran of space combat would risk a tactic like that, and Luis didn't want to get into a shooting match with them. Not only was a light frigate more heavily armed than their caravel, but it was also far more maneuverable than a heavy frigate or a battle cruiser. It might not be as fast as a caravel, but it could give the *Kestrel* a real run for its money.

"They're hailing us, Luis," Junior said.

"Ignore them."

Junior smiled. "That's what I thought you'd say."

The shipwide channel remained open, so he knew the crew in the galley and bridge could hear him. "Quick vote," he said. "Anyone want to bail now before things heat up?"

"No!" Jena said before anyone else could answer. "Leviathan is paying you quite well to do this job, and I expect you to complete it."

Luis wanted to tell Jena to stay out of it. He was this ship's commander, after all. But while Leviathan was a relatively new Guild, it had become a major player in a short time, and that meant he needed to make Jena part of the mission's decision-making process – whether he liked it or not.

"Conditions have changed," Luis said. "The info your Guild gave us was bad. You paid us half up front to take on the job, and that money is ours to keep regardless of how the mission turns out. This ship wasn't designed for combat, and I'm not going to risk my crew's lives without their consent. We're not soldiers. We don't fight for a cause. We fight for profit, and it's hard to spend your earnings if you're dead." He turned away from Jena and faced the bridge crew. "Well? What do you think?"

But Jena interrupted once more. "I'm authorized to double your fee if you continue."

Luis looked at her once again. "Seriously?"

"Yes, but don't go getting any ideas. I can't increase your fee after this. I'm not authorized to go any higher."

Having the woman's word was not the same as having a binding contract, but the cyborg *was* recording this, and that might be good enough.

"All right. Everyone still in for double our fee?"

Junior grinned. "Let's get to work."

Sirena nodded, Lashell smirked, and Dwain gave a thumbs-up.

"How about everyone in the galley?" Luis asked.

A woman's voice came over the bridge's speakers. It was Sidney Cheun, the scientist Jena had hired to accompany them on this mission.

"We're good down here, commander."

"OK, then let's do it. Lashell, set a course for the largest of Penumbra's three moons."

"You got it, boss."

"Sirena, get a jump beacon ready to launch."

"I get what you're going for," Sirena said. "Good idea."

"What are you planning to do?" Jena asked.

Luis smiled. "Disappear."

"They're increasing speed," Lazara said.

So, they're running, Aisha thought. Big surprise.

"Are they heading for Penumbra?" she asked.

Lazara worked the sensor controls for a moment. "Not quite. It looks like they're making for one of its moons."

"Let me guess. The larger one."

"Yes."

"Why would they do that?" Sal asked.

Jason answered. "The largest moon is dense enough to block our sensors. Once they're behind it, we won't know what they're doing."

"My bet is they're planning an ambush," Lazara said. "They'll attack as soon as we come around to their side of the moon."

"Perhaps," Jason said, "but even though the *Stalwart* has seen better days, a caravel is no match for our weaponry. My estimate is that once they're hidden from our sensors, they'll make a run for it at top speed, hoping to put enough distance between us that we won't be able to catch up. They know we won't risk another engine burn, or an inner-system jump, for that matter."

"Maybe," Aisha said. But the ploy was too obvious. Anyone with the balls to sneak into an off-limits system like PK-L had to be smart enough to know the tactic wouldn't fool the crew of a Coalition vessel. Her gut told her the caravel's commander had something else in mind, but what? Still, she needed to be cautious and proceed as if they intended an ambush.

"Sal, plot a course to swing us wide around the moon. If our sensors can't detect them, then theirs can't detect us. I want to make sure we're out of their weapons range when we first set eyes on each other."

"Yes, captain."

"Lazara, send all the data we've gathered on the ship so far to Command. They should know what's happening. Route it through one of the satellites around PK-L7. It'll get there faster."

Aisha and her crew might not have been allowed access to whatever data the satellites collected from Hellworld, but they were permitted to use their powerful communication array to transmit and receive signals, thereby speeding up the flow of information to and from Command by a factor of five. However the confrontation with the caravel turned out, she wanted Command to know about the situation in the system sooner rather than later.

"Eke out whatever extra you can get out of the engines without blowing them up."

"Yes, captain."

Sal sounded doubtful, but Aisha knew he'd do his best. He always did.

"Jason, get a couple missiles prepped and ready to fire."

The android nodded and went to work.

Aisha wanted to be ready to blast the caravel into atoms in case its crew did attack. Command's orders were clear: any ships trespassing into the PK-L system were to be rendered inoperable and their crews taken into custody for questioning. If this wasn't possible, then the ship and its personnel should be destroyed. No exceptions. Aisha didn't consider herself a cold-blooded person, but she had her orders, and she'd carry them out to the letter if she had to. She hoped it wouldn't come to that, though. She'd rather not kill unless she had no other choice.

The pursuit continued, and the caravel slowly began to draw away from the *Stalwart*. Soon Penumbra came into view – a dull yellow planet with brown sandstorms raging across its surface. It had three moons, each larger than the last, all variations of the same color as Penumbra, although none appeared to be plagued by sandstorms like the planet they circled. The moons were unnamed, unless you counted their Coalition designations: PK-L10.1, PK-L10.2, and PK-L10.3. Aisha wondered when the Coalition would finally start employing some stellar cartographers with imagination. True to Lazara's prediction, the caravel headed for the largest of the three moons, PKL10.3, and from the look of things, the vessel would be well concealed before the *Stalwart* caught up. All Aisha and her crew could do now was keep going and wonder what awaited them on the moon's other side.

As Aisha had ordered, once they reached the moon, Sal began to curve around it in a wide arc.

Aisha kept her gaze fixed on the viewscreen. "Jason, if you think you need to take a shot, do it. Don't wait for my order."

The android nodded. His reflexes were machine-swift, and he could respond more rapidly than Aisha could think. If she made him wait for her command, the caravel might get off the first shot, and while the *Stalwart* was well armored, it was always better not to take damage.

They came around the moon and saw...

Nothing. The caravel wasn't there.

Lazara worked the sensors without waiting to be told. "I'm picking up an ion trail that leads directly into a spatial distortion. It looks like they've jumped."

"Whoever they were, they were desperate to get away," Sal said. "They couldn't have had much time to plot a course, though, which means they likely did a blind jump."

Jumping was a relatively new technology, and blind jumps were risky as hell. The massive gravitational fields of stars affected Underspace, creating tidal forces that drew jumping ships toward them. If you didn't take these extradimensional currents into account when plotting your course, you were liable to jump yourself right into the heart of a star – not that you'd ever know it.

"Lazara, can you tell where the ship jumped to?" Aisha asked.

"No. The rift is already closing, and our sensors can't penetrate it."

That was what Aisha expected, but she'd had to check.

"So not only have we lost the caravel, odds are it's been destroyed and is no longer a problem." Aisha thought for a moment. "Seems awfully convenient, doesn't it?"

"Perhaps," Jason said, "but not out of the realm of possibility. Although I suggest scanning for other ion trails in the vicinity."

Lazara did so. "Bingo! There's another faint trail leading around to the other side of the moon."

Aisha smiled. "Their commander is one crafty son of a bitch, no doubt. They probably used a jump beacon to try and fool us into thinking they made a jump themselves. Then they got the hell out of here, going as slowly as they could so they wouldn't leave a significant ion trail, and then went around the moon to keep it between us and them so our sensors wouldn't detect their ship."

"It's an impressive tactic," Jason said.

"Sal, follow the second ion trail, fast as we can manage."

As Sal worked the navigation controls, he said, "I don't get it. Why would such a small craft have a jump beacon? The things are so expensive that only the most elite Coalition ships have them."

The problem with jumping – aside from its imprecise nature – was that the energies unleashed played hell with the hardware. Most jump drives were only good for three jumps, maybe four if you got lucky, before they were ruined and needed to be replaced. Ion engines were fine for traveling within a star system, but jump drives were beyond the financial reach of most Coalition citizens, save of course for the obscenely wealthy. Faster-than-light technology had allowed the human race to leave Earth, expand out into the galaxy, and ally itself with other intelligent species, and jump-tech – while not always reliable and with its own large share of problems – had only accelerated that expansion. But despite the Coalition putting the word *Galactic* before its name, it encompassed only a comparatively small fraction of the Milky Way. It had taken centuries for the Coalition to grow to its current size, and until a more powerful and efficient means of jumping was developed, the Coalition might never grow much beyond its present size.

Jump beacons were probes equipped to make a single jump. They were sent ahead to a desired location to give a craft something to lock onto and hopefully guide it there more successfully. As Sal said, jump beacons were extremely pricey, and the navigational assistance they provided wasn't so great as to make the cost worth it, even for people who could afford to buy them.

Despite the situation, Aisha found herself becoming more

excited. This was the kind of challenge she'd been longing for since taking command of this vessel.

"The fact they used a jump beacon to try to throw us off their trail tells us something very important about them," Aisha said.

"Indeed," Jason said. "Their expedition into this system is well funded."

"To say the least," Lazara added. "But that means they're liable to have the best of everything – a kick-ass ship, state-of-the-art weapons… "

"Sensor deflectors," Sal reminded her.

"Right," Aisha said. "Whatever they've come here for, it must be damn valuable. It also means that they're far more dangerous than we thought."

"We got them on screen again," Lazara reported.

Aisha looked up to see the caravel in the middle of the viewscreen. Now that the *Stalwart* was closer, the rendered image of the other craft became sharper and more detailed, and she could see how new it was. She wouldn't have been surprised to learn it was the vessel's first flight.

"They've seen us," Lazara said. "They've changed course and are now heading for the planet."

"Follow them," Aisha told Sal. "Hang back a bit, but don't lose them."

If the other crew could afford to expend a jump beacon to throw them off the scent, who knew what other fancy toys they might have? Maybe more prototypes like the sensor deflectors. Aisha couldn't risk treating the craft as a simple caravel anymore. It was clear it was anything but.

"Yes, captain."

Aisha leaned forward in her command chair and fixed her gaze on the caravel.

What do you have for me next? she thought.

FOUR

"They didn't buy it," Junior said.

Dwain grimaced at the image of the frigate displayed on the *Kestrel*'s main viewscreen. "No shit," he said.

Serina glanced back over her shoulder at Luis. "It was a good idea."

He nodded his thanks to her, but good idea or not, it hadn't worked, and that was all that mattered. After deploying the jump beacon, Luis had ordered Lashell to move the *Kestrel* to the other side of the moon. Once they were hidden from the frigate's sensors, he'd had her slow their ship down. The hope was if they remained still enough, the Coalition captain would take the bait and either attempt to follow the beacon into Underspace – with no guarantee they'd exit at the same exact coordinates – or they'd think the *Kestrel* had successfully eluded them, and they'd depart to continue their patrol of the system. But the frigate's captain was no fool. They'd seen through his ploy and followed the *Kestrel* to the other side of the moon.

He expected Jena to complain about wasting the jump

beacon – he wagered that a single one of the things cost more than the entire ship – but she didn't say a word. Instead, she asked, "What do we do now?"

"We can still outrun them."

"Absolutely not. We must make planetfall, at least for a few hours. We've come all this way to get… what we need, and I don't intend to leave without it."

"What *Leviathan* needs, you mean."

"Their desires are my desires," Jena said, without a hint of irony or self-awareness.

Regardless of what Jena wanted, Luis didn't intend to deliver his crew into the less-than-merciful hands of the Galactic Coalition. They'd entered a forbidden system, and he knew from his time in the military what the punishment for such a transgression was – a lifetime sentence at a prison colony if they were lucky, summary execution if they weren't. He was about to order Lashell to set a course out of the system and to hell with what Leviathan wanted, when an idea came to him.

"Junior, can you bring up an image of Penumbra with our landing zone highlighted?"

The man swiftly did so. Luis peered at a dingy yellow planet streaked with brown sandstorms, and in the lower left-hand quadrant, a small red dot indicating where they were supposed to land. Jena hadn't seen fit to tell them what was so important about the location, but that didn't matter right now. What mattered was finding the largest sandstorm in the vicinity of their landing zone, and there was a big one off to the southeast, roughly a hundred klicks distant.

Luis tapped a control on his command console and a black dot appeared in the middle of the sandstorm. "Take us down there, Lashell, into the storm."

Jena's mouth dropped open in surprise. Two of the documentary crew paled. Not the cyborg, though. He just kept recording.

It was a moment before Jena could speak. "Are you *insane*?"

"Maybe. I did agree to take this job, didn't I?"

Lashell didn't question his order. She set the coordinates and angled the *Kestrel* toward the maelstrom. The vessel descended, and on the viewscreen the planet seemed to lunge toward them.

"Those of you in the galley, we're headed planetside, and we're going in fast. Strap yourselves in." He turned to Jena. "You and your film crew should get to the galley as fast as you can. The ride's going to be a rough one."

"We're not going anywhere." Fear shone in Jena's eyes, but her voice remained steady.

One of the documentarians, a young Asian man, said, "Uh, Jena, maybe we should–"

"*Maybe* you should shut up and do what you're told," she snapped.

The man looked to his co-worker, a young woman of Indian descent. She appeared just as scared as he was. Luis hoped Leviathan was paying them well enough.

The cyborg spoke then. Outwardly, he looked like a white man with curly black hair, but Luis knew that inside he was far more machine than man. "I can magnetize my feet to the floor. If each of you takes one of my hands, I'll keep you steady." His voice was human-sounding and calm, but underneath it rumbled the slight electronic undertone that all cyborgs possessed.

His two co-workers hesitated at first – some humans were reluctant to make physical contact with cyborgs – but in the end, they did as their colleague suggested. Luis turned his attention from the documentary crew to Jena.

"Grab hold of my seat. Use both hands. You'll need them."

The woman looked terrified, but she followed Luis' advice.

"We're going to try to get rid of the Coalition ship in the storm," he said. "We're lighter and more maneuverable, and we'll be able to ride the wind currents better than they can. With any luck, they'll crash. Since you say we only need a few hours to complete our work, we'll be gone before they can get to us."

Sirena turned around and grinned at him. "Assuming any of them survive."

Luis had served on similar frigates during his time with the Coalition as a soldier, and he knew their capabilities. He had no wish to kill anyone if it wasn't necessary, and he was confident that when their ship went down, the crew might get banged up, but they'd live. He knew Sirena and Lashell didn't give a damn whether the soldiers pursuing them died, just as long as they could finish the job and collect the rest of their pay. Dwain and Junior weren't quite as cold-bloodedly practical, but Luis knew they wouldn't lose any sleep over the deaths of a few soldiers. His crew knew he had a soft side, and they were happy to tolerate it – as long as it didn't interfere with their profits.

He had no idea what the camera crew thought about the possibility of the Coalition soldiers dying. But then he had no idea why there needed to be three of them when the cyborg was the one who seemed to be doing all the work. As for Jena, she was a Guild woman to the core. She'd probably slit her own throat if she thought it would benefit Leviathan.

"What if they don't follow us into the storm?" Jena asked.

Luis smiled grimly.

"They will."

"They're heading planetside," Lazara said.

"Stay on their tail, Sal."

Aisha watched the caravel grow smaller on their screen as it moved away from them. The ship traveled fast, but not as fast as it should. Sure, the ship needed to reduce speed as they approached Penumbra's surface, just as the *Stalwart* would, but the other craft didn't need to slow down to this degree, not yet.

They're trying to lure us in.

"Are their weapons hot?" Aisha asked, perplexed.

Lazara consulted her console. "They don't appear to be. So, they aren't preparing an attack, at least not an immediate one."

Since power needed to be rerouted from other systems, it took time to charge a ship's weapons. No commander would risk initiating combat until their fighting tech was fully online.

The image of the caravel was growing larger now as the *Stalwart* narrowed the distance between them.

"Jason, what do you think they're up to?"

"They tried a relatively sophisticated tactic to fool us earlier. Since that deception failed, they'll most likely resort to violence. As they haven't activated their weapons yet, my guess is that they're going to use the planet itself against us."

"The sandstorms," Aisha said in sudden realization.

"Yes," Jason said. "And it appears they're heading for a particularly large one right now."

Damn, that commander's good!

"Lazara, how bad is that storm?"

Lazara worked the controls on her console for a moment.

"Bad. The winds are hurricane-force. Even if we could fly in that shit, at that speed debris becomes flying missiles. It would be like withstanding a perpetual assault from a mini mass driver. I'm not sure our thrusters will be able to handle it."

Ion engines were too powerful to use within an atmosphere, so starcraft relied on thruster engines. They were strong enough to deal with all but the most extreme planetary conditions – and this sandstorm definitely qualified as the latter.

"If we can't take it, surely the caravel can't," Sal said. "It's a smaller vessel, less heavily armored."

"True," Jason said, "but they're far more maneuverable than we are, and they might try to skirt the edges of the sandstorm, hope that we follow, and end up sustaining enough damage that we're unable to continue our pursuit. Then – assuming they didn't sustain too much damage of their own – they could escape."

"Risky," Aisha said. "But it could work. All right. Let's back off and keep following them from a distance."

"If I may," Jason began, "I think that at this point we should consider firing on them. Even if they abandon their ploy to draw us into a sandstorm, given their superior speed, odds are high that they'll evade capture. A surgical missile strike would allow us to bring them down without destroying their vessel."

"Their ship might not be destroyed," Aisha said, "but that doesn't mean the crew would survive the crash."

"True," Jason admitted, "but our duty in this situation is clear. Unauthorized access to this system is prohibited, and once someone has come here, they cannot be permitted to leave."

Aisha hated it when Jason reminded her of the rules. She'd learned long ago that a soldier sometimes needed to be flexible in the field if they wanted to get the job done and survive to go home.

Still, he was right.

"Jason, get a missile ready and target their port flight stabilizer."

Damaging the stabilizer would force the caravel to land, and with luck, there would be no casualties.

"Yes, Aisha."

As Jason worked to carry out her command, Aisha looked to the viewscreen once more and saw they'd gotten close to the caravel, a half kilometer, maybe less. The commander had slowed their vessel way the hell down, but why?

"Lazara?"

"Weapons are still offline. I don't know what... wait! Their cargo bay doors are opening."

Most starcraft, even small inner-system shuttles, had space for carrying cargo. A caravel's cargo bay wasn't large – the *Stalwart*'s was much bigger – but you could still fit a good amount of material in one if you were careful about how you packed it. But why would the caravel's crew be opening their cargo bay doors midflight? Were they carrying some kind of contraband that they wanted to dump before they were captured? Or did they simply intend to lighten their load to coax a little more speed out of their engines? An instant later, she had her answer.

"Uh, I'm not sure," Lazara said. "But it looks like they've deployed a grabber."

Aisha wasn't certain she'd heard correctly. "You mean a grabber, as in the mining tool? That doesn't make any sense."

A grabber was used by mining ships to pick up material and bring it into the hold for transport elsewhere. Caravels didn't have grabbers – except this one did.

She saw it on the viewscreen then: a claw-like extension on the end of a thick metal cable. It fell out of the cargo bay and trailed behind the caravel for a moment before shooting toward the *Stalwart*. For a moment, all Aisha could do was stare in horror as the grabber came at them, propelled by micro anti-grav thrusters. She understood instantly what the caravel's commander intended. She couldn't believe it. The lunatic intended to take hold of the *Stalwart* with the grabber and pull it into a sandstorm where the frigate would sustain serious damage. The caravel would then release them and be on its way, leaving them to put down on the surface for repairs or, more likely, crash and die. She couldn't let the grabber attach to them.

"Fire the missile!" she shouted, fear filling her for the fate of her crew. They had to destroy the grabber before it doomed them all.

Jason's index finger stabbed the control, but it was too

late. Even though Aisha felt a shudder through the deck indicating the missile's release, there came a loud *whump* of impact. Her head snapped forward then back as the inertial dampeners struggled to compensate. The same thing happened to Sal and Lazara, but not to Jason. His android body had adjusted to the impact force on its own. Aisha knew what had happened – the caravel's grabber had caught hold of them and sealed itself to their hull with the claw's maglocks. She'd just made a terrible mistake, and she had only seconds to fix it.

"Jason, activate–"

She intended to order Jason to activate the missile's self-destruct function before it struck the caravel, but her words came too late. On the screen, the craft's port stabilizer disappeared in a bright flash of light, and the craft wobbled and drifted to the left – and since the *Stalwart* was now attached to the caravel, where the other craft went, the frigate followed.

"They got our aft stabilizer!" Junior shouted.

Damn it! Luis thought.

The missile's explosion had rocked the bridge, and Jena had lost her grip on the back of the command chair. She lay sprawled on the deck, but the other crew members had remained in their seats. The documentary crew had managed to stay on their feet, thanks to their sturdy cyborg companion. From a quick glance, Luis thought Jena wasn't seriously injured, but he couldn't spare any other help for her. As commander, he was responsible for the lives of everyone aboard this vessel, and he had to act fast if they were to have any chance of survival.

"Veer away from the sandstorm!" Luis ordered.

"I'll do what I can!" Lashell said.

"Sirena, disengage the grabber!"

The *Kestrel* couldn't afford to remain connected to the frigate, not with only one functioning stabilizer, and especially not if they got sucked into the sandstorm. Both crafts would end up crashing, and Luis doubted anyone would survive.

Sirena's hands flew across her console. "Something's wrong. The grabber's magnetic field won't deactivate."

"How's that possible?" Dwain said. "The hold's control systems aren't connected to the stabilizers!"

Everything on a starship was connected, one way or another. "Somebody in the galley get their ass down to the cargo bay and see if you can detach the grabber from there. I don't care who does it or how you do it, just as long as it gets done," Luis commanded, trying to keep his panic at bay.

A woman's voice replied in a New Zealand accent. Felicita Duggan, one of the miners that Leviathan had brought on this mission. "We'll take care of it, captain."

Luis hoped the woman wasn't being overconfident. If they couldn't make the grabber let go of that frigate…

"We're going to hit the storm!" Lashell called out. "In three, two…"

The *Stalwart* slammed into what felt like a miles-thick ferrocrete wall. The *whoop-whoop-whoop* of a warning alarm filled the air, along with the shriek of inertial dampeners fighting to compensate for the winds battering the ship's hull. The command chair's automatic restraining belt deployed seconds before impact, and now wrapped securely around Aisha's waist. Lazara, Jason, and Sal's belts had also activated, keeping the crew members in their seats. Good thing, too, for the storm winds tossed the *Stalwart* as if it was a child's toy, and the bridge became a whirling, spinning blur. Aisha couldn't think, couldn't even remember her name, where she was, or what she was doing here. Everything was blaring sound and chaotic movement, and the sensations drove out all other thoughts. But her training soon reasserted itself, and she gasped a breath to start barking orders.

"Sal, use the atmospheric compensators and get us under control! Lazara, tell the caravel to release us or we're both going down! Jason, try to figure out a way to free us from that goddamned grabber in case the caravel can't or won't!"

Her crew's hands danced across their console controls. All Aisha could do now was hope. If she'd been religious, she would've prayed.

Several moments passed, and Aisha began to fear the worst, but then she felt a sudden lurch. Jason checked the readout on his console and said, "We're free!"

"No," Lazara countered, checking the sensor data on her own console. "The grabber still has us. The other crew released the cable from their end."

With the grabber still attached to their hull, the *Stalwart* wasn't at its most aerodynamic, and while Sal was a good pilot, he wasn't the best they had.

"Sal, switch control of navigation to Jason's console."

Sal glared over his shoulder at her, and she thought he might protest, but then he did as she'd ordered. He knew that Jason could think and move faster than any unenhanced human. If they were going to have a chance to survive the next few minutes, it would be with an android at the helm. Jason's hands became a blur as he fought to free the *Stalwart* from the sandstorm's savage winds, and as the seconds ticked by, Aisha could feel the ship begin to come back under control.

But any optimism she felt was wiped away when Jason said, "It's too late. Brace yourselves, we're going down."

FIVE

Felicita Duggan stood at a console in the *Kestrel*'s cargo bay when the ship landed – if you could call the bouncing, juddering, shimmying disaster a landing. She hadn't been able to make the grabber let go of the frigate, but she'd managed the next best thing: releasing the cable from the *Kestrel*'s end, although she'd done so too late to prevent a crash.

At first, she held onto the console through the initial impact, but she soon lost her grip and was flung to the floor. The bay contained mining equipment – diggers, drillers, blasters, and haulers – and as she slid across its surface, she collided with the front tire of one of the diggers, knocking the breath out of her. She grabbed hold of the tire to keep herself from being tossed about anymore and prayed the maglocks holding the equipment in place wouldn't fail. If they did, there was a good chance she would be crushed by one of the heavy machines. But the locks held, and the ship finally came to a stop.

She braced herself against the digger and rose to her feet. She was a miner, not a space combat veteran, and while she'd experienced a rough landing or two in her time, they'd been nothing like this. She trembled, heart pounding, and she felt cold all over. But at the same time, she felt mentally distant from these sensations. Was she in shock? If so, she didn't have time to worry about it now. Got to keep digging until you have a hole big enough to work with, she thought. It was a miner saying that Felicita's mother had passed on before she'd gone into the family trade, a reminder to take things one step at a time.

The *Kestrel* listed at a ten-degree angle, and Felicita kept her hands on the digger to prevent herself from falling. When she reached the end of the machine, she saw the cargo bay's interior door was on the downward slope from her, and she removed her hands from the digger and half-walked, half-skidded in its direction. She smacked into the wall next to the door, reached for the controls, and opened it. She then gripped hold of the door's edge and hauled herself into the outer corridor. She closed the door behind her – you never left a door on a spaceship open unless you had a damn good reason – and began making her way toward the galley as fast as she could manage.

The caravel was a small craft, so nothing onboard was far from anything else, and she reached the galley in moments. When she'd left, there'd been five personnel sitting in the galley. This was a great ship – newly built and equipped with some fancy toys – but the bridge was too small for everyone onboard to be present at the same time. And since the crew quarters on the *Kestrel* were individual sleeping tubes, that left the galley as the only alternative gathering place.

Felicita wondered why they'd chosen such a small ship

to haul so much gear, but she figured a bigger ship would have made them an easy target for the Coalition to spot and capture. She opened the galley door and stepped inside, fearing she'd find her fellow crew members draped across chairs, lying on tables, or sprawled on the floor, injured or dead due to the ship's harrowing descent and crash landing. Instead, she found five people who were very much alive, if banged up, all talking at once.

"–can't *believe* this–"

"–piece of shit–"

"–the hell kind of landing was–"

"–can someone call the bridge to see what happened–"

"–too serious. I think you'll be OK."

Malik Kruse, a fellow miner, sat atop one of the galley's three round tables, holding out his left arm. Juliana Acosta, another miner, stood on his right, looking concerned. Sidney Cheung, the expedition's sole scientist, examined Malik's arm. Assunta Landis and Bernadine Barbosa – both mercenaries, as well as spouses – studied the broken remains of equipment scattered around. Everyone was doing their best not to lose their footing on the now-sloping floor.

"It's dead!' Bernadine said. The Brazilian had tears in her eyes.

"Um, what's dead?" Felicita asked.

Assunta looked at her. "She's talking about the khavimaker. She clonked her head against the wall when we landed. She should be OK soon – I hope. Come on, honey, you need to sit down for a few minutes."

The tables in the galley were affixed to the floor, but the chairs were scattered around the room, some behind the counter in front of the food preparation area, others lying against the wall at the bottom of the slope. The Filipino woman propped one these latter chairs against the wall, then led Bernadine to it. Since the two mercenaries were occupied, and Dr Cheung and Juliana tended to Malik, Felicita decided it was up to her to check in with the bridge.

"Commander, this is Felicia down in the galley. Is this channel still open? Are you all OK?"

The speakers in the galley remained quiet, and for a moment, she feared the worst. But then Luis' voice crackled through.

"We'll live, thanks to you. If you hadn't released the grabber… At any rate, sensors indicate that our hull wasn't breached, but I'm ordering everyone to put on EVA suits, just in case. How's everyone there?"

"Malik has a wounded arm and Bernadine suffered a head injury, but otherwise I think we're good."

"Malik's one of you guys, right? A miner?"

Felicita nodded. "Yes, sir."

"Do you remember where the EVA suits are stored?"

Felicita might've been a miner, but this was far from her first time traveling on a spacecraft, although it *was* her first time crashing in one. Irritated by Luis' assumption of ignorance on her part, she wanted to snap at him, but she restrained herself. This was hardly the time.

"I do."

"Good. Assunta!"

Assunta stood next to Bernadine. She'd parted the other woman's hair so she could get a better look at her bleeding scalp as she answered the captain. "Yeah, boss?"

"If Bernadine and Malik can't wait, get a medkit and treat their injuries. If they *can* wait, all of you get into EVA suits first, and you can patch them up after that. Understood?"

"Got it."

"The rest of us will put on our EVA suits after you. Once we're all suited up, we'll figure out our next move."

Luis fell silent then, and Felicita knew the conversation was over.

Assunta's fingers were slick with Bernadine's blood. The woman wiped them off on the wall as best she could, then she helped Bernadine to stand and put an arm around her waist.

"You heard the boss. Let's go."

Bernadine looked once more at the broken khavi-maker and a tear ran down her cheek.

"Gone too soon," she said, then she draped her arm around Assunta's shoulders and allowed her fellow merc to help her toward the door.

Bernadine's face was pale, and her legs wobbly, but with Assunta's help, she remained on her feet. Since those two were all right, Felicita went to see if she could help Malik.

"How you feeling, you old hole-shitter?" she asked.

He gave her a weak smile. "Remind me why we decided to take on this job?"

"Money," Felicita said.

"Oh, yeah. I remember now."

Leviathan wasn't like other Guilds. Instead of focusing on a specialty – as the Water, Power, and Entertainment Guilds did – Leviathan wanted to dominate *all* business in the galaxy. Luis and his people were freelancers who'd been hired specifically to do this job, but Felicita, Juliana, and Malik were employees of Leviathan, as, she assumed, was Dr Cheung. When you worked for Leviathan, you did whatever the Guild required of you, and if that meant entering a forbidden system, you did it, no questions asked – *if* you wanted to keep your job, that is. If you refused, your employment would be terminated immediately, and Leviathan would make sure you never worked in your profession anywhere else again. Draconian, sure, but Leviathan paid extremely well, and with what Felicita and the other miners would make from this trip – including the bonus they'd get if they obtained what the Guild wanted – the three of them could live quite well for the rest of their lives. That made the risk worth it. At least, that's what she'd told herself.

Felicita turned to Dr Cheung and asked, "Do we need to break out a medkit now or can we get him into a suit first?"

Cheung smiled. "You know I'm not a physician, right? I'm a biologist. Still, in my decidedly non-professional opinion, I'd say he's sprained his wrist, perhaps even broken it. Donning an EVA suit won't be much fun for him, but he'll manage. We can remove the left glove and treat his wrist after that."

"Good," Malik said. "I came here to work, and I need both hands to do my job."

Assunta opened the galley door and helped Bernadine through. Cheung, Malik, Juliana, and Felicita followed. When they were in their EVA suits, Felicita would go with Juliana to the cargo bay to check on the mining equipment and make sure everything was still in working order. The maglocks might've kept the big stuff from moving around and getting banged up, but that didn't mean their interior components hadn't gotten scrambled.

So far, this job wasn't getting off to a great start, but Felicita told herself not to focus on the negative. Things would start looking up soon, right?

SIX

There were many things Oren Tisdale disliked about being a cyborg but possessing the ability to magnetically anchor himself to the deck of a crashing starship wasn't one of them.

"You guys all right?" he asked.

Tad Hoang and Bhavna Khurana were the other two members of the documentary crew Leviathan had sent along to document this mission. Oren was essentially a living camera, while Tad did voiceover narration and Bhavna produced on the fly. Later, once Oren downloaded the data he'd recorded, Bhavna would edit it into a hopefully watchable holo.

Tad had held onto Oren's left arm as the *Kestrel* crashed, and Bhavna to his right. Although now that the *Kestrel* had come to a stop, the two of them still clung to him. He supposed it was because the ship had come to rest unevenly, and the floor now tilted – he did a quick calculation – 9.92 degrees starboard. He didn't need magnetic help to stand at this angle. Outwardly, he appeared human, but aside from his brain, his body was entirely robotic, and his internal servos would instantly compensate for the ship's tilt, allowing him to walk around the bridge unaided. He was certain the humans could get about well enough, although moving might be awkward for them, but he didn't think Bhavna and Tad continued holding onto his arms because they were afraid of falling. He thought they needed time to adjust to what had happened. Holding onto him was more for security than any real need to keep themselves steady. That was his guess, anyway. He wasn't always good at understanding human psychology, not anymore.

Jena had been the only one on the bridge not secured in some way, and she had been tossed around violently during the crash. She sat on the floor near the weapons station, and Sirena knelt next to her, checking her for injuries. Oren couldn't tell if Jena had been badly hurt, but she was moving, so at least she was alive. This made him glad, not because he cared for her – after all, he barely knew the woman – but because she was Leviathan's representative on this mission, and as such its success depended on her leadership. They needed her to be functional.

Stop it! She's a person, not a piece of equipment.

Right. A person. He had to remember that.

"Oren, sweep your gaze slowly around the bridge," Bhavna directed. "Focus on the commander first, and then continue around until you end up on Jena. Tad, improvise your narration, but when it comes to Jena, play up the 'loyal employee willing to sacrifice all for Leviathan' angle. The Guildmasters will eat that shit up."

"You don't think that's laying it on too thick?" Tad asked.

"If anything, it's not thick enough," Bhavna said.

"OK. Let me know when you're ready, Oren."

Logically, there was no need for all three of them to be here. Outfitted with cybernetic implants that allowed him to capture video and audio, Oren could decide what to record, and overlay narration as well. But Leviathan preferred a team of three so that no one perspective would dominate the final product. To be honest, while Oren technically would be able to do all three jobs, he'd be terrible at it. He had trouble identifying what was and wasn't important to focus on at any given time, at least when it came to humans – to other *people* – and he was at a loss for what to say about them. He was glad to have Bhavna and Tad as coworkers. He needed them.

"I'm ready."

Tad nodded and started a voiceover.

"We had a rough landing, but the *Kestrel* has made it to PK-L10, otherwise known as Penumbra. Everyone on the bridge seems to be unhurt for the most part, but the condition of the ship is currently unknown, as is our precise location. The commander has ordered everyone to put on EVA suits as a precaution, but as of right now, there appears to be no immediate danger."

Luis rose from his command chair, and Bhavna gestured for Oren to focus on him. The commander half-walked, half-slid to the communications/sensors station, and when he reached it, he gripped the back of the chair to steady himself.

"Junior, can you get us a look outside?" Luis asked.

The viewscreen had gone dark during their landing. Oren didn't know if it was broken or had simply shut off due to a power fluctuation. He panned down to Junior working the controls, and the viewscreen flickered to life once more. The view was clouded, and for a moment Oren thought they were still caught in a sandstorm, but then he realized that the *Kestrel* had undoubtedly kicked up a hell of a lot of dust when they landed. The cloud would settle soon, but right now all they could see was a haze of dull yellow. He zoomed out, taking in the whole scene.

Oren spoke without thinking. "If you adjust the sensors to filter out the dust, you'll be able to see what's out there."

Everyone on the bridge looked at him, although he wasn't sure why. It was a sensible suggestion, wasn't it?

Bhavna leaned in close to his ear, although the action wasn't necessary. His hearing was so acute, she could've stood on the other side of the bridge and whispered and it would've sounded like shouting to him.

"We're supposed to remain in the background, remember? We're observers, not participants."

Right. He'd forgotten.

"Sorry," he told her.

Luis turned back to Junior. "Can you do that?"

"I can try."

A moment later the screen blurred, and when it came back into focus, the dust cloud was gone, replaced by a barren yellow landscape beneath a brownish sky. Tad began narrating.

"We're getting our first look at Penumbra, and *desolate* is the word that comes to mind. Rocks and boulders scattered atop a flat plain, mountains off in the distance. Some signs of life, though. Small spiny plants that resemble cactus..."

Junior zoomed in on one of the plants to reveal several tiny insects crawling among the spines. Their carapaces were a striking blue color, and they had ten legs, four more than terrestrial insects.

"... as well as insects. No indication of any larger lifeforms, but if there were any around, no doubt our less than stealthy landing frightened them off. Perhaps we'll see some later."

Oren focused his attention on the blue insects, and although he normally didn't experience intense emotions, he felt overpowering disgust. Images and sounds flashed rapidly through his mind – misshapen things with claws and fangs, people running and screaming, monsters tearing them apart as if they were ragdolls, his mother and father... his mother and father... one of the monsters coming at him, claws swiping toward his face...

The images cut off as swiftly as they'd come, and Oren knew his emotional regulator had kicked in. A human brain in a cyborg body could be dangerous if emotions weren't controlled. A robotic body could respond far faster than a human one, and intense emotions such as fear and anger could cause it to lash out before the human part knew what was happening. Given how strong cyborgs were, they could cause significant damage to people and property if their emotions ran rampant. But even with the emotional regulator doing its job, Oren still felt a distant echo of revulsion at the sight of the insects. They were small, and in all probability no real threat, but they were *alien*, and Oren believed that all alien life, no matter what kind, was a threat to the human species.

After all, he'd seen it firsthand, hadn't he? That was the reason he was a human brain encased in an android body, and as far as he was concerned, the galaxy would be a better place if humans were the only beings that inhabited it.

The plan was for the crew to remain on Penumbra only a short time, a few hours, maybe a day at the most. They needed to get their work done, get off this rock, and leave before the Galactic Coalition caught them. However long Oren was here, though, he'd make sure to step on every goddamned bug he could. Every dead alien, even an insect, meant one less potential threat. And if there were any higher lifeforms here? He'd deal with them, too.

Humanity first, he thought. Always.

"Stop daydreaming, Oren," Bhavna said. "Get your eyes off the viewscreen and focus on the commander."

"Hmm? Oh, sorry." Oren did as his producer directed.

"Where are we at, Lashell?" Luis asked. Oren zoomed in on his grim profile.

The woman consulted a readout on her console.

"I tried to bring us in as close to the predetermined landing zone as I could, but nav sensors are damaged, and I'm not sure what our exact location is."

"Pan around," Luis told Junior, and the crewmember did so.

The view on the screen shifted left, showing a different part of the planet's empty landscape. Then, a moment later, a cluster of white domes appeared, one larger than the others. Junior grinned.

"Nothing wrong with *my* sensors, and they tell me we're less than half a klick away from those buildings."

"Which is a half a klick away from where we wanted to be," Jena interrupted, sounding breathless as she got to her feet.

Now it was Luis' turn to grin. He clapped Lashell on the shoulder. "Lashell, you are a goddamned genius."

She smiled back. "Tell me something I don't know."

"Focus on the screen," Bhavna said. Tad continued narrating.

"Thanks to the remarkable skills of the *Kestrel*'s navigator, we find ourselves having landed at almost the exact touchdown point we were aiming for."

Tad went on, but Oren paid him no more attention. He imagined crushing small blue bugs between his fingers one at a time. The thought brought a rare smile to his robotic face.

SEVEN

Kilometers away from the *Kestrel*'s landing site, in a cavern deep below Penumbra's surface, the Summoner woke and opened its one great eye.

The creatures, clustered on the thick layer of luminescent blue mold that covered its body, sensed their master's return to awareness and became excited, their insect-like bodies quivering, mouth parts clicking and chittering. The Summoner reached into the smaller creatures' minds, scanned their recent memories, and learned that a great disturbance within the earth had occurred, with vibrations so strong they had frightened its children. Some had been so terrified they'd abandoned the nest and fled into the vast network of tunnels that spread outward from it. Now that the Summoner knew why it had been pulled from its deep slumber, it ordered a half dozen runners to flood the tunnels, hunt down the deserters, and slay them for their cowardice.

Runners – smaller and leaner than others of their kind, but no less deadly – leaped off the Summoner and raced into the tunnels, eager to do their master's bidding. When they were gone, the Summoner mulled over the information it had extracted from its children. Had a meteorite struck nearby? Such impacts occurred infrequently on Penumbra, but they were known to happen. It didn't *feel* like a meteorite, though. What's more, there had been *two* impacts, not far apart. What were the odds that two meteorites would strike at the same time so close together? Perhaps a meteor had broken up upon entering Penumbra's atmosphere and the pieces had followed the same trajectory down to the planet's surface. That would account for it, but there was another possibility, remote though it might be, one the Summoner had waited nearly a century to present itself.

A starship – perhaps two of them – landing.

The impacts *had* occurred near the domed nests the humans had built for themselves. The humans that had originally lived in those nests had been gone many years, but perhaps more had come, maybe to learn what had happened to the others or simply to occupy the empty nests. The reason for the newcomers' arrival on Penumbra didn't matter to the Summoner. What mattered was that they were here, and that in order to *get* here, they had to have traveled in a starship. It ordered another half dozen runners to go forth, inspect the impact sites, and report back as swiftly as they could. As had the others, these jumped off the Summoner and raced away into the tunnels.

The Summoner, far too excited to return to its slumber, settled in to wait. The remaining children shared their master's excitement – how could they not? – and they crawled across the Summoner's body, vibrating with anticipation and chittering loudly. Normally the Summoner would've been annoyed by their noise and commanded them to be silent, but not this time. Let them revel in their excitement, for if one or more starships had landed on Penumbra, then the Summoner's time had come at last.

EIGHT

"'Join the military', my father said. 'You'll get to see the galaxy. You'll go places no one has ever gone before.'" Sal sighed. "Why did I listen to him?"

Aisha, Lazara, Jason, and Sal trudged across the surface of Penumbra. Although the planet's gravity was less than Earth standard, their EVA suits were heavily armored combat models, and they each carried weapons. Aisha had a light machine gun and a cattle prod and pistol attached to her suit's magbelt. The four also wore backpacks containing further equipment food, water, medkit, locator, suit-breach patches, a searchlight, flexine rope, and additional ammo. The armor and gear weighed them down to the point where it felt as if the gravity was Earth standard, or close to it. This was a good thing. If they ended up in a combat situation – and there was an excellent chance they would – they'd be able to move faster and easier than they would have on a world with heavier gravity.

"Your dad wasn't wrong," Lazara said, as she adjusted her SMG and cattle prod. "How many people do you think have seen this view before?" She swept out her gun hand to take in their surroundings.

Their voices were tinny coming over the EVA suits' internal comms. As a soldier, Aisha had grown used to the sound, although she'd rarely heard it since taking command of the *Stalwart*. The sound brought her back to her combat days, and while she didn't remember them with fondness, the memories brought up fewer negative associations than she would've expected. She supposed some things didn't look so bad the farther away from them you were.

Some.

"Who would want to look at this?" Sal said. He carried an assault shotgun and a heavy cutter on his belt as a backup weapon. "This has got to be the ugliest planet I've ever been on. Piss-yellow ground, shit-brown sky... No wonder there's no sign of life. What the hell would want to live here?"

"There are abundant signs of life," Jason said. He wielded a heavy shotgun and a chainsword, one in each hand.

"Weeds and insects," Sal countered. "They don't count."

Silence followed Sal's statement as they continued walking.

We got lucky when the *Stalwart* came down, Aisha thought. Damn lucky.

Jason had been able to bring the ship in for a relatively controlled crash landing, and none of them had suffered any serious injury. The same, unfortunately, couldn't be said for the *Stalwart*. The frigate had sustained several hull breaches, one of them quite serious, and they'd had to race to get into their EVA suits. They might not have been able to do it in time if it hadn't been for Jason. He wore an EVA suit to protect his body – from combat, a planet's harsh environment, or both – but as an android, he didn't need to breathe, so he'd been able to help them into their suits before donning his.

"Our situation looks pretty damn bleak," Lazara said.

"Bleaker than bleak," Sal added. "Our jump engine's toast. The damn things are so temperamental they go offline if you look at them wrong, so the crash *really* messed it up. And one of the ion engines can only operate at twenty-three percent power now. The thrusters are damaged, and while they might be able to get the ship airborne, no way in hell can it reach escape velocity."

Before leaving the *Stalwart*, they'd sealed the ship's breaches and activated a distress beacon. Aisha knew, given how far off the beaten path the PK-L system was, the fastest a Coalition ship could get there was a couple days, but it could take longer. They had more than enough oxygen on the *Stalwart* to last that long, so they'd be in no immediate danger of dying. But they still had a job to do – capturing the crew of the caravel.

"According to the *Stalwart*'s sensors, the other craft came down only a few kilometers away," Jason said, "next to a station of some sort that, as far as Coalition records in the ship's computer were concerned, doesn't exist."

"That doesn't mean it's not a Coalition station," Lazara said. "The Coalition keeps as many secrets as the Guilds do, maybe more."

"Whatever it is, it's our duty to check it out," Aisha said. "The station is likely the reason the caravel's crew came to Penumbra in the first place. After all, what are the odds of the caravel making landfall almost right on top of the station when it had an entire planet to crash on? No, the crew were already heading for the station when they tried to lose us. I want to know why."

"We could easily be walking into a trap," Sal pointed out. "The other crew will be able to see us coming from a klick away, and there are enough boulders for them to hide behind and ambush us. They could start shooting before we even know they're there."

"Jesus, Sal," Lazara said. "No wonder you ended up pulling shit duty in this system. No one could stand to listen to all your whining."

"Yeah, and what about you? What brought you to the ass end of the galaxy?"

"A general got too handsy with me, so I shot his dick off. The docs managed to attach an artificial one, but the guy was so pissed, he sent me packing."

"I'm surprised he didn't have you court martialed," Jason said.

Lazara grinned. "It wasn't the first time he'd tried it, so I made sure to record the whole thing. When Command saw the holo, they demoted him. Since he couldn't act directly against me, he had a friend reassign me to PK-L. I've got my own friends working on getting me out of here, though. Hopefully, I won't have to stay here much longer. No offense to you guys."

Jason turned to Sal. "If it's any reassurance, I have a locator built into my system, a quite sophisticated one, actually. I've been scanning our surroundings ever since we left the ship, and I'll detect anyone lying in wait for us long before we reach them. We won't be taken by surprise."

Sal *hrumpf*ed, but otherwise made no reply.

Aisha felt good to be walking on a planet again. None of them had been off the *Stalwart* for a year and a half, and it was a relief to be in a place where she wasn't surrounded by walls and ceilings. As one of the jokes in the military went, *go to space, get no space.* Even the most luxurious of starships couldn't devote much room to human occupancy and recreation. Even though they'd been walking for only ten minutes, Aisha's legs started to feel sore. She exercised regularly on the ship, but she supposed you used different muscles when you were actually walking somewhere, especially when you had to trudge in an EVA suit. Once again, she was glad for Penumbra's lighter gravity.

"What about you, captain?" Sal said. "You think you'll be getting out of this shithole of a system soon?"

That was a question she couldn't answer. Since it touched on the reason why she'd been sent to PK-L in the first place, she didn't want to talk about it. But before she could find a way to change the topic, Jason did it for her.

"I'm picking up something on my internal locator. Something coming our way."

Aisha paused, her body tense, senses on high alert. She raised her machine gun into firing position and swept her gaze across the area in front of them. She saw nothing.

Lazara, Jason, and Sal all stopped and held their weapons at the ready. They formed a staggered line, ready for action.

"See anything?" she asked.

"Nope," Lazara said.

"Same," Sal said.

"I have no visual confirmation of my locator's findings," Jason said.

Sal snorted. "A simple *no* would've done it."

Jason's brow furrowed. It was such a human thing to do that it momentarily took Aisha by surprise. "I believe that whatever it is, it's underground. Five meters or so."

Aisha didn't like the sound of that. Perhaps the rogues were using mining gear to tunnel? They'd used the grabber on the *Stalwart*, after all. Did they have some specialty tunneling tech she didn't know about?

"How close to us?" she asked.

Before Jason could answer, the ground in front of them exploded and a blue creature swiftly crawled upward and emerged into the light.

"Very," Jason said.

The thing was human-sized and bipedal – two arms, two legs, both with long curved claws – but it also possessed insect-like qualities. Large compound eyes studied them, and ant-like mandibles jutted from the sides of its fang-filled mouth. Its chitinous armor was covered with sharp spines, the tips glistening with a thick, clear substance. Its color was a bright, almost metallic blue, and its limbs were long and lean. This was a creature built for both speed *and* killing, Aisha thought. Despite her military training, she was absolutely terrified of it.

The creature made no move to attack. It stood and regarded them, mandibles clicking together, clawed fingers flexing and unflexing. Aisha had the impression the thing was trying to decide what sort of creatures they were and whether they presented any threat.

Sal answered the latter question a second later when he fired his shotgun. His round struck one of the creature's eyes, and its head burst apart like an overripe melon. Its body spasmed, fell to the ground, and the limbs curled inward as the creature died.

Aisha whirled around to face Sal. "Who gave you the command to fire?"

Sal's eyes went wide, his face pale, and the shotgun shook in his hands. "I… It… Did you *see* that thing?"

"A being's appearance is no reason to kill it," Jason said. "It demonstrated no hostile intent."

"I don't know," Lazara said. "With those claws and spikes, it *appeared* pretty goddamned hostile to me."

Aisha put her hand on Sal's arm and forced him to lower his weapon. "You've never encountered an unfamiliar alien species in a potential combat situation before, have you?"

Sal shook his head.

"For all you know, that creature was intelligent. You may have just killed a citizen of this world because you couldn't keep your cock in your pants."

"I don't see any buildings around," Lazara said.

"There are the structures near where the caravel landed," Aisha reminded her. "They could've been built by this being's race – and not all intelligent species build things. The Ghevraeth on Echorix 4 are sentient trees whose entire civilization is a communal mental construct."

"It didn't make any attempt to communicate," Lazara pointed out.

"That's because Quick-Draw here blew its damn head off," Aisha said.

"Just playing devil's advocate," Lazara said with a scowl.

"Well, cut it the hell out!"

Jason looked at Aisha appraisingly. "Your heart rate is significantly elevated, and the strain in your voice indicates a heightened emotional state. Has the creature's death brought up some... unpleasant memories for you?"

Aisha glared at him. She didn't think Jason was purposefully goading her, but she was about to tell the android that he could detach his head and shove it up his artificial ass anyway, when Lazara said, "There's another one!"

Everyone looked toward the hole where the insect-creature had emerged. A second crawled partway up, only its head and chest visible, its arms flat against the ground, claws dug in to anchor it. Aisha and the others trained their weapons on it, but none of them fired, and Aisha hoped Sal had learned a thing or two. The creature regarded them with compound eyes for several moments, paying no attention to its dead companion. Then it pulled its claws free, sank down into the hole, and disappeared. Aisha watched the hole, but when the creature didn't reappear, she said, "Jason, with me. Lazara, Sal, cover us."

Lazara and Sal spread out so they both had clear lines of fire in case another creature emerged. Aisha slowly approached the hole, Jason at her side, both holding weapons at the ready.

"My locator isn't picking up any signs of movement," Jason said.

That was a hopeful sign, but locators detected motion – vibrations in the ground, disturbances in the air. Jason's locator wouldn't pick up something if the creature was careful to remain very still. Nothing happened as they drew closer, and when they reached it, they peeked inside. Aisha couldn't see far, but Jason's android vision was much sharper.

"The tunnel descends at a thirty-degree angle for five meters, then levels out and presumably continues on from there. I see no sign of life. Would you like me to go down and examine the tunnel further?"

"No." Given his physical, mental, and technological capabilities, Jason was the one indispensable crew member they had. Aisha didn't want to risk losing him to an attack by pissed-off human-sized bugs. She motioned for Lazara and Sal to join them, and the two lowered their weapons and approached. All four of them then grouped around the dead creature's body for a closer analysis.

Even without its head, the thing looked dangerous as hell.

Jason frowned. "That's odd."

"What is?" Aisha asked.

"Its body is more asymmetrical than I would've expected. Nothing in nature is completely symmetrical, of course. Even android bodies are built with a certain amount of asymmetry in mind to make them appear more natural to humans. But the limbs on the left side of this creature's body are significantly longer than those on the right, and its right shoulder is higher on the left side. Its carapace is different thicknesses in places as well."

Now that Jason had pointed out these details, Aisha could see it herself. The asymmetry added to the monstrousness of the creature's appearance.

"What does it mean?" she asked.

"I don't know. This species might have more variety in its physical form than most. The asymmetry could be natural for its kind."

Aisha frowned. After working in close quarters with Jason,

Aisha had learned to read the android's voice. It sounded emotionless on the surface, but it wasn't completely, not if you knew what to listen for. "You don't sound convinced," she said.

"I don't have sufficient data to extrapolate from to draw any real conclusions," Jason said. "It could be a sign of rapid, almost chaotic growth, I suppose. I am unsure why this should bother me, but it does. It doesn't feel right."

"Since when are androids intuitive?" Sal asked.

"Our brains may be more complex than yours, but they function similarly. Intuition is merely when one senses a connection between several data points, but that connection is not yet clear to me. My subconscious will continue working on identifying the connection, and hopefully I'll understand it soon. In the meantime, I'm recording visual data on the creature, and I'll transmit it to Command when we return to the ship."

Aisha tilted her head and examined the creature further. Patches of a mold-like substance clung to its body. The mold was the same color as its carapace, making it difficult to discern at a distance, but upon closer inspection she detected that the mold glowed slightly.

She pointed to one of the patches. "What do you think that stuff is?"

"Could be a parasitic lifeform," Jason suggested. "Like fleas on a dog. Or it could be a natural part of its body. Whatever it is, I don't have the equipment to safely take a sample. I suggest we don't touch it."

"No shit," Sal said. "What do you think they wanted?"

"Probably just wanted to check us out," Lazara said. "Our

landing drew their attention, and they wanted to see if we were a threat."

"Or if we were good to eat," Sal said.

Lazara smiled. "That too."

Aisha couldn't help feeling it was more than that. She might not be an android, but she was no slouch when it came to drawing connections between data points, either.

"The first creature came all the way onto the surface, but it didn't attack us," she mused. "It was almost as if it wanted to test us, see what our reactions would be, discover what our capabilities were. The second observed us, then left."

"You think they were scouts?" Lazara said, more serious now.

"Maybe. If they were, the fact that one of them was willing to die to provide information for the others tells us something important about their species."

"What's that?" Sal asked.

"That they're not afraid to die to achieve a goal," Jason said.

"Or maybe they're just following orders," Aisha said. "Like us."

"You think they're soldiers?" Lazara asked.

Aisha shrugged, although no one could see her make the gesture in her EVA suit.

"We know they can be killed," Sal said, "so they're no problem for us."

"Two of them weren't a problem," Aisha said, a bit harder than intended. "But there's only four of us and we don't have an infinite supply of ammo. How many of them do you think there are on this planet?"

Her question hung in the air for several moments, but no one responded.

"Come on," she said. "Let's keep moving."

They continued trudging forward, each alone with their thoughts.

While the two runners assessed the humans, another pair emerged from the ground close to the *Stalwart*. They approached the ship cautiously, alert to any indication that it might attack. But the large metal contraption remained still, and they moved toward it, emboldened. They circled the ship, touched it with their claws, licked it with long, slime-covered tongues, crawled across its surface, compound eyes searching for the most minute flaws.

The runners possessed only the most rudimentary sentience and had no conscious awareness of what they were looking for, but that didn't matter. The information they collected would be delivered to the Summoner, and their master would know what to do with it. The Summoner knew all, *was* all, and the runners existed only to serve.

When they'd finished gathering all the data they could, they scuttled off the *Stalwart*, crawled into the hole they'd made, and began running toward their master's den as fast as they could.

NINE

"I've got life support up and running," Sidney reported. "You can take your helmets off, but I recommend leaving your suits on for the time being. The outside temperature is far below freezing, and it'll take some time to warm up in here. And don't leave this dome. The research station's generators are online and seem to be in working order, but they haven't been operative for nearly a century. I don't think we should overtax them by attempting to restore power to all the domes. At least not right away."

"Agreed," Luis said. "All right, everyone. Take off your helmets and conserve your O_2."

Everyone did so, even Oren. It was common knowledge that cyborg bodies didn't require the use of an EVA suit, but the organic brains encased in their skulls still needed oxygen to survive, so they breathed like any other human, although via artificial lungs. As a biologist, Sidney found cybernetic organisms fascinating, but as a person, she thought they were a perfect symbol of human resilience. Even the lack of a physical body couldn't stop humans. Their tenacity – the drive to keep going, no matter the obstacles they encountered – was what she admired most about them.

But too often, this tenacity manifested in humans not fully thinking through their actions and considering the consequences. As one of their ancient sayings went, "Damn the torpedoes and full speed ahead". They'd caused a good deal of harm in the galaxy because of such tenacity. That was the reason she was here – to prevent *this* group of humans from hurting Penumbra and whatever lifeforms inhabited it.

Her body twinged, sore, and she had a headache. Since the *Kestrel* didn't have private quarters, she'd had to maintain this female human form during the entire journey to this system to maintain her cover. The Empusa needed to reassume their natural shapes from time to time in order to rest and restore themselves, and she wouldn't get the needed privacy until this mission was completed. She had medicine to help with the symptoms of what her people called shape-lock, but it could only do so much.

Sidney stood in front of a computer terminal in what she believed to be the center of operations for this station, which was comprised of a half dozen domes joined by enclosed corridors. The dome design was popular for planetary outposts a century ago, before the advent of aeolian routing tech, especially on worlds like this one, where violent windstorms were a problem. The dome's inner shell glowed with soft light, and numerous workstations lined the curving wall. She found it hard to believe that so many had been necessary, but modern computer systems came equipped with AI's that handled much of the work, reducing the need for flesh-and-blood users. Several tables and chairs, presumably for workers to collaborate face to face or perhaps sit and take breaks, filled the room. Otherwise, the rest of the place was spartan. Facilities like this were designed for function, not aesthetics, something that hadn't changed in the last century.

Sidney thought it was a shame. From her observations, humans needed personal touches in their work environment – such as family pictures or pieces of art – to maintain a healthy psychological outlook and maximize productivity.

Once everyone had removed their helmets and placed them on the floor, Luis ordered the injured crew members – Malik, Bernadine, and Jena – to sit at one of the tables. As they did so, Assunta removed a medkit from her backpack and tended to them. Sidney went over to help. Her people were extremely empathic, and she couldn't stand to see a living being suffer.

Jena waved Assunta and Sidney away, though.

"I'm fine. Just a twisted ankle." She stood, none too steadily, Sidney thought, and addressed the group. Oren's eye gleamed green while he filmed her, and Bhavna and Tad stood at his side. The mercenaries and miners gathered around her to listen.

"We've made it this far," Jena said, "so congratulations are in order. Our landing could've been smoother–" she glanced at Luis "– but we survived, and that's the main point. Before we left the ship, I sent an encrypted signal to Leviathan headquarters informing them of our situation. They will dispatch a ship to come for us in case we can't get the *Kestrel* spaceworthy again."

"You can bet the Coalitionists did the same thing," Sirena said.

"If they survived," Jena pointed out. "But yes, just to be cautious, I'm assuming they sent a message to their people as well."

"So, it's a race to see who arrives here first," Junior said. "Leviathan or the Coalition."

Jena nodded. "Which is why we need to get our work done, repair the *Kestrel*, and leave as soon as possible." She looked at Luis. "What's the state of the ship?"

"Thanks to Lashell's piloting and Felicita uncoupling the grabber's cable in time, we landed with minimal damage. The Coalition vessel's missile took out one of our stabilizers. We'll see if we can jury-rig a replacement that can last long enough to help us achieve escape velocity. What do you think, Junior?"

"I need to get a close-up look at the damage, but my guess is that we can build something that works within say, five hours. Maybe less."

"Shoot for less," Jena said.

"You said we need to get our work done," Dwain said, "but you've been tight-lipped with the specifics up to now. What exactly is it that we're supposed to do?"

Jena scowled at Dwain, clearly displeased with his attitude, but she answered his question.

"One hundred years ago, an energy-rich element called Xenium was discovered on PK-L7. Xenium possessed qualities no one had ever seen before, and early tests indicated that it contained so much energy it could not only power jump drives, but it could also extend both their range and lifespans. Instead of making only a handful of jumps, a single engine powered by Xenium could make a hundred jumps, maybe more, before needing to be serviced or replaced. And the jumps such an engine could make would be ten times farther than any our ships are capable of now."

This news stunned everyone, including Sidney. If what Jena said was true, no longer would the Coalition be confined to a relatively small portion of the galaxy. New regions of the Milky Way would open up for them to explore, to learn from…

…and to colonize.

She imagined it with dread. The humans would discover new planets and find new ecosystems to exploit. In the centuries-long history of the Coalition, 52,784 different animal and plant species in the galaxy had gone extinct thanks to its exploration. This ghastly number haunted Sidney and now she knew it would only keep increasing and only strengthened her resolve.

After all, Sidney belonged to a group called the Safekeepers, an interspecies organization that believed in protecting native habitats from Coalition predation. She'd adopted the guise of Sidney Cheung and gone to work for Leviathan in order to spy on the new Guild for the Safekeepers. When she'd been approached to be part of the mission to the PK-L system, she'd jumped at the chance. Something had happened on PK-L7 to earn the nickname of Hellworld and render it off limits to the rest of the galaxy. Rumor had it that the Coalition had completely destroyed the planet's ecosystem, and they'd quarantined the system to conceal their crime. She'd hoped she might learn something about PK-L7 by visiting its sister world, something that she could use to bring justice to the wronged ecosystem, but Jena's revelation was terrifying. Could the Coalition and the Guilds – with their large population of *tenacious* humans – be trusted with enhanced jump capabilities? She feared she knew the answer. The Guilds, with their profit at all costs mentality, would be especially dangerous to the rest of the galaxy.

Jena went on.

"The research station on PK-L7 met with some… difficulties and had to be shut down. The Coalition forbid travel to the planet, and for a hundred years they've debated in secret about what to do with its large storehouse of Xenium."

Sidney glanced at Luis to see how he processed this information. Had the commander not been informed of the particulars of this mission? From the dark expression on his face, she guessed not, and he was none too happy about it.

"That doesn't make any sense," Lashell said.

"Yeah," Malik said. Sidney had placed a regen-wrap on his left wrist, and he could already move his hand better. "Why would anyone leave an element that powerful just sitting there for a hundred goddamn years?"

Luis finally spoke. "It's because of those *difficulties* she mentioned."

Jena looked at him with suspicion. "What exactly do you know?"

He shrugged but he bit his lip as if finally putting some puzzle pieces together. "Just rumors, really. But there's a reason the planet came to be called Hellworld."

"You're right. The personnel working at the station on Hellworld were attacked by some kind of native lifeform, one so deadly that almost none of them survived," Jena said.

"And the Coalition then put up a satellite defense network around the planet and started patrolling the system to keep people like us out," Luis finished.

"That's essentially correct," Jena confirmed.

"So, what does this have to do with us coming to Penumbra?" Bernadine asked. The regen-patch on the woman's headwound had given her a fast-acting painkiller and anti-inflammatory. Her eyes were clear now, and she sounded lucid.

"After PK-L7 was placed off-limits, the Coalition sent survey teams to explore the rest of the planets in this system in the hope of locating additional Xenium deposits. Penumbra was one such world. That's why they built this station. They intended to mine the element." Jena paused and cleared her throat. "Although, this was a different variety of the element with somewhat different properties. Because of this, they called it Neo-Xenium."

"Let me guess," Luis said. "Neo-Xenium wasn't the only thing they found here."

Jena nodded. "They discovered a similar hostile lifeform as on PK-L7 – or one close to it. They attempted to destroy the creatures, but there were too many and they were too savage. And unlike on PK-L7, the Neo-Xenium deposits here were far fewer. The Coalition decided it wasn't worth the trouble, so they left their research behind and withdrew their personnel."

"Those that were still alive," Dwain said.

"Yes," Jena confirmed. "Why the Coalition didn't place satellites around this world, I can't tell you. Perhaps they thought the small amount of Neo-Xenium here didn't make the effort and expense worth it. Whatever their reason for leaving Penumbra unmonitored, it worked to Leviathan's advantage."

"So, the miners are here to get the Neo-Xenium," Luis said, "and we're here to protect the miners."

"Again, yes. Leviathan doesn't expect us to bring back a vast quantity of the element, just enough for them to analyze and, with any luck, learn how to synthesize. But that's only half of our mission. The other half is to obtain samples of the native lifeform to bring back for study. If Leviathan can find a way to… *pacify* these creatures, they can sell the technique to the Coalition – for quite a pretty penny, I might add – and then they'll be able to mine the Neo-Xenium on PK-L10 and even PK-L7." Jena spread her hands. "And everybody's happy."

Sidney knew that Jena was spewing what humans called bullshit. She had no doubt that Leviathan's motives were far more self-centered. She frowned, knowing that obtaining samples of this deadly lifeform was the real reason she'd been sent on this mission, and not to *assess the native ecosystem*, as she'd been told. She didn't like being lied to this way, but what else should she have expected from humans?

There was no way Leviathan would want to help the Coalition obtain Neo-Xenium, not if there was the slightest chance that the Guild could synthesize it and corner the market. It would instantly make them the most powerful force in this sector of the galaxy. Leviathan wanted samples of the hostile lifeform so that they could find a way to exploit it, too. This was precisely the kind of situation that the Safekeepers had been created to prevent. Only now that she was here and knew Leviathan's true intentions, what could she possibly do about it? Whatever these lifeforms were and however aggressive they might be, odds were they'd simply been defending their territory from what they – rightly in her mind – viewed as invaders. Now a new invasion force had arrived, and she had no doubt the natives of this world would defend themselves as ferociously as they had before.

"All right," Luis said. "We have four main tasks: take stock of what supplies remain on this station, repair the *Kestrel*, obtain Neo-Xenium samples, and obtain samples of this alien lifeform, whatever it is."

"You forgot one," Dwain said. "Don't get killed in the process."

"Right," Luis said. "*Five* main tasks." He clapped his hands together. "Let's get moving, people. The sooner we get started, the sooner we can get out of here. Mercs, we need to fix the ship before anything else."

Luis sounded upbeat, but Sidney noticed the way his eyes narrowed when he looked at Jena. He was *not* happy that he and his team hadn't been informed of the true nature of their mission. She shook her head, a very human gesture. What had he expected from a Guild? To them, people were assets to be used as needed and then discarded. Leviathan had leveraged the promise of a big payday to lure Luis and his crew on this mission, and the money had been so good that they hadn't asked many questions. Same for the miners.

They might be regretting their choices now, but there wasn't anything they could do about it.

Junior was the closest thing the mercenaries had to an engineer, and Luis put him in charge of the *Kestrel*'s repairs. Junior selected Lashell to help him, and Sirena and Bernadine would accompany them to stand guard as they worked in the event any of Penumbra's "hostile lifeforms" appeared. He also warned them to be on the lookout for Coalition soldiers in case any of them had survived the crash and felt like causing trouble. Sidney intently listened as he told the miners to search the station's database for information on Neo-Xenium deposits and directed Sidney to look for records of the planet's native species. Luis assigned Dwain to be her bodyguard. Sidney winced, unhappy with this development, as it would make it difficult for her to do her real work with someone looking over her shoulder, but she had no choice but to accept the situation. She understood that to Luis, her expertise in biological matters was of great importance to tackle one of the five tasks.

This dome would serve as the group's base of operations, where Jena would remain to oversee things. Right now, she huddled with the documentary crew to discuss who and what they should record. Sidney found the human need to manage the perception of events fascinating. Even as such events occurred in real time, humans shaped them into a narrative that would suit their needs. The Empusa shifted their forms, but humans shifted their reality, and not always to their benefit.

Junior took a seat at one of the workstations and searched the station's system to see what sort of tools and parts might be stored that would be useful in repairing the *Kestrel*. The ship had the materials necessary for basic maintenance and repair, but they didn't have a spare stabilizer lying around. Junior and Lashell would have to build a replacement from what they could scavenge. Malik sat at another terminal, Felicita and Juliana at his side. All the while, Sidney chewed on the few scraps of information the Safekeepers had picked up about Xenium over the years. No one had any idea what effects, if any, Xenium had on organic life, but if the element contained the kind of energy Jena claimed it did, Sidney doubted it would be easy to use safely. All the intelligent races that comprised the Galactic Coalition had flirted with nuclear power in the past, and its long-term effects were ruinous to the environment. How much worse might Xenium – or Neo-Xenium – be?

As Sidney pondered these things, Luis and Dwain came toward her. She still stood by the table where she'd tended to Malik, and when she saw them, she walked over to meet them halfway.

"What would you like me to look for specifically, commander?" she asked. Luis was an even-tempered man, but during her time masquerading as human, she'd learned that authority figures of the species responded best to proactive displays of deference. Or, as a human might put it, got to keep the boss happy.

"See what you can find out about this lifeform Jena spoke about. I want to know how dangerous they are and what the most efficient way is to deter them from attacking us – and, if necessary, how to kill them. We can't take the chance that they'll greet our arrival in a peaceful manner."

If Sidney had truly been human, she would've felt a chill ripple down her back at Luis' words. Instead, she felt a tingling in her jaw, the Empusan equivalent. All too often, the human response to being confronted by something alien was to shoot first and keep shooting until the threat, real or imagined, was nullified. What would Luis think if he knew that she wasn't human and more, that she was a spy for the Safekeepers? Would he shoot her? She liked to think he was more evolved than that, but he *was* human, and ultimately, she'd found there was no way to predict for certain what they might do.

Luis continued.

"When Jena said she wanted a sample of the creature, my guess is she wants a living specimen. I'd prefer not to transport an unknown lifeform. I'd rather we collect blood and tissue, or better yet, just data. It seems likely the people who worked here would've done research on these creatures, so the information we need may already be in the station's computer system. They may even have collected samples, some of which might still be on site. If they did, that would save us time and effort."

"You really think any samples would still be good after a hundred years?" Dwain asked.

Sidney answered. "Possibly. It depends on how they were stored. If stasis tech was used, the samples could be preserved indefinitely."

"Let's hope that's the case," Luis said. "If not, I'll need a plan to find and capture one of the things. I'll leave you two to get to it."

Luis walked off to speak with Jena, who was still discussing matters with the documentary crew. Dwain looked at Sidney, resigned. "No offense, doc, but babysitting duty isn't my thing."

Sidney smiled. Even after all the practice she'd had pretending to be human, the expression still felt awkward to her. "Look on the bright side. If we can't find any samples onsite, I'm sure Luis will be more than happy to let you go out and look for some."

Without waiting for a reply, Sidney headed for the dome's main console. She'd search for the information Luis wanted, but as she did, she'd think about how she could protect Penumbra's species from the aliens that had invaded their world.

TEN

"I'm picking up some strange readings on my locator," Jason said.

Aisha, Sal, Lazara, and Jason had been walking across Penumbra's desolate landscape for what seemed like a very long time, and still there was no sign of buildings or the other starship. Aisha knew that time always seemed to drag when you were in an EVA suit, since you couldn't move naturally, and nothing occupied their attention in the dull vista surrounding them.

Aisha had grown up in a colony on Vore H-31, a world very much like Earth, and the first time she'd set foot on another planet as a new military recruit, she'd been dazzled with wonder. Since then, she'd lost track of how many different worlds she'd visited, and the thrill had long since worn off. Each planet's particulars might be different – atmosphere, gravity, colors of the sky and ground, flora and fauna – but they were all ultimately places where you had to schlep your ass from one location to another to get the next shitty job done. Penumbra was no different.

"Strange in what way?" Aisha asked.

"I'm sensing movement beneath us–" Jason looked at Sal "–and it's *not* caused by the creatures we encountered. It appears to be geologic in nature, but I can't determine… Everyone stop, *now!*"

Aisha hadn't heard Jason shout before, and her surprise, more than the android's actual tone, caused her to cease moving. Sal and Lazara stopped as well, and both stared at Jason in puzzlement.

"What is it?" Aisha asked.

"There's no way to gauge how many tunnels the lifeforms we encountered have dug throughout the area, but it's safe to say that it's likely there are many that comprise a highly intricate system."

"So?" Sal asked, irritated.

"So, the impact of our landing sent shockwaves radiating through the ground in all directions, damaging the tunnels' structure. I'm sensing instability in the earth beneath us, and I fear we may have caused a chain reaction that–"

The soil beneath their feet gave way. Aisha gasped as she fell. Her first reaction was to tighten her grip on her machine gun so she wouldn't lose it. Her second reaction was to draw her knees to her chest and bend her head forward to protect her helmet's faceplate. After that, all she could do was let gravity take her where it would. She landed hard on her back, weapon still in her hands, faceplate intact. She couldn't see anything because of all the dust in the air. She had no idea if the others had fallen with her and, if so, where they were.

"Sound off, everyone! Let me know you're still alive!"

Jason responded first. "I am undamaged."

"I'm good too," Lazara said.

"I think I just shit myself," Sal groaned.

Aisha smiled, relieved. "Be glad your suit has a waste processor."

Rocks shifted beneath her as she worked to sit up. The dust began to settle, and she saw a large gap in the ground, maybe twenty meters above them. A long fall, but the EVA suits were tough, and Penumbra's lower gravity had made their descent and landing easier on their bodies and equipment. Jason came toward her, deftly picking over stone and soil, and he helped her rise to her feet. He then moved off to help Lazara and Sal. A moment later, the four of them stood together. After checking their suits' integrity and finding them undamaged, they took in their new surroundings. They were in what appeared to be a large cavern, although now that it lacked a ceiling, Aisha supposed it qualified as a small canyon. Glowing blue rocks were scattered about them, and a similarly colored mold-like substance grew on the walls. It glowed as well, but its light was much fainter than what the rocks put out.

The EVA suits didn't contain sensors to examine the glowing rocks' mineral and chemical composition, but they could detect radiation levels, and Aisha was relieved to see that the rocks posed no threat. She, Lazara, and Sal were safe from radiation poisoning, and Jason didn't have to worry about his circuits getting fried. Of course, who knew what other kinds of energy the rocks could be emitting and what it might do to them? Best not to think too deeply about that, she decided.

Lazara toed a small glowing rock with her boot. "I've never seen anything like this before."

Sal pointed at a mold-encrusted wall. "That's the same crap that was on the insect-monster. You think it's connected to the rocks? They share the same color."

"That would seem to be a logical supposition," Jason said. "But we would need to do rigorous testing to be certain. After all, a banana and a squash are both yellow, but that doesn't mean they're the same."

"You think these rocks are the reason someone built a station near here?" Lazara asked. "So they could study them?"

"It's a distinct possibility," Jason said. He swept his gaze around the chamber, assessing it with his superior android vision. "There are indications of artificial marks on the walls and floor – presumably the ceiling too, if it still existed."

"Could the marks have been made by the claws of those ugly aliens we saw?" Sal asked.

"They're too precise. I'd say they were caused by tools, most likely mining equipment."

"So, the people that were here before us weren't just studying the rock," Aisha said. "They were taking some of it too."

"For all the good it did them," Sal said. "We've never heard of this mystery element, and no one but Coalition patrols have been in this system for a century." He kicked one of the glowing rocks and it bounced away. "If there was any use for this, they'd have found it long before now."

Aisha wasn't so certain. "One of the rumors about Hellworld is that a fabulous new power source had been discovered there, but it was impossible to mine it. Maybe the Coalition hasn't done anything with it because they were unable to get enough samples to work with."

"What would make mining it so hard?" Sal said. "I mean, it's right below the surface. You could practically dig it up with a shovel."

"Maybe *they* were the problem," Lazara said.

Everyone turned to look in the direction she pointed. Six blue-shelled creatures emerged from the darkness, clawed fingers spread wide, mouth parts clacking softly, compound eyes unreadable.

"Looks like the one that got away from us found some friends," Sal noted.

"More than you think," Jason said. "According to my locator, there are another six behind us."

Even now, with a dozen of the monsters closing in, Aisha was reluctant to fire on them. They *could* be intelligent. They could be responding to beings they perceived as threats, instead of confronting them out of simple animal aggression. But she couldn't afford to think like this, not if she intended to keep her crew alive, or in Jason's case, functional.

"Jason, you take the ones in back. Lazara, Sal, we'll deal with the ones in front. Don't–"

She was about to tell them to be cautious, but the aliens raced forward, making her instruction moot. The creatures emitted a high-pitched screech, the cries amplified by the cavern walls. Aisha raised her machine gun, set the selector switch to full auto, and started firing. At the same instant, Sal let loose with his shotgun, and Lazara with her SMG. The gunfire was loud as thunder in the cavern, and it countered the creatures' screams to a degree. Their rounds tore chunks out of the aliens' carapaces and broke off a number of spines, but they didn't penetrate further, and they certainly didn't slow the creatures down. If anything, the things sped up, clawed feet flying across the rubble of the cavern ceiling's collapse, the uneven terrain no impediment to their advance.

As Aisha's gunshot slammed into a creature's carapace, she remembered Sal reflexively shooting the alien at their crash sight. One round to the head, and the creature had gone down like a machine that someone had flipped the off switch. No, not the head. The *eyes*. The creatures' large compound eyes were completely unprotected, making them a prime target.

"Go for the eyes!" she shouted.

More blasting gunshots with a specific target sounded and they were rewarded with the sight of two alien heads exploding. Horrifyingly, their bodies lurched forward for several more steps, claws swiping the air as if determined to inflict whatever damage they could before death fully claimed them. But soon the bodies fell to the rocks. God, that was close – and there were still plenty more of the things to deal with.

Aisha had been dimly aware of Jason firing his shotgun, and the ratcheting hum of his chainsword as he swung it in vicious arcs through the air. With his android speed and precise aim, Aisha was confident Jason could handle the aliens attacking from the rear. That left four for her, Sal, and Lazara to deal with.

Either the surviving aliens were smarter than they appeared, or their instincts were razor-sharp. Instead of rushing them head-on, they veered off – two the right, two to the left – and hunched over, using the larger rocks from the cave-in as shields. Sneaky bastards. The pair on the left turned and launched at them again, heads down and zig-zagging. Aisha, Lazara, and Sal kept up the barrage of gunfire. The accumulated damage they inflicted finally began to have an effect. One of the aliens lost control of its right arm, and the appendage flapped uselessly at its side. The other's left leg was injured, and it dragged behind the creature, slowing it down. No zig-zagging for that one anymore, and Aisha took it out with a burst of gunfire to the head. Just as the second alien was in arm's reach of Sal, he managed to blow its head off with a shotgun blast. He jumped to the side to avoid the creature's swiping claws as it fell to the ground and died.

Four down. Where were the other two, the ones that had veered right? Aisha swept her gaze back and forth, but she didn't see them. The alien screeching had stopped. Had they been wounded more seriously than it had seemed, causing them to retreat? As fast and savage as they attacked, running away didn't seem like a natural tactic. They pressed their attack until their bodies were no longer capable of movement, so where…

Above.

With dread, Aisha looked up in time to see the last two aliens dangling from the edge of the cavern's ceiling. They dropped.

"Look out!" she yelled and aimed her machine gun skyward. The aliens could do nothing to evade the rounds slamming into their bodies as they fell. Both of their heads burst apart before they were halfway down. They were dead – or near to it – but like the others, their bodies continued attacking, claws swiping the air. Aisha realized that one of the aliens was falling straight toward her. She started to get out of its way, but her boot slipped on a section of loose gravel, making her stumble. In a moment, the dead alien – somehow still functioning – would be on her.

She felt the flat of a hand slam against her shoulder and shove hard. As she tumbled toward the side, she instinctively turned her body to protect the oxygen tank on her back, and she saw Lazara standing where she'd been an instant before. The headless alien crashed onto the woman, claws scratching frantically. Lazara was knocked to the ground with a cry.

An instant later, something slammed Aisha into the ground. She lay there, stunned, listening for the telltale hiss of air that would indicate a rupture in her EVA suit, rapid gunfire, or the screech of an alien, but she heard nothing. Was it over?

One of the rocks from above must have been dismantled and smacked into Aisha. Getting up in an EVA suit after a fall was a four-step process. First, you needed to get onto your knees, then raise one leg, plant your boot firmly onto the ground, then push. She had reached step three when Sal came over and held out a hand to her. She took it and he helped her the rest of the way up.

"You OK?" she asked him.

"Yeah. Damn things almost landed on me, but I managed to knock it out of the air with the butt of my shotgun. Felt like I almost broke my arm. Those things are *solid*."

Aisha lumbered over to where Jason tended to Lazara.

She lay on the ground, face up, with the headless alien – motionless now – only a meter from her.

"Lazara?"

"She's unconscious," Jason said. "Her faceplate is cracked. The alien's claws penetrated the right arm of her suit. Some patches of blue mold have attached to her – most likely transferred to her from the alien when it landed on her – but they don't seem to be causing any harm. The damage to the suit isn't serious, and I should be able to patch both breaches easily." In fact, he was already doing so, working as he spoke. Aisha noted that he was careful not to touch the mold clinging to Lazara's suit. Good.

"Any broken bones or internal injuries?" Aisha asked.

"Unknown. It appears the creature only struck her a glancing blow. I believe her suit protected her from the worst of the impact, but we won't know for certain until she wakes."

"All right. Sal and I will stand guard while you finish helping her."

Sal edged behind her, and the two soldiers stood back-to-back, weapons at the ready, and scanned the cavern's gloom for any sign of further alien attack.

Soon, Jason said, "Her suit is repaired. I'm going to administer a stimulant to wake her, along with a painkiller, an anti-inflammatory, and a broad-spectrum antibiotic, just in case the alien's claws broke her skin."

Soldiers in combat situations couldn't always count on a medic reaching them in time, so their EVA suits had a built-in mini medkit which could inject various drugs into their bodies in an emergency. The controls were on the EVA suit's left wrist. Jason tapped the plasteel plate there twice, and it popped open. He pressed several buttons, then closed the plate. He continued kneeling next to Lazara as they waited for the drugs to kick in. It didn't take long.

Lazara's eyes flew open. She gasped and sat up, wobbling to the side. Jason put a hand on her shoulder to steady her.

"Damn, that *hurt!* It was like having a ton of bricks land on your head."

"Thanks for pushing me out of the way," Aisha said.

Lazara smiled weakly. "Got to protect the mission leader, right? It's regulation."

"Still, I appreciate it. Run a quick medcheck on yourself."

Lazara nodded. "Computer, run medical diagnostic." She sat for several moments, and then a readout appeared on the inside of her faceplate. She skimmed it quickly. "I've got a bruised kidney and a strained ligament in my left shoulder. Nothing serious. The suit's computer says I'm still good for active duty."

There was something in Lazara's tone that made Aisha think she wasn't telling the whole story about the medcheck results. If the results recommended that Lazara be removed from active duty, her EVA computer would've sent a message to Aisha, informing her of that fact, since Aisha was the commanding officer. But no message arrived.

Even if Aisha had received a recommendation to remove Lazara from active duty, how the hell could she do that here? Given the situation, Lazara needed to keep moving with the rest of them.

Aisha extended her hand and helped Lazara stand. The woman had dropped her SMG when the alien struck her, and Aisha picked it up and returned it to her.

"What's the plan?" Lazara asked, tucking the SMG tight to her body.

Aisha glanced up at the hole in the cavern's roof. "Jason, can you climb up there?"

The android stood with his back to Sal, watching for aliens. "Of course. Assuming the walls are stable enough."

"They should be," Aisha said. "The aliens were able to climb them. Once you're up there, you can drop a flexine line and haul us up one by one."

Jason paused for a moment, and Aisha knew he was mentally reviewing her plan and judging its strengths and weaknesses.

"This plan has a better than even chance of success," he said at last.

Sal sighed. "I suppose that's better than nothing."

Jason raised an eyebrow. "It's significantly better than nothing."

Jason placed his shotgun and chainsword against his magbelt – one on each hip – and the weapons snicked tight to the metal. Then, without another word, he strode toward the closest wall and began climbing. Aisha, Lazara, and Sal watched as he ascended. Aisha wondered how many more aliens they might encounter on their way to where the outlaws were holed up, or for that matter, if they'd experienced any alien encounters of their own. If so, she hoped they'd managed to survive, and if they hadn't… well, their deaths wouldn't have been painless, but from what she'd seen of the aliens so far, at least they'd have been swift.

Jason reached the hole in the cavern roof, climbed onto the surface, and quickly lowered a flexine rope. He was strong enough that he didn't need to anchor it in the ground, and he'd be able to pull them up quickly, one at a time.

"Lazara, you're up," Aisha said when the rope reached her.

Lazara shook her head. "You first, captain."

"I agree," Sal said, grim. "Up you go, captain."

Aisha knew she'd been outvoted and wouldn't waste time arguing. She wrapped the rope around her magbelt a couple times, then gave it a yank to signal Jason that she was ready. The android pulled, and as she began to rise, she looked down at Lazara and Sal. They took up positions back-to-back, weapons raised, alert for any sign of alien attack. Lazara rubbed her right arm with her free hand, directly over the place where the alien's claws had penetrated her suit. She rubbed vigorously, as if the arm itched, and Aisha told herself not to worry. If Lazara had contracted something from the alien, the antibiotic that her suit had administered should take care of it.

She hoped.

Aisha had fought alien lifeforms before, but she'd never gone up against anything as vicious and powerful as these creatures. She and her crew had been lucky to escape with their lives. If they encountered more of the things, there was no guarantee their luck would continue to hold.

If you wanted guarantees, you shouldn't have joined the military, she thought.

When the twelve runners attacked the four humans, a thirteenth held back, concealed by the shadows. When the last of the humans had been pulled free of the cavern, the thirteenth runner dashed back to the den. It raced through tunnels created by the last humans that had come to Penumbra, then turned off into side tunnels created by its kind. A short time later, it emerged into the cavern where the Summoner laired.

It leaped onto its master and crawled over the others until it found an open place. It then settled in and waited. The Summoner reached into its mind and reviewed the memory of the runners' encounter with the humans. The thirteenth runner quivered with ecstasy at being in communion with its master's mind, and when the Summoner finished and broke the link, it felt a sense of profound emptiness.

The Summoner had taken the measure of the new arrivals to its world. They appeared weak, their fragile bodies needing the protection of artificial shells to survive, but in truth they were highly dangerous, just like the humans that had preceded them. The Summoner had expected no less, but it was good to have its suspicions confirmed. But now the time for gathering information had passed.

Go.

The Summoner's children – thralls, runners, slayers, and ravagers – detached themselves from its body and hurried off to do their master's bidding. Once they had gone, leaving the Summoner alone, it began to replace those that had been lost. The Summoner reached out mentally to the blue mold that covered its body and activated it. As new children began to form, the Summoner decided it might be best to make several dozen extra. They would most certainly be needed before all this was over.

The Summoner closed its one great eye and dreamed of sailing among the stars as its new children grew.

ELEVEN

"Go easy now. Sensors indicate that the tunnel's unstable."

Felicita sat behind the wheel of a driller, while Malik and Juliana trailed behind her in a hauler. The driller's headlights illuminated the shaft before her, revealing ferrocrete beams that had been placed every five meters on the walls and ceiling. The shaft was large enough for both vehicles to fit, one after the other, with room to spare, and visually it *looked* stable, but the readout on the digger's console told a different story.

This shaft was a century old, which was concerning enough, but other signs indicated smaller tunnels that had been dug alongside the shaft, sometimes intersecting it. The miners that had been here before them had done good work – which was why the shaft hadn't collapsed before now – but there was no telling how much longer it would last. It could remain intact for years to come, or it could collapse on them at any moment.

This is why they pay you the big bucks, she thought.

Malik's voice came over her EVA suit's comm. "We'll keep it smooth."

The electric engines made almost no noise as the vehicles rolled through the winding tunnels. The machines had been designed to create as little disturbance as possible within a shaft. The wheels were outfitted with ultra-shock absorbers to minimize vibrations, and the vehicles also possessed low-level inertial dampeners that further reduced unnecessary motion. One thing about Leviathan – they didn't skimp when it came to equipment.

Finding information about the mine in the research station's computer system hadn't been difficult – once Felicita had adjusted to the old tech – and she found the location easily. She'd also learned the station's previous occupants had left a good deal of mining equipment behind.

Unfortunately, all of it was too old to be of any use to her and her team. She'd hoped there might be some Neo-Xenium samples stored onsite, but she'd found no record of any. Data about Neo-Xenium filled the system – how much of it had been mined, what they'd learned about its properties – but most of that information had been protected, and she couldn't access it.

Not that it would have done her much good if she'd been able to. She was no geologist or physicist. She went underground, dug stuff up, then brought it back to the surface. There was always a risk that unknown elements might produce harmful radiation, but the miners' EVA suits were equipped with sensors, and if the Neo-Xenium was dangerous, they'd know ahead of time and would take necessary precautions as they worked.

Felicita wasn't worried about that, though. There'd been nothing in the computer records to indicate Neo-Xenium was radioactive. She was more concerned about encountering any of the hostile lifeforms that inhabited this world. Neither the driller nor the hauler possessed any weaponry, but the miners had brought along shotguns and cattle prods for protection. She hoped they wouldn't need them.

Before leaving the station, she asked Luis how much Neo-Xenium he wanted them to bring back. It was Jena who'd answered, though.

"As much as you can."

Luis had amended that to as much as they could get *in an hour*. After that, he wanted them to return to the station and looked frustrated that his team needed to stay behind to fix the ship and secure organic samples of the planet's lifeforms, rather than dedicate efforts to join the mining team. Felicita didn't mind... too much.

She would leave the driller behind and ride back with Malik and Juliana. They'd no longer need the driller, and the machine's weight would be replaced by the Neo-Xenium, so the *Kestrel* would be roughly as heavy as it had been when they'd landed, if not lighter. Weight was always a prime factor when traveling in space – or within an atmosphere, for that matter – and if they wanted to get off Penumbra, they'd need to be careful not to overburden the ship.

They soon reached a place where the shaft broadened into a cave. The ceiling was still reinforced with ferrocrete beams. Obvious signs of mining covered the space – the walls had large divots in them, and the floor was scored by marks left by the wheels of heavy machinery. At first, she feared the cave had been tapped out and they'd have to search for a new deposit of Neo-Xenium, but one wall had thin veins of glowing blue running through the stone. She grinned. She'd seen images of Neo-Xenium on the station's computer, and they'd had the same telltale color and glow. Jackpot!

"Is that what I think it is?" Malik said over her suit's comm.

"Sure as hell looks like it." Felicita checked the radiation readings on her suit's inner-helmet display and saw they were minimal, well within the safety range. "There's hardly any rads to speak of," she said. "I think we're good to get started."

"We'll hang back while you work. Let us know if you need any help."

"Will do."

Malik moved the hauler close to the far wall and angled the vehicle so its headlights would provide additional illumination for Felicita. The light caused the veins of Neo-Xenium to glow more intensely, as if they were drawing power from it. Maybe they were. Who knew what this shit could do?

The driller was a four-wheeled vehicle with an extendable trautium laser drill on top which could move in any direction. Felicita worked the controls, and the drill powered up and swiveled toward the Neo-Xenium vein. She extended the metal tip until it was only centimeters from the glowing blue line of Neo-Xenium, and then activated the lasers. Now came the nerve-wracking part. No matter how quiet the machine was designed to be, it would still create vibrations as it bored into the rock, and there was nothing she could do about that. If the cave roof was as unstable as the rest of the mine, she could bring the entire thing down on them. The vehicles were designed to withstand a cave-in, so they wouldn't be killed, but Luis had stressed how little time they had to complete their mission. Would the others, lacking mining expertise, try to rescue them? Or would they say screw it, depart the planet before Coalition soldiers could arrive, and leave the miners trapped to slowly run out of oxygen and die? She knew what plan of action Jena would suggest.

She fired up the drill. Once the bit spun at top speed, she eased it into the cave wall. The rock made a grinding, rumbling sound combined with the drill's loud whine. Felicita kept one eye on the drill and another on the console's sensor readout. The vibrations further destabilized the rock, but not to the point of any danger, yet.

"Stay that way," she said softly. If Malik or Juliana heard her, they made no comment.

Rock dislodged from the wall and fell to the cave floor, quickly piling up around the front of the driller. A good amount of Neo-Xenium came with it, enough to make a good start. She shut down the drill and backed the vehicle away from the mound of rubble.

"Your turn."

Malik brought the hauler forward and activated the scoop arm at the vehicle's rear. It extended downward, picked up a hefty load of Neo-Xenium with only a few rocks mixed in, rose, swiveled, and dumped the material into the hauler's bed. There was no way to make this process quiet, and the rocks and Neo-Xenium sounded like thunder as they struck the plasteel bed. Felicita held her breath as she watched the console readout, but the cave structure remained solid. She released her breath in relief. She was now cautiously optimistic this place would hold together long enough for them to finish their work and get out of here.

Malik sent the scoop back down for another load, but before he could drop the Neo-Xenium into the bed, Felicita caught motion in her peripheral vision. She turned and was gripped by terror as she saw a mass of bipedal creatures with clawed hands and armor-shelled bodies flood into the cave. The creatures were blue, like the Neo-Xenium, and sections of their bodies glowed like the element as well. Felicita had worked on several worlds, and she'd encountered her share of non-human lifeforms, but she'd never seen anything like these monsters before. They looked like huge insects that had evolved humanoid form, some larger, some smaller, all deadly as hell. They let out terrifying high-pitched screeches as they approached, the sound so loud Felicita could feel the inside of the driller vibrate.

"Malik, Juliana! We're under attack!"

"I see them," Malik said, sounding determined.

"God, they're hideous!" Juliana said. She sounded as if she might throw up any second. Felicita knew exactly how she felt.

The creatures swiftly clambered onto the two mining vehicles and began pounding and scraping the hulls. The driller and the hauler had both been designed for working on deoxygenated worlds, and thus had no windows. Like starships, they had viewing screens inside that reproduced an image of the vehicle's outer environment. So, while it looked like the creatures were trying to break a window to get inside, it was an illusion. Of course, that didn't mean the things couldn't find a way in if they worked at it hard enough. This was a driller, not a goddamned warship.

Felicita tapped controls on her suit's right wrist to open a channel to the research station. She hoped someone would be able to hear her. With all this rock between them and their crewmates to block the comm signal, she figured her chances of reaching them would be low. Most likely, they were going to die down here, torn to pieces by alien monsters. Still, she had to try.

"This is Felicita! We're in the mine, and we're being attacked by a crowd of pissed-off two-legged bugs! Can you send assistance?"

No reply.

"Luis?"

Nothing.

They were on their own.

"Screw it."

Felicita activated the trautium drill. Since her view was obstructed by the creatures, she couldn't see to direct the tool's course, so she operated it blindly, swinging it around, jabbing it outward, up, down, side to side, hoping to hell she hit something. She was rewarded with solid *thunks* and shrieks of alien pain, but without a clear view she couldn't tell whether she caused any significant damage to the creatures.

"Malik, use your scoop as a weapon!"

"I'm trying, but I can't get it to work. I think the bastards sliced through the control cables!"

"Roll over the goddamned things then!"

Vibrations rumbled up through the floor of the driller, and she knew Malik had gotten the hauler moving. Was its viewscreen blocked like hers? If so, that meant Malik couldn't see where he was–

The impact jolted her out of the driller's seat and knocked

her into the console. She felt something crack inside her – a rib? – and then she fell backwards onto the floor. The miners' EVA suits weren't as heavily armored as the mercenaries', but no alarms sounded to indicate a breach, so that was something. She sat up, wincing at the pain in her chest, and saw that her viewscreen image was now clear. She remembered something her grandmother had told her. *Bad luck can turn to good, sometimes sooner than we think.* Smart woman.

Felicita hauled herself back into the driller's chair and adjusted the viewscreen to focus on the hauler. The creatures were clustered thick on the machine, almost covering it completely. Malik had likely drawn their attention when he'd collided with the driller, indicating to them that his was the more dangerous of the two machines, and the creatures on hers had jumped over to attack his. They struck the hauler's cab with their clawed hands, screeching in rage when they failed to break through its plasteel hide. Numerous dead and wounded creatures were scattered on the ground – some Malik had run over, some Felicita's drill had skewered – but far more still lived. If the miners weren't able to get control of this situation, it would only be a matter of time before the monsters managed to crack their enemies' shells to get at the tender morsels inside.

One of the creatures was much larger and bulkier than the rest, and it lumbered toward the hauler like a tank. The thing was insect-like but bipedal, with compound eyes, mandibles, fangs, and spine-covered blue armor – a monster built for sheer destruction. It placed its huge, clawed hands on the side of the machine, seemingly oblivious to the smaller creatures it crushed in the process, and shoved. The hauler rocked, but it didn't go over. The behemoth tried again, with the same result, but then pushed harder the next time. The hauler finally tipped all the way and fell onto its side with a loud crash. Most of the creatures leaped off before the machine hit the ground, but not all of them made it. Blue ichor shot out from beneath the hauler and splattered the monsters standing close by. Their screeching went up an octave, though whether from anger, excitement, or both, Felicita didn't know.

The hauler's door was pointed toward the ceiling now, and the big creature pounded furiously on it with its gigantic fists – *bam-bam-bam-bam-bam-bam-bam* – and while the door held, it gave a bit with each strike. Felicita knew that within moments, the door would burst open. The big one might have trouble reaching inside to get at Juliana and Malik, but it wouldn't need to. The smaller creatures would plunge through the opening and tear her friends apart within seconds.

She stared at the nightmarish aliens on the viewscreen, frozen into immobility by horror and indecision. What could she hope to do against creatures like these? She was a miner, not a goddamn soldier. She was trained to dig shit out of the ground, not battle monsters. They were going to die down here, not in a cave-in or an explosion of volatile gasses released by digging – deaths every miner was prepared for – but slaughtered by demons straight out of some alien hell.

Unless…

Trautium bits could overheat if a driller operator wasn't careful, and this would cause one hell of an explosion. Before that happened, an operator could eject the drill to get it away from their machine, as well as anyone else in the immediate vicinity. This safety feature wasn't all that safe in practice, however. How much room did you have when working underground? And an explosion in a mine tended to be bad regardless of where it occurred. Plus, when the drill bit was ejected, it shot off with the speed and force of a miniature missile. Felicita had known miners that used the driller's ejection function for target practice when they were topside, cracking boulders or splitting tree trunks with trautium bits for the fun of it. Felicita could use the ejector function to fire the bit at the creatures, but she knew she'd only kill a few that way.

There's got to be a way. Think… Think!

She grabbed the machine's controls, raised the drill until it was pointing at one of the ferrocrete beams directly above the hauler, then activated the ejector function. Trautium was one of the hardest substances known to the Coalition, and the bit cut through the beam as if the latter was sheerest gossamer. The bit slammed into the rock behind the beam, dug in, and became embedded there. If this cave had been structurally sound, that's all that would've happened, but this cave was *not* sound, as the driller's sensors had shown Felicita. Cracks began spreading outward from the bit's point of impact. Weakened, the beam sagged, and fissures opened in the ferrocrete, small at first, but rapidly becoming larger.

"Come on," Felicita said. "Come on…"

All at once, the beam snapped and the ceiling caved in. Tons of rock fell onto the creatures, splitting their carapaces like fragile eggshells, blue blood and internal organs bursting from their broken bodies. Rock fell atop the hauler too, of course, but the machine – like the driller – had been built to withstand a cave-in. Felicita hoped Malik and Juliana would remain safe inside. Rocks struck the driller too, but the ceiling's collapse was focused above the hauler, and only a few chunks of the roof were knocked free to fall onto Felicita's machine. The rocks struck the driller hard, but its roof held, and after a moment, the sound of stones clanging on the machine's surface stopped.

Felicita glanced at her viewscreen, but the air was filled with dust, making it difficult to make out any detail. Shafts of sunlight shone down, and she knew she'd opened a hole to the surface, maybe more than one. She saw several blue lights glowing through the dust, and knew it had to be more Neo-Xenium that had broken loose when the ceiling collapsed. The sight made her laugh. Talk about mining the hard way!

"Malik? Juliana? Can either of you hear me? Are you all right?"

The dust began to settle, and she saw that the collapse hadn't killed all the creatures, although most of them had at least one broken limb, if not more. The big one that had pushed the hauler over stood among a pile of Neo-Xenium rich boulders, its shell cracked and oozing blue blood. It trundled forward, but it wasn't dead, and that meant it was still a threat. She tried to contact her friends again, this time shouting their names.

"Malik? Juliana?"

After what seemed like a lifetime, Malik responded. "That

was probably the craziest goddamned thing I've ever seen anyone do."

Felicita almost wept with relief, but they weren't out of the shit yet.

"Are either of you hurt? Are your suits intact?"

"We're a little shook up," Juliana said. "OK, *more* than a little, but we're good. That was fast thinking, Felicita. Thank you."

"Don't thank me yet. We still need to…"

She heard the sound of creaking metal. She jumped up from her chair. Turning toward the noise, she saw the driller's door was bent partway open. When had that happened? When the hauler had rammed into her? When the roof caved in? The how didn't matter, though. A pair of long-clawed hands gripped the edge of the door and struggled to force it the rest of the way open. Cold fear shot through her, and for a moment all she could do was stand and watch as those hands widened the gap centimeter by centimeter.

Get moving, dumbass!

She looked for her shotgun and cattle prod. She'd placed both close by on the floor near the control console. But since then, the driller had been knocked, and the weapons were no longer where she'd left them. She couldn't see them.

The door creaked, and the gap widened. A sliver of the creature's face now peered at her, one mandible and a compound eye.

The driller's cab wasn't large, but she was on the verge of panic. She wasn't a warrior. The only fights she'd ever been in had taken place in dive bars, and those had consisted primarily of shit-talking and one or two sloppily thrown punches. She'd never had to fight for her life before, never had to try to think straight in the midst of battle. Up to now, she'd been able to function because she'd felt protected within the driller. But now one of those damn things was trying to get inside, and if it succeeded – *when* it succeeded – there would be nowhere to run. She'd be trapped.

Stop it, she told herself. You're a goddamned miner! You've dealt with tunnel collapses, explosive charges that went off earlier than they were supposed to, catastrophic equipment breakdowns that almost got you killed... You've helped dig to find trapped miners and return them to the surface and their families. If you can do all those things, you can do this.

Her mind cleared and she spotted her weapons. The cattle prod was lined against one wall, the shotgun tumbled against the other. She grabbed the cattle prod first, then the gun. Holding the prod in her left hand, she activated it. Energy crackled at its tip, and she stepped forward and jammed the rod through the opening the creature had created. She felt the rod strike something solid, heard the loud *zzzttt* of energy discharging, followed by an inhuman shriek of pain. *Take that, you sonofabitch!*

And the creature did so. It gripped the other end of the rod and pulled, slamming Felicita hard against the door. It was her turn to cry out in pain. She lost her grip on the shotgun and it fell to the floor. She still had hold of the cattle prod, though. The monster outside gave it another yank. She slammed into the wall again, this time so hard that a burst of white light went off behind her eyes. She released the prod, staggered backward, and would've fallen if she hadn't backed into the driller's chair and used it to prop herself up.

"Felicita! What's happening?"

Malik's voice.

"I'm... One of them is trying to get in."

Red covered her right eye, and it took her a second to realize she was bleeding from a head wound. It took her another second to see the crack in her faceplate and hear the soft hiss of escaping oxygen. She needed to get a breach seal out of her pack, but she couldn't afford the time. The creature had dropped the cattle prod and was once more attempting to pry the door open. It slid several more centimeters, becoming wide enough for the alien to reach inside. It thrust its arm through and swiped a clawed hand at Felicita, but she kept beyond its reach. It made two more attempts to claw her, and when it realized it couldn't get her this way, it withdrew its arm and resumed cranking open the door. Felicita knew it would succeed, and soon.

"Hold on!' Juliana said over the comms. "We're going to try to get to you!"

Felicita knew they'd never make it in time.

She lunged for the shotgun as the door finally slid all the way open. She didn't think. With a two-handed grip on the weapon, she raised it to her shoulder, and as the insectoid came at her, she fired. The shotgun roared and the creature's head disintegrated in an explosion of blue. The impact knocked the thing backward, and it fell to the driller's floor, arms and legs twitching. She watched as its limbs drew inward as it died, and she smiled in grim satisfaction as she lowered the shotgun.

"Screw you."

But the driller's door was still open, and the monster she'd just killed wasn't the only one who'd survived the cave-in. She raised the shotgun once more, only to face a mass of swiping claws and clacking mandibles as more creatures fell upon her.

She had no idea she could scream so loud.

TWELVE

The hauler lay on its side, surrounded by rocks deposited by the cave-in. The passenger-side door of the cab, which now faced the open gaps in the ceiling, was badly dented, and Malik strained to open it. His injured wrist hurt like hell, he'd hit his head on the cab's control console when the machine was overturned, and he had a raging headache. His vision blurred around the edges as well, and he wondered if he'd sustained a concussion.

He didn't have time to worry about the state of his health, though. He needed to get himself and Juliana out of there.

He climbed halfway out of the cab and shouldered his shotgun, ready to blast the shit out of anything that moved. Nothing rushed him immediately, and he realized that was because the surviving monsters had flooded into the driller to go after Felicita. Her dying screams over his suit's comm still rang in his ears. She'd given them a chance to live by bringing down the cave roof, and he and Juliana needed to move fast if they didn't want her death to be in vain.

The big monster that had pushed over the hauler remained next to the vehicle, buried in rock up to its waist.

It was within reach of Malik, but it made no move to attack him. Malik understood why when he saw its head had been cracked open, a thick blue substance oozing from the wound. The creature wasn't dead – its arms moved listlessly, and its broken head lolled from side to side – but it was stunned, and Malik had no idea how long it would remain that way. He briefly considered finishing the job the falling rocks started by blowing its goddamned head off, but if the thing wasn't a threat, he didn't want to waste ammo on it. He'd need the rounds to fight off the monsters in the driller when they'd finished with Felicita and came out in search of new prey. Plus, he worried the sound of the shotgun firing would alert and draw them to his presence. Better to keep a close eye on the big one and fire at it only if it became necessary.

He quietly climbed the rest of the way out of the cab, and then he held the shotgun in his left hand while he reached in with his right – the one that hadn't been injured during their less-than-elegant landing on Penumbra – to help Juliana. His head hurt so much that he thought the strain of pulling her up would cause him to pass out, but he managed to hold onto consciousness. Soon, Juliana crouched on the side of the cab with him. He didn't want to make any more noise than he had to, so he tapped his gloved fingers to his faceplate, then pointed to her. He was asking if her EVA suit had sustained any damage. She gave him a thumbs-up to let him know she was OK. She stood and then helped Malik to his feet. She pulled the pistol affixed to her magbelt free, flipped the safety off, and was ready to rock and roll. Malik gripped his shotgun with both hands, and the two of them surveyed their surroundings, looking for an easy escape.

The cave-in had broken both of the hauler's headlights, but one of the driller's headlights still shone. That, plus the sunlight filtering through the holes in the roof, gave them enough illumination to see through the settling dust. The entrance to the cave was now blocked, and the openings in the roof were ten meters above them, too far to jump up and reach, even with Penumbra's lower gravity. Insect creatures littered the cave, broken limbs sticking up between rocks, and while some of those limbs twitched, most were still. Juliana pointed to the hauler's scoop. Its arm was bent out of shape and the control cables had been slashed by the creatures, but Malik knew what Juliana was suggesting. If they could repair the cables, or rig a bypass, they might be able to swivel the scoop toward the ceiling and extend it far enough that they could climb up it and jump the rest of the way to reach one of the openings to the surface.

It was a good idea in theory, but impossible in practice. The monsters inside the driller would emerge long before they could complete the repairs, and even if they did somehow manage to jury-rig the scoop and get it working, the sound of the arm moving would draw the creatures out to attack them.

He wished he and Juliana could actually speak to one another without fear. Maybe then, together, they could brainstorm a way out of this mess. What if they whispered? Surely the monsters' hearing couldn't be that good, could it? He was about to suggest this to Juliana when the huge tank insectoid turned its head in their direction and released an angry shriek. It reached for them with both hands, and Malik and Juliana both cried out in fear as they fired their weapons. The twin blasts struck the creature's injured head, and it exploded in a gush of thick blue fluid. Despite not having a brain to direct its motions any longer, the body continued reaching for them. They ducked as the huge, clawed hands swiped the air, and then the body trembled and fell still.

"The driller!" Juliana yelled.

Malik spun in the direction of the other machine. Smaller insectoids climbed out of the cab's open door. So much for staying quiet. He and Juliana began firing, and although neither of them was a trained shooter, there were so many creatures that almost every round struck one. A hit didn't mean a kill shot, though, and most of the creatures continued coming at them. Malik knew they didn't have enough ammo to take out all the bastards, but he was determined to end as many as he could before he and Juliana were torn to bits. Every dead monster was one less that could threaten the others.

One of the human-sized insectoids got close enough to shred the right sleeve of Malik's EVA suit before he blew its head off. His suit's alarm sounded, indicating a breach.

No shit, he thought.

He was a dead man – the only question was whether he'd run out of air before one of the monsters could finish the job its companion had started.

"You were a pain in the ass to work with, you know that?" he said.

Juliana grinned. "Love you too, dumbass."

The two fired as the creatures kept coming. Then, an unfamiliar voice came over their comms.

"We're sending a line down. Grab hold and we'll bring you up."

What the hell? Malik couldn't believe it. Someone had come for them. He laughed in surprise and relief.

Malik and Juliana blasted the creatures, but now their gunfire was joined by rounds from above. Insectoids jerked and shuddered as bullets tore chunks out of their carapaces and penetrated their compound eyes, killing them instantly. A flexine line dropped down in front of Malik and Juliana, and without pausing to question their good fortune, Malik threw his shotgun – which by this point was out of ammo – wrapped the line around his magbelt, grabbed hold of Juliana, then gave the line two quick tugs. They were yanked up in the air and rapidly ascended toward one of the gaps in the ceiling, leaving the screeching creatures behind.

When they were pulled all the way into the light, Malik saw that a lone man in an EVA suit held the other end of the line.

Android, has to be.

Two other people in suits – one man, one woman – reached out and pulled them fully onto solid ground. A fourth person stood at the edge of one of the holes, firing a light machine gun at the insectoids below. Once she saw that Malik and Juliana were safe, she stopped and stepped back.

"Jason, cover us while we reload," she said.

The android dropped the flexine, picked up a heavy shotgun off the ground, and aimed it at the hole while the other three removed ammo from their backpacks and reloaded. When they finished, they guarded the hole while the android reloaded. Smooth. Practiced.

Malik let go of Juliana. She dropped her pistol, swiftly removed a breach patch from Malik's backpack, and sealed the rent in his sleeve. Malik had been holding his breath and breathing shallowly, but now he took several sweet gulps of oxygen and he felt better, despite his pounding headache. He unwrapped the flexine from around his waist and stared at their saviors. Even though he'd left his shotgun behind, Juliana made no move to retrieve her pistol.

Not only were their saviors' EVA suits heavily armored, they wore the emblem of the Galactic Coalition on their shoulders.

"Well, shit," Malik said.

THIRTEEN

"We picked up your call for help on our comms, and we got here as fast as we could," Aisha said. "I'm sorry we weren't in time to save your friend."

The two they'd rescued — miners, Aisha assumed, given the large machines down in the cave – said nothing. They didn't seem defiant, though. Just weary and in shock.

Sal peered at the pair of holes in the ground. "Two cave-ins in one day," he said. "At least we didn't fall in this time."

"We still may," Jason said, "unless we leave the immediate area. I believe the ground here is quite unstable."

The four soldiers walked a dozen meters from the holes, and the miners followed without having to be told. What else could they do? It wasn't as if there was anywhere to run. Aisha wondered how far they had traveled from their ship's crash.

"Lazara, Sal, keep watch on the holes. Blast any bugs that come out."

"You got it," Lazara said. She shouldered her weapon and Sal did the same.

Aisha then turned to the miners. Time to find out who these people were and what they'd been up to out here.

"What are your names?" she asked.

They hesitated, but then the woman answered. "I'm Juliana." She looked at her companion, who said, "Malik." Up to this point, he'd avoided making eye contact with Aisha, but now he met her gaze. "Thanks for saving us."

"You're welcome. I'm assuming you were crew members on the ship we were chasing."

Juliana and Malik exchanged uncertain glances. Sweat dotted Malik's brow and his eyes were bleary. A reaction to stress? He was a civilian, and likely not used to battle. But even a military veteran would be shaken at having to fight those insect creatures. He rubbed the place on his arm where his sleeve had been repaired, vigorously, and the action reminded her of the way Lazara had rubbed her arm after she'd been clawed by one of those alien monsters. Aisha frowned.

"Lazara?"

The woman turned to look at her. "Yeah, boss?"

Her face was sweaty too, and she had the same glazed look in her eyes. Aisha wondered how long she'd been like this. Aisha had been so preoccupied with their situation, she'd forgotten to check in with her teammate.

"Have you done a medcheck on yourself recently?"

"I'll do it now."

Aisha turned back to Malik. "Your suit got a built-in med function?"

"No. Those don't come standard on mining suits."

"Too bad. Guess we'll have to get antibiotic in you later."

Even though these two had broken Coalition law and had become her prisoners, not to mention that their ultimate fates would likely be imprisonment or even execution, as long as they were in her custody, Aisha intended to treat them as humanely as possible.

"Lazara, how are you?"

"The scan is finished. The results say I'm still fine."

Aisha frowned. "You don't *look* fine."

Lazara pursed her lips in irritation. "OK, my BP and pulse are elevated, but we *were* blasting bugs a minute ago, remember? I'm sure my vitals will return to normal once the adrenaline wears off."

Aisha wasn't so certain, but wouldn't make an issue of it at the moment. She'd have to remember to keep a closer watch on Lazara's condition. She turned back to Malik and Juliana.

"So, what brings a couple miners to a shitty planet like Penumbra?" she asked.

Once again, Malik and Juliana exchanged glances. Juliana sighed.

"Screw it," she said, and told Aisha and the other soldiers everything.

"I'm not sure this is a good idea," Lazara said.

Aisha and her three crewmates walked behind the two miners. The soldiers had their weapons in hand and ready to use, not so much because they thought the miners were dangerous, but because Penumbra's insectoids most definitely were.

After Juliana informed them about the reasons for Leviathan's clandestine expedition to Penumbra, Aisha had asked them if they'd be willing to lead the Coalition crew to the research station where the mercenaries were holed up.

"Are you asking us or telling us?" Malik had said.

"Does it matter?" Aisha had answered. "We'll all need to replenish our O$_2$ sooner rather than later."

Now, she wondered about Lazara's concerns. "What don't you like about it?" Aisha asked.

"For one thing, you should've let Jason hack into their suits' systems and disable their comms. That way, they wouldn't be able to contact the mercenaries and warn them about us."

"It's OK if they tell them. I *want* them to know that we're coming. We're going to propose a truce."

She knew the others – apart from Jason – thought she was out of her mind. Not only had the mercenaries broken the law by coming to this planet, but their actions had resulted in the *Stalwart*'s crash and current predicament. How could the Coalition soldiers trust them? But after what had happened at Janus 3, she was determined to prevent *any* unnecessary loss of life, whether among her crew or the mercenaries. A truce was the best way of making that happen until they managed to find a way off this planet.

She explained further. "Both groups stand a better chance of surviving until rescue arrives if we work together. Besides, if the miners told us the truth about their group, we're outnumbered. They've got seven mercenaries, along with five others who, while they might not be trained warriors, are still capable of holding a gun and aiming it in the right direction. If we tried to take them into custody, a firefight would break out, and odds are we'd lose."

"Yeah, but we'd take some of them with us," Sal said.

"To what end?" Jason asked. "It would be a purposeless waste of life – for both sides. Aisha's plan is sound."

It had been fifteen minutes since they left the cave where they'd rescued the miners, but Lazara's face was even more sweaty than when they'd set out. Aisha began to fear that her suit-administered antibiotic wasn't strong enough to counteract whatever shit had been on the claws of the alien who'd tagged her. One of the other reasons she wanted to make a truce with the mercenaries was so they'd let them enter the station the miners had told them about. She wanted to get Lazara out of her EVA suit as soon as possible and pump stronger medicine into her. Malik, too. The last time Aisha had seen his face, he'd looked just as bad as Lazara – if not worse – and he was having trouble raising his feet off the ground. Sometimes, he swayed as if he was dizzy and might fall.

"What if they betray us?" Lazara said.

Aisha smiled. "Then you have my permission to shoot them."

"Maybe if we used the miners as hostages ..." Sal began.

"We're Coalition soldiers," Aisha said. "We don't *take* hostages. We *free* them."

Sal barked out a laugh. "What military are *you* in? It sure isn't the same one I joined."

"Maybe it isn't," Aisha said softly. Once more, she thought of Janus 3.

The miners had reported the mercenaries were attempting to repair their ship, which made sense for their lack of protection, but if they failed, it wouldn't matter. The mercs had undoubtedly contacted Leviathan, just as Aisha had contacted Coalition Command. Rescue ships were already en route, and all that mattered was which arrived first. Regardless of which it was, Aisha intended to let the mercenaries go free. The idea rankled, and doing so would most likely lead to her court martial, but the mercenaries' freedom was all she had to bargain with to help her own crew survive. If she could make a deal with them, she would honor it, even if her crew didn't approve of her choice. She may have been captain of a rickety old starship working one of the dullest postings Command had to offer, but she was a still a *captain*, goddamn it, and she intended to behave like one.

Malik let out a loud groan and fell to his knees. He hunched over, hugging himself, and began shaking.

Juliana leaned down and put a hand on his shoulder. "What's wrong? Are you sick? We're close to the station now, and you only need to walk a little farther, then we can–"

Malik's EVA suit started to swell. Aisha feared his oxygen unit had malfunctioned and was madly pumping out air, causing his suit to inflate like a balloon. But that didn't make sense when his suit started to rip and tear apart. Without the suit's protection, he'd be dead within minutes. Not only couldn't he breathe in the carbon dioxide atmosphere, the temperature was below freezing. It would be a race to see what killed him first: lack of oxygen or the cold.

Juliana stepped away from Malik and spoke quietly over her comm. "No... No..."

She sounded terrified.

Malik stood up abruptly. He spread his arms and legs wide. His EVA suit fell off him in tatters, revealing a body hideously transformed. His muscles had become massive, and his hands and feet now terminated in a pair of curved, sharp claws. He was bald, and his hairless skin had a blue tint, with patches of brighter-hued mold clinging to it. The muscles on his back flexed, and a pair of large scorpion-like stingers burst outward and curved over his shoulders, pointed tips glistening with venom. He turned around to reveal a face out of nightmare – no nose, mouth filled with tusk-like teeth, and worst of all, eyes that still looked human, but which now burned with a desire to kill.

Juliana screamed, and the thing that had been Malik spun toward her. His stingers shot forward and buried themselves in her shoulders, the tips piercing the EVA suit's material as if it were the thinnest of cloth. She screamed again, louder and higher this time, and when Malik retracted the stingers, she went down on her knees.

Malik turned back to Aisha and her crew and started running at them, his hook-clawed feet tearing chunks out of the ground. Aisha didn't give the command to fire, but she didn't have to. This was one of those combat situations where soldiers didn't need to be told what to do. The four of them fired endlessly on Malik. His blueish hide was tougher than human skin, but not nearly as strong as the insectoids' chitin, and he took significant damage as he drew near. He bled blue just like the bug monsters did, but while his wounds slowed him down, they did not stop him.

"Hold your fire!" Jason suddenly shouted.

Everyone did so, and the android activated his chainsword and stepped forward. Malik's stingers lanced toward him. Moving with inhuman swiftness, Jason dodged to the side and swung the weapon at Malik's neck. As the chainsword bit into Malik's flesh, his stingers lashed out, this time striking Jason's shoulders. Unlike the miners', his suit was armored, but even so, the stingers dented the metal. Jason's chainsword dug further, and Malik's head went flying in a spray of blue. Even so, his body kept fighting. His hook-clawed hands tore at Jason's armor, and his stingers shot forward again, attempting to find a weak spot. Jason swung his chainsword in a backward strike, and the ratcheting blade cut into Malik's chest. Malik's body didn't die until the chainsword cut halfway through his torso. Only then did it shudder and fall, slipping free of the chainsword as it went down.

The soldiers stared at Malik's headless corpse and struggled to process what they had just witnessed. Julianna screamed again, this time so loud it sounded like the effort tore her throat to pieces. They ran to her, but she fell onto her side before they could reach her. Aisha got to her first, and she turned the woman over, was about to call her name, when she saw only a fleshless, eyeless skull looking back at her. Seconds later, the skull fell away to dust, leaving the suit empty. Aisha jerked her hands away and took a reflexive step back.

"Jesus," Sal said, "what the hell happened to her?"

Jason responded. "It would seem the venom from Malik's stingers induced extremely rapid decay in Juliana's body."

Aisha had seen chemical weapons in action before, but she didn't know anything that worked as fast as the stinger venom had. An alien weapon that could reduce a human body to nothing in mere seconds was absolutely devastating.

"Uh, guys," Lazara said. "I don't feel so good. Maybe… maybe you should get away from me."

Oh, no, Aisha thought. Not you too.

Lazara let out a moan that sounded too much like Malik's. Her body began to shake all over. Her muscles swelled and her face began to change – nose shrinking, teeth growing. Aisha understood what was happening. Lazara had been infected by the insectoid mold too, but the antibiotic her suit had administered had kept the change at bay until now. A guttural voice came over their comms, one that could barely form words, but Aisha still comprehended them.

"Kill... me... "

Aisha, Jason, and Sal raised their weapons and honored their crewmate's last request.

After Lazara had fallen, the Coalition crew trudged toward the research station in silence.

It had all happened so fast, Aisha thought. Crashing onto the planet's surface, the appearance of the alien creatures, their fall into the cavern, the attack by the insect monsters, the rescue of the mercenary miners, and now the horrible transformation and death of both Lazara and Malik.

Nothing in her military training had prepared her for a situation like this. She'd never engaged in such savage hand-to-hand combat before. Did she have what it took to get her crew through this safely, let alone negotiate a peace with the outlaws who had violated Coalition law and made landfall on Penumbra? Unsure of herself, she was tempted to turn command over to Jason. The android was the most competent member of the *Stalwart*'s crew – smart, strong, fast, and always in control of his emotions. He would be far better suited to leadership.

She turned to Jason, intending to ask him to assume command, but she hesitated.

You can do this, she told herself. More than that, you *need* to do this.

After Janus 3, she needed to prove to herself that she still had what it took to be a soldier. A Coalition soldier didn't turn away from her duty. She did it without fear and without complaint.

Suck it up, buttercup. Whether you like it not, this is war, and you're the boss. Better start acting like it.

She tightened the grip on her weapon and kept walking.

FOURTEEN

"That's disgusting," Dwain said.

"Looks formidable," Luis said.

Jena shuddered but smiled as she did so. "It's deliciously creepy, isn't it?"

The four of them stood before a cylindrical tube made of transparent plasteel. Mere moments before, it had been concealed by a ferrocrete wall, but Sidney had hacked the control console and the wall had slid open to reveal a recessed area where the tube – and the creature – had been stored. Sidney still had her EVA suit on, but she'd removed the gauntlets so that her hands were free to work. The longer Empusans remained in a single shape, the more uncomfortable they became, and when that shape was enclosed within the hard, unchanging shell of an EVA suit, the more they came to feel trapped. Even something as simple as uncovering her hands made her feel less confined. It was still cold inside the research station, but the heat had come on when she'd activated the power, and it would warm up before long.

"This is just fantastic," Bhavna said. "Oren, stay focused

on the alien, but make sure to keep Jena, Dr Cheung, and Dwain in the shot. Tad, let's go for interview-style here. Ask the doctor to fill the audience in on what they're looking at, etcetera."

When Sidney had discovered the existence of this lab, located two domes away from the central one, powered it up, and snuck off to investigate it, she hadn't been surprised to discover leads bringing her to uncover a lifeform confined in stasis. The more different a species was from humanity – especially if it deviated from their standards of what they thought was pleasing to the eye – the more likely they considered it a monster. This specimen was a symbol of everything the Safekeepers stood for: preventing humans from treating other beings the way they'd treated this one. In retrospect, perhaps she should've tried harder to keep her discovery quiet. But after cataloguing the evidence, she'd been foolish enough to inform Luis, which meant Jena overheard, and she'd tasked the documentary crew to tag along. From the expression on Luis' face, he wasn't thrilled to have them join, either, but Leviathan was footing the bill for this mission, and since Jena represented the Guild, she got what she wanted.

Once again, Sidney would never understand the human need to document experiences via holos. Perhaps it had something to do with how poor their memories were. Empusa never forgot anything, didn't even have a word for it in their language. When you were a species that could change shape, you needed to recall a massive amount of information if you wanted your disguise to truly fool anyone.

"Is it alive?" Jena asked.

"Yes and no," Sidney said. "It's currently in stasis and has been for the last hundred years. This lab has its own power supply, likely to keep our friend here from reanimating. As long as the power isn't shut off, it won't be any threat to us."

Luis looked doubtful, but he said nothing.

Tad cleared his throat. "Dr Cheung, what can you tell us about this alien lifeform?"

Sidney had read through a number of files before finally coming across a reference to this lab, and while she hadn't gone over all the information the previous occupants of this station had gathered about Penumbra's creatures, she knew the basics.

"This lifeform is known, colloquially at least, as a Xeno. Based on the information I've been able to obtain from this station's computer system, these creatures were responsible for the quarantining of PK-L7, as well as the entire system, a century ago. An energy-rich mineral called Xenium was discovered on PK-L7, and early tests suggested that it could be used to create far more powerful and durable jump drives, as Jena confirmed earlier. But when the Galactic Coalition began to mine the mineral, Xenos appeared and savagely attacked. Almost all personnel were killed, and after the few survivors escaped, the Coalition placed a quarantine on PK-L7."

"Is that how the planet came to be called Hellworld?" Tad asked.

"I would assume so. Apparently, something similar happened here on PK-L10. The Coalition surveyed the other planets in the system, hoping to find a world with Xenium but no Xenos. The only planet that contained Xenium – or at least a mineral similar to it – was this one, but it has far less than what was found on PK-L7. Still, there were no signs of Xenos, at least at first, and a mining operation was set up here. They also established laboratories to study Xenos, and we are standing in one of them now. Whether the Xenos were native to this world or brought here from PK-L7, I haven't been able to determine yet. From what I've been able to gather, while Penumbra's Xenos share certain qualities with Hellworld's, such as high aggression and a biological caste system, there are a number of differences. Because of this, they've been catalogued as Neo-Xenos. With a more insect-like appearance than PK-L7's Xenos, they possess blue coloring, similar to that of a native species of insect, although I don't know if there's any link between the two."

So far Luis had taken all this in quietly, but now he spoke. "What kind of Neo-Xeno are we looking at?"

"This is the lowest-ranking caste, equivalent to a drone in an anthill. The scientists at this station dubbed its caste thralls."

"Are you saying that thing is the *weakest* type of Neo-Xeno?" Jena asked.

"Yes," Sidney said. "The other castes are larger and more powerful, and each possesses its own unique strengths. In ascending order, the station's scientists named them thralls, runners, slayers, and ravagers. Devastators are humans who've been transformed into hybrid Neo-Xenos, but information on these is sparse and I don't know anything about their physiology. There may be more types, but those are the only ones I've run across in the records so far."

Luis looked thoughtful, digesting Sidney's words. Dwain

appeared a little green around the gills, while Bhavna and Tad had expressions of terrified awe on their faces. Jena gazed at the Neo-Xeno with naked greed. Oren's expression remained neutral. As a cyborg, he had artificial equivalents of all the facial muscles necessary to produce the full range of human emotions. But the longer someone was a cyborg, the more they lost touch with their humanity. It didn't happen all at once, of course, but one of the first symptoms was a flat affect, which was exactly how Oren looked now. The condition was called *inversion,* and in extreme cases the organic mind turned so far inward that the sufferer became permanently catatonic.

The Empusa had something similar called *kesh'k'dor,* which roughly translated into Coalition standard meant *broken.* It was when an Empusa became locked into a single form – whether their native one or one they'd assumed – and could no longer change shape. Most Empusa who became broken chose to end their own lives rather than be imprisoned in a single form for the rest of their days.

As an Empusan, Sidney was a keen observer of human expression – she needed to be if she expected to pass for one – and while Oren might appear devoid of emotion, she sensed otherwise. A slight narrowing of his eyes, a mild tightening of his lips, his skin tone reddening the merest fraction – all of these things told Sidney that Oren was overwhelmed with rage by the sight of the Neo-Xeno specimen. She wondered why.

"Those spikes look nasty," Luis said.

With the exception of its head, the Neo-Xeno was covered with two-centimeter long spines.

"They are," Sidney said. "Obviously they can cause damage in and of themselves, but like the Neo-Xeno's claws, they secrete a toxin of some kind. I have yet to discover what effect it has."

"What are those strange growths on its body?" Tad asked.

"Mold of some kind. The records are unclear whether it grows naturally on the creatures or if they contract it from their environment somehow. What purpose it serves, if any, is unknown."

"*Xeno* sounds a lot like *Xenium*," Luis said. "Is there any connection between the two? I want to know if any insect monsters are going to pop out of those blue rocks the miners are obtaining before I put any samples of them in the *Kestrel's* hold."

"As I said earlier, the mineral on this planet shares some characteristics with Xenium, but not all. But as for the two root words – Xeno and Xenium – the records I've reviewed so far made no mention of the origin of either name. Nor do they indicate any relationship between them. Besides, it's almost unknown for organic matter to rise naturally from inorganic matter."

"Almost isn't the same as completely," Luis said.

Tad cleared his throat again, as if irritated that the conversation had been continuing without his direction.

"If Neo-Xenos – even lower-caste ones – are as dangerous as you say, how was this one captured?" he asked.

"I have no idea," Sidney admitted. "The body appears undamaged, so I doubt force was used."

Jena spoke then. "One of the mandates of our mission is to return with a Neo-Xeno sample. It looks as if the personnel who originally worked at this station have saved us the trouble of capturing one ourselves. If a portable power source was rigged up so the stasis field wasn't interrupted, could we move the tube and the Neo-Xeno onto the ship?"

Sidney wanted to say it wasn't possible. Now that she had a better idea how dangerous Neo-Xenos were, she didn't want so much as a single Neo-Xeno cell leaving the planet. To humans who held positions of power, *dangerous* meant *useful*, and regardless of whether it was Leviathan, some other Guild, the Galactic Coalition, or simply an independent entrepreneur with a complete lack of scruples, someone would be determined to turn Neo-Xenos into bioweapons of incredible power and ferocity.

For years, there had been rumors that Coalition Command desired to use her people as bioweapons, and while this hadn't yet come to pass, she considered it a real danger. As a member of the Safekeepers, Sidney didn't want Neo-Xenos exploited, but as a being who valued all forms of life, the thought of the creatures being used as weapons made her sick. She doubted it was possible to control the Neo-Xenos, but based on the data collected, if they escaped and increased their numbers, they would decimate the population of any world they were on. Entire planets could become wastelands in a short time.

Just like PK-L7 and Penumbra were.

But Sidney had to play the role she'd assumed, whether she wanted to or not – at least for now. Perhaps later she could free the Neo-Xeno and return it to the wild so the humans couldn't exploit it. But if that proved too difficult, she might be forced to destroy it. She was loath to take life, no matter what kind of life it may be, but if she had to kill one being to safeguard the lives of trillions, then she would, although she'd take no pleasure in it.

"We might be able to adapt the stasis tube to make it portable," she said. "We'd need to consult with Junior, though. He knows far more about the technological side of things than I do."

Jena clapped her hands together in glee. "Excellent!"

"I'll check with Junior," Luis said. "What about weaknesses? Do the Neo-Xenos have any?"

Trust a human to ask how to kill a lifeform before finding out if it was sentient or not.

"From the reports I've read, the original Coalition soldiers were stationed here to protect the scientists and miners, and they had a number of encounters with Neo-Xenos. Their carapaces are tough to penetrate with projectile weapons, especially at a distance. Chainswords do a better job, but you have to get close to use them, which gives a Neo-Xeno ample opportunity to kill you. Explosives work well, but if you're in proximity to the blast, you risk injuring yourself. The best tactic is to shoot them through the eyes and hope the round penetrates their brain."

Oren hadn't spoken the entire time he'd been in the lab, but he did so now, not taking his eyes off the Neo-Xeno specimen.

"What happened to the personnel who were stationed here originally?"

His tone seemed normal, but Sidney detected the tension in his voice. She'd hoped none of them would ask this question. It would solidify the humans' response to these Neo-Xenos being enemies.

"The soldiers were all killed fighting the Neo-Xenos, as were the miners. The final report I found was from the only survivor, one of the scientists. It said simply, 'No rescue coming. I'm going outside.'"

No one said anything as they let Sidney's words sink in.

"OK," Luis said, "let's try not to end up like them. Doctor, stay here and check out the stasis tube, see if you can get a better sense of whether it can be moved or not. Dwain, stay here and keep guarding her. If that thing—" he nodded toward the Neo-Xeno "– so much as blinks, kill it."

"It has no eyelids," Oren said. "How can it blink?"

Everyone looked at him. It was difficult to tell if he was joking, but Sidney thought he wasn't.

Luis continued as if Oren hadn't spoken. "I'll speak to Junior about rigging up a portable power source for the tube… once I check on the miners. We haven't heard anything from them, and after what you just told us, I'm starting to worry." He looked at Jena. "Coming?"

She continued staring at the Neo-Xeno, but then she turned to him and nodded. Together they started toward the door that led back to the research station's central dome.

"Come on," Bhavna said to Tad and Oren. "We need to see what Luis finds out about the miners. I hope something terrible has happened to them!" She looked at Sidney then, as if she'd momentarily forgotten she was there. "Sorry. Sometimes it's hard for me to remember that the stuff we record is real life, you know?"

Sidney did *not* know what the woman was referring to, but she smiled and nodded anyway.

As Bhavna and Tad started to go, Oren said, "I'm going to

stay here for a minute. I want to get footage of the Neo-Xeno from different angles. I'll catch up."

Bhavna frowned, clearly unhappy, but she said, "Don't take too long." Then, she and Tad departed.

When they'd left the dome, Oren focused his gaze on the Neo-Xeno and walked from one side of its tube to the other.

"I know what you are, Sidney."

Sidney's jaw began tingling.

"I see more than normal humans do. A *lot* more."

He finished recording, turned, and walked toward the door. Sidney stared after him, her jaw tingling so badly that it was quickly becoming numb. For her species, this sensation was akin to terror in humans. Had Oren meant to intimate that he knew she wasn't human? Would he share his suspicions with Luis? And if he did, how would the commander react to learning that one of his crew was a shapeshifter who'd been lying about both her identity and her true reason for becoming part of this mission? Not well, she suspected.

"What the hell was *that* about?"

She'd forgotten about Dwain. She turned to her bodyguard and gave him a bemused smile.

"I have no idea. Probably fabricating more drama for his viewers."

Dwain didn't respond. She didn't like the way he looked at her, and she knew Neo-Xenos weren't the only threat she needed to be concerned about now.

FIFTEEN

Oren needed to pass through another dome to return to the station's main one. The power had been turned on so people could see, but the light was unnecessary for him. His cyborg eyes allowed him to see quite well in the dark. He didn't know what function this dome served and wasn't sure he cared. There were workstations along the walls, with round tables and chairs arranged in the middle of the structure, just as in the central dome. While his brain had certain hardware installed that allowed his mind to interface effectively with his robotic body, he didn't possess augmented intelligence or memory. He had no vast storehouse of information to consult to help him determine what this dome had been used for, and really, what did it matter? The people who had once worked here were long dead by now. Humans were made of meat, and eventually meat spoiled – if it wasn't eaten before that.

The sight of the Neo-Xeno in the stasis tube had shaken him badly, not that the others had noticed. Well, the doctor might have. His cyborg eyes were far keener than mere organic ones, and they'd detected numerous differences in

Sidney's body language from that of ordinary humans. Slight differences, to be sure, ones that anyone else wouldn't have noticed, let alone recognized. But not Oren.

Sidney might *pretend* to be human, but he knew she was something else. He'd had his suspicions on the ship, but he hadn't had the opportunity to spend much time around her during the trip to the PK-L system. But now, he was positive. She was an alien. He didn't know what species or why she was posing as human, but it didn't matter. She was a thing, no different than that monster in the tube.

The common attitude in the Coalition was that sentient species were simply variations on the common evolutionary theme of intelligent life. They were all equal, all *people*. But Oren knew better.

He had been five. His parents worked for the Coalition as planetary surveyors, part of a team exploring a newly discovered world in a distant star system. The planet had been given the official designation of XR-G4, but the survey team had taken to calling it the Orchard because rich plant life covered the landmasses. Oren's parents had taken him with them on that job – it had been the first time he'd accompanied them – and he had been thrilled to really travel in space instead of merely visiting worlds in his home system. He was proud of his parents, too, because they did important work. What job could be more important – or more awesome – than exploring a whole world?

The first time he'd set foot on the planet had been a magical moment for him. The sky was bluer than on the planet where his home colony was located, the flora greener. The flowers' colors were breathtaking, and there were so many different hues! His mother told him the botanists on the survey group had to create new names for some of the colors because they didn't exist on any other planet in the Coalition. They eventually named one after him: Oren Red.

The team had been on the planet's surface for less than a week when the monsters attacked. An entire army rushed out of the forest one night and killed every man and woman on the survey team, including his parents. They'd nearly killed him, too, but security officers from the Coalition transport ship in orbit landed and found him – or rather, what was left of him – before he died. They'd put him in stasis, and the Coalition decided to leaven the news about the survey team's deaths by saying that the one child that had accompanied them had survived. The Coalition paid for his android body – an adult-sized one, and hadn't *that* been weird to wake up in? – and for a time he became the face of the single bit of success the Coalition had managed to pull out of what was otherwise a screwed-up bloodbath of a mission.

For a brief time, Oren had been something of a celebrity, and eventually the Upholders contacted him to recruit him. They were a human-centric organization who believed *Homo sapiens* were the pinnacle of evolution, and that it was their right to rule the galaxy. Considering what had happened to his parents, the Upholders' views made sense to Oren. Soon he became a full-fledged member, and in the Upholders, he found a new family, one that still accepted him as human no matter what technological enhancements had been made to his body. His *soul* was human, and that was all that mattered to them.

He whispered the Upholders' slogan to himself, as if it was a comforting mantra, or perhaps a prayer.

"Humanity first. Always."

The attack on Orchard had been over twenty years ago, and Oren still didn't know any details about the things that had killed his parents, other than what he'd seen that night. The Coalition sealed all records pertaining to that mission, and they put the Orchard on the no-travel list, much as they had with PK-L7. The Neo-Xeno in the tube looked different from the creatures that killed the survey team and destroyed his original meat body. It was blue for one thing with insectoid features. But he had no doubt it was the same species. There were too many similarities to ignore, including that disgusting mold caked on its body. On Orchard, he had learned that aliens were monsters, and while ones like Sidney might smile and pretend to be your friend, they were merely waiting for the chance to reveal their true selves.

He was tempted to tell Luis about her, but he decided to wait. He needed proof before he could approach the commander. And if he couldn't get that proof? Then he would be forced to deal with Sidney himself. And if that meant killing her, so be it.

His emotional regulator activated, and suddenly he felt a wave of shame. If Sidney really was an alien in disguise, he had no proof of ill intent toward the others on her part. Was he really contemplating murdering her? What the hell was wrong with him?

Oren believed in the Upholders' mission of humanity first, but he wasn't always comfortable with their methods, especially their use of force. He'd witnessed violence first hand when he saw his mother and father killed by alien monsters, and when those same monsters had ravaged his body and nearly killed him. They were responsible for the life he now lived, an organic brain trapped in a cold, inorganic form. Yet he understood the pain that violence brought – both physical and psychological – and he was reluctant to visit that pain upon any living being. But he also understood that sometimes violence was the only language aliens understood, and when that was the case, you had no choice but to speak it if you wanted to obtain your goals.

Detached as cyborgs were from the experience of physical human existence, they could have difficulty feeling anything at all, or their emotions could start running wild, becoming unpredictable and difficult to control. In the worst cases, the condition was close to a form of madness, and cyborgs needed to make sure their emotional regulators were always in working order.

But could he afford to feel sympathy toward Sidney? What if she'd come on this mission to sabotage it? What if her whole goal had something nefarious to do with these Neo-Xenos? Better to make sure nothing alien left Penumbra.

If he needed to kill her, would he be able to bring himself to do it? Not as long as he still experienced emotion. He might hesitate, and in that moment, Sidney could gut him before he could kill her. What would the Upholders ask of him? The answer was simple.

He couldn't afford the luxury of emotion, and so the best course of action was to deactivate his emotional regulator. Living without emotion would be psychologically damaging long term, but he should be fine for a few days. Long enough to stop Sidney and prevent the Neo-Xenos from leaving the planet. If he survived, he could have his emotional regulator replaced. And if he didn't… well, it wouldn't matter then, would it?

He concentrated and sent a burst of power into his emotional regulator, attempting to overload it. His automatic system defenses kicked in. He fought to override them, continuing to flood the regulator with power. He felt it beginning to shut down, felt something break inside it, and then… it was over. He performed a quick diagnostic, and found that while he'd damaged the regulator, it was still partially functional. He would continue to experience emotions, but erratically, and there would be no way to tell when and how intense they would be. He had no choice but to hope that he could keep his emotions under control while he kept humanity safe. If he couldn't… No use in thinking about that now. He had to work with what he had and hope for the best.

All aliens were monsters of one kind or another, but none of them were as dangerous as the Neo-Xenos. Maybe this was why fate had spared him on Orchard – so he could be here at this place and time to stop the Neo-Xenos from becoming a threat to the entire galaxy. If so, he would die here, and gladly, just so long as he could take the bugs with him when he went.

SIXTEEN

Luis was worried.

He'd known this was a high-risk mission when he and his crew accepted it, but he hadn't known the risk was going to be *this* high. If the Neo-Xenos were even half as dangerous as Dr Cheung made them out to be, his people were going to have their work cut out for them. Yes, his team of skilled professionals could handle themselves in combat situations, but they'd never gone up against anything like Neo-Xenos before – after all, the brethren of these were the damn creatures that kept the Coalition from mining Hellworld's rich deposits of Xenium. Before hearing what Dr Cheung had to say about the Neo Xenos, not to mention seeing one in the stasis tube, Luis' greatest concern was Coalition soldiers arriving before they could get the *Kestrel* flying again. Now, soldiers were the least of his worries.

As soon as he and Jena returned to the central dome – which he'd begun to think of as their base – he tried to contact the miners with his suit's comm. When no one replied, he sat at one of the workstations and routed his signal through the computer to boost it. Still no reply. It might not mean anything, he told himself. The miners might be too far underground to send or receive comm signals, and given Neo-Xenium's massive energy-producing capabilities, the element might be interfering with communication, too.

On the other hand, Neo-Xenos might've torn the miners to shreds. The coldly calculating mercenary part of him knew they needed the miners alive to acquire the Neo-Xenium samples Leviathan wanted. But the part of him that had once been a Coalition soldier – and maybe always would be – wanted to make sure the miners were safe simply because they were people. More so, they were members of his crew, at least for this mission, and that meant he was responsible for them. He should've allocated more resources for them.

He couldn't stay here any longer. He had to get out of this damn dome.

He'd left his helmet on the floor by the workstation, and he picked it up and stood. He carried it at his side as he walked over to Jena. Once they'd returned to the dome, she'd removed her EVA suit – which Luis considered a huge mistake – and sat at one of the tables, talking with Bhavna, Tad, and Oren. All of them looked toward him as he approached.

"I'm going out to talk to Junior and see how the repairs on the stabilizer are going," he said. He didn't want to share his concern about the miners, not yet. No need to make them any more worried.

"Do you think we'll be able to get the Neo-Xeno on the ship?" Jena asked.

"I don't know, but if it's possible, Junior can do it." He didn't like the idea of taking a living creature aboard the

Kestrel, but if Malik thought they could get the tube's stasis field to hold, it might be doable.

"Very good. And how are the Neo-Xenium samples coming? The miners have been at work for a while now. Have they given us a progress report?"

He wished she hadn't asked. "Not yet. I don't expect we'll hear from them until they have a full load to bring back."

"Odds are they're all dead." Oren's voice was flat and emotionless.

Everyone looked at him, shocked.

He shrugged. "You were all thinking the same thing. If there are Neo-Xenos in the vicinity–"

Luis interrupted. "There's a saying in the military: 'Don't count casualties until they're confirmed'. I intend to proceed on the assumption that there *are* Neo-Xenos around, but as of this moment, none have been sighted, and we have no evidence to believe that anything bad has happened to the miners."

"But we don't have any evidence it hasn't, either," Oren said.

Luis felt like decking the kid, but he knew he'd only break his hand on the cyborg's metal jaw. He directed his attention to Jena.

"No wonder Leviathan was willing to risk an illegal mission to this system. Penumbra has two big prizes – Neo-Xenium *and* Neo-Xenos. A lot of money to be made there."

Jena slowly smiled. "Tons and tons."

"You should've told us about the Neo-Xenos," Luis said, voicing the anger that had been stirring inside him. "It would've changed our approach to this mission."

"How so?"

"For one thing, I would've insisted you bring more personnel and *hell* of a lot more weapons."

"Are you telling me you and your team can't handle this job on your own, with the tools you've been given?"

"I'm telling you that holding back intel from your people in the field is one of the surest ways to sabotage your own mission."

"I think you're forgetting that as Leviathan's representative on this mission, *I* am in charge. You'll do what I say when I say it."

"You *were* in charge, but once the Neo-Xenos showed up and tried to slaughter us, everything changed. This isn't about profit anymore. This is about survival. I'm not about to let some Guild functionary with no battle experience call the shots. If you want to live, you'll shut up and do what I say. If you don't like it, you know where the door is. Maybe you'll have better luck with the Neo-Xenos if you negotiate with them personally."

He turned and started toward the dome's exit.

"Hold up a moment, *commander*," Jena said, a sneer in her voice. "Give my holo crew a chance to get their helmets on. They're going to accompany you."

While Bhavna, Tad, and Oren retrieved their helmets, Luis took the opportunity to don his. He locked it into place, and as his oxygen unit activated, a realization struck him. He turned back to Jena.

"Leviathan didn't send them to record the mission for PR purposes. They're really here to capture images of Neo-Xenos in action that you can show to potential buyers.

They'll be so excited at the prospect of owning such deadly bioweapons, they'll pay any price you want."

Jena smiled, but she didn't respond.

There were a lot of things Luis wanted to say to her, but he knew none of them would have any effect. She was the boss, and he was the employee, and bosses always got what they wanted.

He turned and headed for the door, Jena's walking holo studio following close behind him.

Jena watched Luis leave and shook her head. She was determined to make this mission a success, no matter what. After all, she'd been raised as a Guild brat. Her mother and father had been midlevel managers in the Water Guild, and when she was old enough, Jena had joined them in the Guild's service. She proved far more adept than either of her parents at Guild politics, and she was colder and more calculating in her business decisions than both her parents combined.

She rose swiftly through the Guild ranks, ruining the careers of anyone who stood in her way. She'd heard that a new Guild – one that intended to replace all the others – was coming into power, and she kept track of it, watching as it extended its reach further into the galaxy. Leviathan, it was called, and its monstrous ambition appealed to her. When she contacted them, she demanded – not requested – an interview.

She was a perfect fit and left the Water Guild for her new career. Leviathan's personnel matched her cunning and conniving ways, so advancement proved to be slower than it had been in the Water Guild, but she thrived on the challenge.

Now, she had risen to a position roughly commensurate with what her parents held in the Water Guild – a midlevel manager – and she found herself stuck. Determined to do whatever it took to continue her ascent in the Guild hierarchy, when she got wind Leviathan was planning a clandestine mission to the PK-L system, she fought to be assigned command of it. She'd had to call in every favor, use every secret to blackmail the right people, but in the end, she'd succeeded. She'd been elated. She'd known if she could pull off the mission successfully, she could write her own ticket at Leviathan.

But the mission had started to go downhill before they'd even reached Penumbra, thanks to those damned Coalition soldiers – and Leviathan's lousy sensor-cloaking tech. It made her wonder if someone else in Leviathan had it in for her. After they'd crash landed, she thought she'd still be able to pull off the mission. All she had to do was make sure the *Kestrel* was repaired and that they left with some Neo-Xenium and at least one Neo-Xeno bio-sample. But somewhere along the line, she'd lost control of the mission. *That's what you get for hiring freelancers.* The mercenaries were concerned only with profit. She understood that, even respected it, but they had no loyalty to Leviathan to get the job done.

No matter. She wasn't about to let anyone screw up her chance to rise in Leviathan's ranks, even if that meant she had to kill every last mercenary and soldier herself.

SEVENTEEN

Luis noticed four things as he approached the *Kestrel*.

One, Junior and Lashell had adjusted the landing gear to compensate for the uneven terrain, and the caravel now sat evenly on the ground, making it easier to work on. Good.

Two, both Junior and Lashell stood on top of the ship, but instead of tools they held weapons – a heavy shotgun in Junior's case and an SMG in Lashell's – pointed in the same direction, away from the domes. Great.

Third, Sirena and Bernadine, who stood on the ground, had their weapons in firing position as well, and aimed in the same direction as their crewmates. Sirena had a light machine gun, as did Bernadine. Suspicious.

Four of his people had their weapons trained, not on a ravening horde of oncoming Neo-Xenos, but on three beings in armored EVA suits standing thirty meters from the *Kestrel*. From this distance, he couldn't tell if they were human, but they *were* bipedal, and armed with light, heavy, and assault machine guns. Two carried cattle prods, while the one with the heavy machine gun held a chainsword as well. Luis couldn't make out their facial features through their faceplates, but he had no trouble seeing the insignia of the Coalition military emblazoned on the shoulders of their armor. There was one other important detail: all three of the soldiers held their weapons at their sides.

"Talk to me, Sirena," he commanded over comms.

"They say they're the crew of the frigate that damaged our ship. Their craft is wrecked and beyond repair – or so they claim."

"What are they doing here?"

"They say they want to talk. I told them to put their weapons on the ground, but they refused."

"Did they say why?"

An unfamiliar voice came over Luis' comm then. Most likely the Coalition's commander.

"If you'd seen the goddamned monsters running around out there, you wouldn't put down your weapons either."

Fair point, Luis thought. He asked, "Why should I trust you? You're Coalition, and we're lawbreakers. It's your duty to take us into custody. If we don't go with you peacefully – and trust me, we won't – you're authorized to execute us on the spot. Of course, you're seriously outnumbered. If you start shooting, it won't end well for the three of you."

"You don't have any reason to trust us," the commander admitted. "But by the same token, we don't have any reason to trust you. But it's not a matter of trust. Our ship is damaged, and so is yours, and there are hostile lifeforms on this planet which have already killed some of your people and one of mine. Right now, it's a matter of survival for both sides."

Luis felt sick, knowing now that the mining expedition had

been a failure. He considered the Coalition commander's argument.

"I'll talk to you. You put your weapons on the ground. I'll do the same with mine. Our people will keep theirs, and if either of us tries something cute, they can all start blasting. Deal?"

No hesitation. "Deal."

The woman, who he assumed was the soldiers' commander – most likely a captain – put her gun and cattle prod on the ground.

"I'd tell you this was a bad idea," Sirena said to him, "but you wouldn't listen to me anyway."

"Correct."

Luis' weapons – an assault shotgun and reaver sword – were still affixed to his magbelt. He pulled them off one at a time and placed them on the ground.

Bhavna's voice came over his comm.

"This is awesome! Oren, make sure you stay focused on Luis and magnify the view, make it look like you're right beside him. Tad, make your narration real dramatic, this is like an ancient Wild West showdown, all right?"

"You got it." Tad cleared his throat. "Two enemies prepare to parley on what may soon become a blood-soaked field of battle. The commanders of each side may have relinquished their weapons, but there are still plenty of guns in play. Will–"

"For hell's sake!" Luis snapped. "Can the three of you switch to a different channel?"

"What was *that*?" the Coalition commander asked.

Luis sighed. "You wouldn't believe me if I told you."

•••

"I was afraid something like that would happen."

The man – Luis – closed his eyes and lowered his head. He looked tired. Aisha knew exactly how he felt. "I should've sent someone along with the miners to guard them," he whispered.

"From what you've told me, you had no idea how dangerous these Neo-Xenos were. And if you *had* sent guards, they'd have died too. There were just too damn many of the things."

"You're probably right. But still..."

The two commanders stood out in the open as they talked, but Luis' people no longer had their weapons trained on the Coalition members. Now, they all kept watch for Neo-Xenos. After the first few minutes of conversation, Aisha and Luis had decided that, given the severity of the threat posed by the Neo-Xenos, it was foolish for either of them to remain unarmed while their people stood guard, so they'd retrieved their weapons and held them at the ready. As they spoke, they continuously swept their gazes back and forth, keeping an eye out for any hint of Neo-Xeno activity.

Aisha suspected Luis might be former military. There was something in his bearing that spoke of more self-discipline than she expected in a mercenary. Then again, it wasn't as if she got up close and personal with soldiers of fortune on a regular basis, so what did she know?

"Is the one with the chainsword an android?" Luis asked. "I can't make out his facial features from here."

"Yes. His name's Jason. What tipped you off if you couldn't get a good look at him?"

"Androids are still as statues until they move, and when they do, there's a precision and fluidity to their motions."

"What about your holographer? He moves like Jason. Is he an android, too?"

"Cyborg," Luis said.

Aisha had noticed the holographer sneaking occasional glances at Jason. At first, she thought it might be a case of one android recognizing another, maybe the two of them even chatting via some cybersignal she was unaware of. She supposed they were like different branches of the same species in a way. She'd served alongside both androids and cyborgs in her career, and weirdly, it was the androids who seemed more human.

"I'm sorry about your miners," Aisha said.

"I'm sorry about your loss. What was her name again?"

"Lazara."

"And you think the mold the Neo-Xenos carry is what changed her and Malik into, well, whatever it was they turned into?"

"It's just a theory, but it's our best guess."

"Great. So not only do we have to worry about the Neo-Xenos killing us, they can turn us into monsters too if we're not careful. This must have been the devastators Dr Cheung spoke about."

"Which is why I think we should call a truce and work together for as long as we're stuck on this planet."

"And what happens when we're finally off world again? You try to arrest us?"

"No. You go your way, we go ours. I'll have to report what Leviathan did here, but I'll keep your names out of it."

"We've broken some serious Coalition laws by coming to this planet," Luis said, "and you expect us to believe that when this is all over and done with, you're going to turn your back on your duty and let us go? Assuming any of us survive, of course."

"I've given you my word. What else can I do? I don't blame you for being skeptical. Hell, if I were you, I would be too. For the time being, why don't we concentrate on dealing with the Neo-Xenos, and if we do live through this, we can sort out our situation later?"

Luis studied her before he responded. "Just so we're clear – we're going to keep a close eye on you, and if it so much as *looks* like you're going to screw us, we'll kill you."

"Same for me and my crew."

"You're outnumbered. You can't defeat us."

"Maybe so, but how many of your people do you think we can take with us when we go down?"

Neither of them spoke after that. Finally, Luis broke the silence.

"You don't seem like the type to falsify reports to Command."

"I wasn't, until I saw what the Neo-Xenos in that cave could do. I have to protect my crew. If that means working with people like you, then so be it." She paused. "You don't seriously plan to take any bio samples of the things back to Leviathan, do you?"

She hoped he'd answer honestly. The stakes were too high for either of them to lie.

"No. And at this point, it looks like we're not going to have any Neo-Xenium to bring back, either. We've found some records left by the research station's staff and we'll take them to Leviathan. They'll have to be satisfied with that. My reputation as a mercenary will take a hit, but I'll have to live with that."

She was fairly certain now that he was ex-military, and he still had a lot of years left in him before he reached mandatory retirement age. She wondered why he'd left the service and taken up life as a warrior-for-hire. She wouldn't ask him, though. It was none of her business.

"How about my people – I mean, Sal and me, since Jason doesn't breathe – go into the station and resupply our O_2. Then we can come back out and help guard your ship while..."

"Junior and Lashell," Luis supplied.

"Junior and Lashell finish repairing the stabilizer. Jason could help them, if you like. He served as the *Stalwart's* engineer, and if he could keep that piece of crap running, he surely can get the *Kestrel* going again."

Luis offered her a small smile. "That sounds good. Give me a few minutes to talk to my people and sell them on the idea of a truce. They don't exactly have a lot of trust in the Coalition, especially Command, but I think I can convince them to go along with it."

"Sounds good. I'll tell Jason and Sal what we–"

Aisha broke off when she saw a mound of soil bulge upward behind Luis.

"Behind you!" she shouted.

Luis spun around, and Aisha stepped to the side, so she had a clear line of fire. A Neo-Xeno burst out of the ground and lunged toward them, clawed hands stretching outward.

Aisha and Luis fired simultaneously, and the Neo-Xeno's head disappeared in a shower of blue ichor and carapace fragments. The headless body swiped at them one last time, but they stepped aside to avoid its claws, and it fell to the ground and died.

"Jesus," Luis breathed.

At the sound of more gunfire, Aisha turned to see that other Neo-Xenos had emerged from the ground and were attacking the mercenaries and soldiers. The two mercenaries on top of the *Kestrel* – Junior and Lashell – stood back-to-back, firing upon Neo-Xenos clambering up the sides of the starship. The creatures coming at them were leaner than the one she and Luis had killed, more agile and swift, and the mercenaries were hard-pressed to fight them off. Sirena and Bernadine stood on the ground – Sirena on the port side of the *Kestrel*, Bernadine on the starboard – and they blasted away at the Neo-Xenos attempting to get on top of the ship. Some of the creatures leaped off the craft to attack them, but the women cut them down in midair.

"We're under attack by Neo-Xenos!" Luis shouted over the open comm channel. "Dwain, Assunta, stay at your posts. I'll call you if we need you."

Aisha wasn't sure who Luis was talking to, but she assumed it was personnel who remained in the central dome. She shouted over the comm then.

"Go for the eyes! And don't get any of that mold on you!"

Jason and Sal had their own Neo-Xenos to worry about. They were surrounded by a group of creatures similar to the one she and Luis had killed. They were stockier, slower, but stronger than the ones assaulting the *Kestrel*, and equally as vicious. Jason and Sal stood back-to-back, moving in a tight circle as they fired their weapons, cutting down one Neo-Xeno after another. But for each one that fell, another emerged from freshly dug holes in the ground. Aisha didn't know how long her crew could hold out against the waves of monsters. At the rate they were firing, they would be out of ammo soon.

The holo crew stood off to the side, the cyborg moving his head back and forth as he recorded the action taking place around him, camera eye glowing green. None of the Neo-Xenos made a move toward the three, and Aisha wondered if the creatures could sense that they posed no immediate threat to them. The Neo-Xenos almost seemed drawn to the loud gunfire.

"Aisha!" Luis shouted.

Another Neo-Xeno emerged from the hole nearby, and Aisha turned to help Luis blow it away. More came after that, and she stopped thinking and fell back upon her training and experience, in a way becoming as much of a machine as Jason or Oren, spraying rounds from her machine gun, as dead Neo-Xenos piled up around them. At one point she pulled her cattle prod from her magbelt and wielded it with her left hand while she continued firing with her right. Luis drew his reaver sword and swung it in deadly arcs as he continued blasting away with his shotgun. Before long, both of their EVA suits were covered with blue Neo-Xeno blood, and Aisha had enough on her faceplate that it was difficult to see. In other circumstances, she would've spared a second to wipe it off, but the Neo-Xenos kept coming. If she stopped fighting – even for an instant – she'd knew she'd be dead.

"We can't keep this up much longer!" she shouted. "We should retreat to the station!"

"They'd slaughter us before we could get inside," Luis said. "We should have everyone get in a circle and fight back-to-back."

"No way! That'll just make us a bigger and easier target for the goddamn things!"

Bernadine's voice came over the comm system then. "No! Let go of me, you bastard!"

Then she cried out, more in frustration than fear, Aisha thought. After that, the woman was silent. Aisha couldn't see Bernadine from her current angle, but she feared the worst.

She *could* see the holo crew, though. While the Neo-Xenos left them untouched, Tad broke away from his companions and started running toward the research station's central dome. She'd seen new recruits do this during combat sims. They panicked, forgot their training, and fled, obeying animal instincts telling them they needed to get *away*, wherever away was. And Tad was a civilian; he had no military training to fall back on. At least the poor sonofabitch was running in the right direction.

Unfortunately, he passed within arm's reach of one of the thicker-limbed Neo-Xenos, and the creature – perhaps attracted by the man's movement – swiped out with its claws and laid open his gut. Tad screamed and managed to run several more steps before his intestines spilled out in a slick, bloody mass. One loop wrapped around his foot, and he tripped and went sprawling. The Neo-Xeno that had disemboweled him leaped onto his back and with several swift claw swipes tore the man to shreds.

It was too late to help Tad, but Aisha swiveled her machine gun in the Neo-Xeno's direction. Its head exploded in a geyser of blue. Its body fell onto Tad's, twitched several times, then went still.

Aisha stood for a moment, stunned. She'd never seen anything so horrific.

Junior and Lashell managed to keep the Neo-Xenos from climbing on top of the *Kestrel* up to this point, but one of the leaner ones got past their fire and lunged toward Lashell. Junior fired his shotgun at the creature and blasted its head off. The creature fell, slid a meter toward Lashell, then was still.

"On your six!" Lashell shouted.

Junior spun in time to see another Neo-Xeno coming at him. He tried to fire his shotgun, but the weapon clicked empty. He flipped it around, gripped it by the barrel, and swung it like a club. There was a satisfyingly loud *crack*, and the Neo-Xeno staggered backward, blue blood leaking from a newly made fissure in its head.

Come on, Aisha thought. Finish the bastard off.

Junior stood between the Neo-Xeno and Lashell, but the woman couldn't get a clear shot. She started to maneuver herself into a better position, but when another Neo-Xeno made it onto the roof, she turned and fired on it. Junior wasn't defenseless, though. He dropped the shotgun and pulled a heavy cutter off his magbelt. The Neo-Xeno he'd struck was stunned, and Junior stepped forward to kill the alien monster before it attacked again.

But as he swung the cutter, the Neo-Xeno ducked and lunged at him. Junior had been so caught up in the battle, that he hadn't noticed the Neo-Xeno had been standing in front of the damaged stabilizer. The cutter slammed into it the same instant the Neo-Xeno struck Junior, and the device exploded in a shower of components. The Neo-Xeno knocked Junior onto the ship, climbed on top of him, and clawed wildly at his faceplate. Lashell screamed in frustration. She was too busy dealing with yet another Neo-Xeno who'd climbed onto the roof and couldn't aid him.

"Cover me!" Aisha shouted to Luis, then she aimed her machine gun at the Neo-Xeno attacking Junior and fired. Rounds of ammo shot toward the creature and its head jerked back as the bullets hit home. Aisha fired until the Neo-Xeno's head was obliterated, but its body wasn't dead, yet. With the last ounce of life remaining to it, the body slammed a hand onto Junior's faceplate. This time the layer of clear plasteel shattered and the Neo-Xeno's claws sank into Junior's face. The man's scream was brief, before the headless Neo-Xeno slumped forward onto Junior, alien and human both dead.

Then, as if heeding some unknown signal, the Neo-Xenos began to withdraw. They ran toward the holes they'd emerged from, and while the soldiers and mercenaries continued firing as they retreated, they made no move to defend themselves. A number died escaping, but others scurried down the holes and were gone.

"Cease fire!" Luis called. "Don't waste your ammo!"

Everyone listened to him, the soldiers included, although they kept their weapons up, alert for any sign that the Neo-Xenos might return. Aisha wiped enough blood off her faceplate to see, then she scanned the area to take stock of the situation.

Neo-Xeno bodies were scattered all around the area, with the greatest number lying around the *Kestrel*. The caravel was covered in Neo-Xeno blood, and the soldiers' and mercenaries' EVA suits, hers included, were splattered with the blue muck. Lashell still remained atop the *Kestrel*, standing over Junior's body and weeping. Sirena stood on the ground next to the ship, seemingly uninjured. Sal sat on the ground with Jason beside him, placing a breach seal on the man's right leg. The android gave her a thumbs-up, indicating that Sal hadn't been contaminated by Neo-Xeno mold. The other holographic team, Bhavna, as Luis had told her, wept, her arms wrapped around the cyborg, Oren, for support. The cyborg held her stiffly, and Aisha wondered what, if anything, he felt about the death of his colleague.

She turned to Luis. "You hurt?"

He shook his head. "You?"

"I'm good."

"Junior's gone. I don't see Bernadine," he said.

"Me neither."

"Her weapons are lying on the ground, though."

"Think the Neo-Xenos took her?"

Luis paused. "Yeah."

They walked to one of the holes where the Neo-Xeno that had first attacked them emerged, their weapons up and ready to fire if any of the bastard's friends decided to return for more carnage. The hole was gone, though.

"They filled it in behind them as they retreated," Luis observed.

"That's what it looks like. Bet the others are filled in too."

"Bet you're right."

They lowered their weapons and looked at each other, a bit at a loss.

"Why do you think they took Bernadine?" Aisha asked.

"I don't know, but whatever it is, it can't be good."

"Want to mount a rescue mission? I'll go with you."

Luis sighed. "I appreciate the offer, but where would we look?"

"Maybe the Neo-Xenos have a main nest somewhere. They could be taking Bernadine there."

"Maybe, but we can't follow them into their tunnels. They probably filled them in behind them as they went. Even if they'd didn't, we'd be at a massive disadvantage if they attacked us on their home ground. And if we *did* manage to locate their nest, we are woefully unprepared to take on an army of them. We'd need a strategy, and a hell of a lot more firepower than we have. As much as I want to save Bernadine, if we went after her right now, it would be a suicide mission."

Aisha didn't disagree with him, but she wondered what his people would think of his logic. He hadn't switched to a private channel as they spoke, and she knew the other mercenaries had heard him.

"Come on," he said. "We should all get inside before those things come back. We need to figure out what the hell we're going to do now."

"Sounds like a plan," Aisha said. They each gave the order to their respective people, and all headed back to the central dome.

Bhavna ran – or rather shuffle-hopped in her EVA suit – to Aisha's side.

"What about Tad? We can't just leave him out here!"

Aisha turned to the woman and saw the pain on her tear-streaked face. Her heart went out to her, but there was nothing she could say to make her feel better.

"We have to leave him, at least for now. He's dead, and we're alive, and every second we remain exposed, we're under threat of another attack. We need to get inside, refresh our suits' O_2, and reload our weapons. Once we've figured out how we're going to survive, then we can worry about taking care of our dead."

Fresh tears flowed from Bhavna's eyes. "You're a monster, do you know that?"

"Maybe," Aisha said, wondering why Bhavna had approached her and not Luis. "But there are bigger and meaner ones than me on this planet, and if we don't get tough fast, we're all going to end up like Tad."

Bhavna opened her mouth, and Aisha thought the woman was going to yell some more, but instead she nodded and turned back to rejoin Oren.

Aisha took in the carnage around them, her heart heavy. "That was a rough one," she said.

"Sure was," Luis agreed. "Nothing they teach in basic training can prepare you for something like that, huh?"

"Not even close."

They resumed walking toward the dome.

EIGHTEEN

Bernadine fought like hell to escape the Neo-Xeno, but the creature held her too tight. When they'd grabbed her on the surface, they'd knocked her weapons out of her hands, and she wished to God she had them now. That way, she could at least kill a few of the damn things before they did whatever they were going to do to her.

The tunnel they carried her through was cramped, but their bodies were far more flexible than humans, and they navigated the constrained space with no problem. As bad as it was to be captured by killer space bugs – and no mistake about it, it was *bad* – she hated being in the tunnel just as much, if not more. She'd suffered from claustrophobia all her life, to the point where she wasn't exactly comfortable in starships, given their efficient use of space.

She'd never told anyone about her fear, though. A big bad merc like her, afraid of being cooped up in a small space? She'd be teased mercilessly. She couldn't see anything in the tunnel, but she could feel her EVA suit scrape the narrow sides as they traveled. When this happened, she let out a sharp, startled cry, and was glad no one else was around to hear it. No one human, anyway.

She tried calling on her comm for help, but no reply came. She assumed she was too far underground for the signal to get through, but she continued trying, just in case.

It felt like the Neo-Xenos carried her for hours, but the display on the inside of her faceplate said only twenty minutes had passed since she'd been taken. She wondered how the others had fared against the Neo-Xenos back at the ship. Had any of them died in the battle? Had anyone else been taken as she had? She wondered if she would live long enough to find out.

Eventually the tunnel widened, and she became aware of a faint blue light. She thrashed back and forth, trying to twist herself free from the Neo-Xenos' grip, but it was no use. The creatures were simply too strong. The light grew brighter, and while it was still somewhat dim, it was enough to see by. She had a sense that they were nearing their destination, and that whatever it was, it was larger than this tunnel. She was relieved at the prospect of having more space around her, but she dreaded what might await her up ahead.

She was right to be afraid.

The Neo-Xenos that had her – one holding her feet, one holding her arms behind her head – carried her out of the tunnel and into a cave. The same blue mold that encrusted the Neo-Xenos' bodies in scattered patches covered the entire chamber, and its glow illuminated everything within.

Like Luis, she was former military, and when she'd been a raw recruit in basic training her sergeant once told her squad that fighting at night was ten times worse than fighting during the day. *Sure, in daylight, the enemy can see you, but you can see them too. You know who's firing at you, and you know what to fire at. But at night, you can't see shit, and if it's dark enough – I mean dark as the bottom of a goddamned ocean – you could be facing anything, and it could be only centimeters in front of you, and you wouldn't know it.* Now, in this cave, looking upon the giant monstrosity that filled most of the space, Bernadine knew her sarge didn't know what the hell she was talking about. Bernadine would have given anything for it to be dark, because sometimes seeing was far, far worse.

A gigantic mold-covered orb rested in the center of the cave. Neo-Xenos – dozens upon dozens of them – clustered around it or clung to its surface, so many she could barely see the creature beneath. She recognized the two types of Neo-Xenos that had attacked them by the *Kestrel,* but there were two other kinds, larger in form but less numerous than the others.

One type seemed twice the size of the smaller ones, more thick-limbed, and the spines that covered its body were more like thick spikes. The other was larger still, also thick-limbed, but it possessed four arms, and instead of spines, its body was covered with mold, making it seem as if it had been sculpted out of the stuff. The mold on the big ones seethed and bubbled, as if it were animate and possessed a life and will of its own.

The gigantic orb split horizontally in the middle, and as the gap widened Bernadine was horrified to realize she was looking at a single massive eye, and what was worse, it wasn't an insectoid eye – it resembled a human's, the iris the same blue color as the mold covering its outer surface. The huge black pupil widened, and she could feel the weight of the thing's monstrous gaze on her.

The two Neo-Xenos which had hold of her carried her closer to the eye. They put her on her feet, and then one of them moved away while the other wrapped its spine-covered arms around her and pulled her back against the spines on its chest. The message was clear: if she struggled again, the Neo-Xeno would press her against its chest and skewer her. She resolved to remain as still as an android.

For a long time, nothing happened. The Neo-Xeno that held her captive remained as motionless as she did. The other Neo-Xenos in the chamber, from the smallest to the largest, were equally still, as if they all waited for something to occur. She wanted to turn away from the eye's horrible unblinking scrutiny, wanted to close her own eyes and break off contact with the thing, but she couldn't do either. It was as if the eye projected some kind of psychic force that prevented her from resisting it. That, or it was simply her own terrified fascination which made her unable to look away.

Finally, the great eye blinked, the motion so unexpected that it startled her. As if it was a signal, the Neo-Xeno holding her spread its arms. At first, she thought it was letting her go. But then it started slashing its claws into the back of her EVA suit. It took a fair amount of force for the Neo-Xeno to cut through the suit's armor, but eventually it did so, and she screamed as its claws raked her flesh.

She knew at that moment that she was going to die.

Her body tried to draw in air, but the tunnel's atmosphere couldn't nourish her lungs, and they began to ache, starving for oxygen. She glared at the eye, and although she had no idea if it was intelligent or had access to her thoughts, she sent it a mental message. *I hope Luis and the others kill every last one of you bastards!*

Did the eye's pupil narrow slightly? She couldn't tell.

The Neo-Xeno didn't dig its claws any further into her flesh, though. Instead, now that her EVA suit was open in the back, the creature took hold of the edges and pulled them apart. It tore the rest of the suit off her and tossed the pieces aside. Frigid air slammed into her like a thousand ice hammers, and she shivered uncontrollably. She supposed she could now add freezing to death to the list of ways she might die here.

The eye closed its moss-covered lid, as if her audience with the terrible thing was over. One of the larger Neo-Xenos stepped toward her. It grabbed her by the upper arm, lifted her, and then hurled her toward the eye as easily as if she were a child's toy. She smacked into the lid, but rather than bouncing off, she stuck fast. Everywhere her bare flesh touched the mold she experienced a searing pain, as if she was being burned alive. She took in a deep breath of the atmosphere, and while the carbon dioxide gas didn't feed her lungs, it still allowed her to scream.

The pain grew more intense. She had the sensation that she was sinking into the eye, that her substance merged with it, and as this went on, she felt tendrils of thought coiling their way into her mind, sifting through her memories, taking what was needed, discarding the rest. And then, when the pain had become so intense that she lost all sense of self, had become nothing but a nervous system in agony, it vanished.

But the pain didn't just end – it was replaced by an ecstasy beyond anything she could have ever imagined. She'd never been a religious person, had never subscribed to the idea of a transcendent afterlife, but if she had been, she would have felt as if she was on the verge of entering paradise. She would've smiled if she still had lips.

Then the mold absorbed the last of her and she was gone.

The Summoner pondered what it had learned from the human woman as it added her substance to its own, just as it had done with the surviving members of the humans that had originally inhabited the planet's research station. Those humans, long gone, had been brought into the presence of their new master by the Summoner's children and granted the great honor of becoming one with it so they could add to its storehouse of knowledge, just as Bernadine had now done.

Thanks to her, the Summoner now knew *two* ships had landed on Penumbra, but only one was salvageable. That was all right, though. It only needed one. Yes, the craft needed repair, but the humans believed that they could fix it with minimal difficulty, and the Summoner would allow them to complete this task.

It couldn't, however, leave them alone entirely.

From the Neo-Xenos' encounters with the humans, along with the memories it had extracted from the one called Bernadine, the Summoner knew that these were formidable foes, well trained in the art of dealing death. They were stubborn, too, and would not relinquish their ship without a fight. If the Summoner wished to gain control of... it consulted Bernadine's memories... the *Kestrel*, it needed to reduce their numbers drastically. Only a few humans were necessary to pilot the ship, perhaps only one, depending on who the Summoner selected.

The mold was the key to the Summoner's connection with its children, as well as how it had absorbed the human woman's body and gained her memories. Through the mold, all things were possible. The Summoner could sense the presence of some within one of the domes that had been built by the first humans to visit this world. The mold clung to the body of one of its children that had been taken captive and placed within a stasis tube. The child might not be conscious, but the mold was. It had remained in stasis with its host, waiting through the long years, biding its time, and now the Summoner was ready to make use of it.

The Summoner considered its plan, found it good, and ordered its children to go forth and carry out its will. It sent the ones which had recently been grown as well, and when they had left, only a handful of children remained behind to attend it. The Summoner was well protected in its den, so a small group would suffice for its needs. Still, it would continue to produce more children. There had been casualties in the battle with the humans, and there would undoubtedly be more. The Summoner would need as many children as it could create in order to claim its rightful place among the stars.

Most, if not all, of those children would end up sacrificing their lives so their master could achieve its destiny, and they would do so with joyous hearts – at least as joyous as semi-sentient creatures were capable of being. A century of waiting would soon be over, and as new Neo-Xenos rose from the mold covering its body, the Summoner thought about what the galaxy would be like when it was master of all, and another memory of Bernadine's supplied a name for its dominion to come.

Heaven.

NINETEEN

Sidney was reviewing the data the station's research team had gathered on the captive Neo-Xeno when Luis' voice came over her suit's comm.

"Everyone to the central dome. We need to talk."

Despite her real mission, Sidney was glad to hear the man's voice. For the last few minutes they'd been listening to the sound of weapons fire coming from outside. Listening to the team battle Neo-Xenos had been agony for Dwain, who'd wanted to assist his comrades, but Luis had ordered him and Assunta to remain in the domes as protection for Sidney and Jena. Now that the battle was over, Dwain seemed relieved.

"You heard the boss," he said. "Come on."

"You go on ahead. I need a few minutes to finish going through this data. It may help us fight the Neo-Xenos."

It looked for a moment like Dwain might protest, but then he nodded and walked off. When he'd exited the dome, Sidney bowed her head over the computer console. She knew the humans had only been defending themselves from attack, but had they even attempted to communicate with the Neo-Xenos? Had they once considered what the situation might look like from their point of view? Of course not, and how many Neo-Xenos and humans had died because of this shortsightedness? Such a waste.

Sidney believed in the Safekeeper mission with all her heart. Humans had an innate tendency to claim and use whatever resources they found in their environment, a legacy from their origins as tool-using hominids. If an object was in reach, they grabbed hold of it and found a use for it. And once they had it in their possession, they would fight and kill to keep it for themselves and for their tribe – another legacy of their primitive origins.

That's what had happened when humans first encountered her people well over a century ago. At first, they viewed the Empusa as shapeshifting monsters, little more than animals. But humans soon realized that if they could exploit the Empusa's ability to change forms – whether by enslaving them or duplicating their abilities – they would have a formidable weapon. Many Empusa were captured and experimented on, but it was not a simple thing to keep shape changers imprisoned – especially when they were intelligent – and some managed to escape. They masqueraded as humans, learned their ways, mastered their technology, and acquired starships. They returned to the Empusan homeworld and evacuated the rest of their people. Thus, the Empusa moved out into the galaxy and hid among humans.

Eventually, humans recognized the Empusa as sentient beings and laws were made forbidding their exploitation. The Empusa were invited to join the Coalition as full-fledged members – at least on paper. In reality, the races of the Coalition didn't trust the shapeshifters, and the Empusa's relationship with the galaxy's other sentients was rocky at best. There were rumors that clandestine experiments on Empusa still continued to this day, and Sidney feared they were true. Because of how the humans had attempted to use the Empusa, her people created the Safekeepers, and over time, members of other races joined, and in many ways, the organization became the peaceful multicultural force that the Coalition pretended to be.

But despite the history between the Empusa and humans, Sidney didn't hate their species. In her time posing as one of them, she'd gotten to know them well – from the inside out, you might say – and she knew them capable of heeding what they sometimes called their better angels. They could demonstrate honor, compassion, loyalty, mercy, self-sacrifice, love…

The Safekeepers operated in secret, and while she acknowledged the practicality of this, she also understood that it was based in deceit. How could humans and the other races in the Coalition ever come to trust her people if they kept themselves hidden and operated in the shadows? They couldn't, and sometimes Sidney thought the Safekeepers should approach the Coalition openly, try to convince them to join forces to preserve the galaxy's native species.

But then there were times like now, when humans encountered a species even more bloodthirsty and ruthless than they were, and the humans' first response was to kill and keep killing. Sidney wondered if humans would ever be able to leave the savagery of their animal ancestry behind, or if it would follow them forever, eventually despoiling everything they met.

There was no denying that the Neo-Xenos presented a serious threat, though. From what she could determine, they seemed to live solely to destroy, and they killed for its own sake, not even bothering to feed upon the bodies of those they'd slain. They were like living machines that had been programmed for a single task – to bring death to any lifeform in their sight.

If Jena managed to get even a single specimen off the planet, Leviathan would find a way to breed the monsters, and they would inevitably lose control of them. Once the other Guilds learned what Leviathan had done, they'd be desperate to capture their own specimens, as would the Coalition. It would only be a matter of time until someone managed to acquire specimens from both PK-L7 and Penumbra, and an arms race unlike any the galaxy had ever seen would result. Xenos of various types would spread throughout known space, destroying everything in their path. She feared that despite her best efforts, she would be unable to prevent the species' exploitation, and the galaxy would pay a heavy price for it.

History, it seemed, was doomed to repeat itself.

A wave of sorrow cascaded over her; the emotion so powerful it almost brought her to her knees. Empusa were highly empathic – a quality which helped them blend in more effectively with the species they imitated – and she quickly realized the sadness she experienced originated from outside herself. She raised her head and looked at the Neo-Xeno in the stasis tube. Could the emotion she sensed be coming from there? According to the console computer, the Neo-Xeno showed no life signs, but that didn't necessarily mean anything. The sensors had been designed by people who had never encountered a member of its species before. What did they know about what sort of life Neo-Xenos were or how a stasis field might affect them?

She stepped out from behind the console and approached the tube. Her people weren't telepathic per se, but their empathic abilities could be used as a form of communication, and she reached out with them now.

"Are you awake? Can you hear me? Did you feel the deaths of the Neo-Xenos outside, is that why you're so sad?"

The Neo-Xeno's body didn't move, but the feeling of sorrow intensified. The patches of mold on the creature's body began to pulse with glowing blue light. Sidney continued toward the tube, the strength of emotion coming from it compelling her forward. She stepped into the recessed area that housed the tube and examined it more closely.

There were several small apertures on the sides designed so researchers could insert instruments to take closer sensor readings and gather bio samples. She placed a hand over one of the apertures, as if by doing so she could be closer to the Neo-Xeno and perhaps establish an empathic connection to it. If she could find a way to communicate with the creatures, perhaps she could establish a truce between them and the humans. If the Neo-Xenos left them alone so they could get off this planet, Sidney could go to the Galactic Coalition and make a case for why Penumbra should be guarded as closely as PK-L7. Penumbra's Neo-Xenos were just as deadly as the ones inhabiting Hellworld and should also be isolated from the rest of the galaxy. If the Neo-Xenos were left in peace, no one would attempt to exploit them.

She closed her eyes, relaxed, opened her mind to the Neo-Xeno. *You can talk to me,* she thought. *I mean you no harm.*

The sorrow the Neo-Xeno exuded changed to surprise, bewilderment, then curiosity. She felt it reaching out to her, but she quickly sensed frustration. The connection between them wasn't strong enough. The Neo-Xeno couldn't communicate.

It's the stasis field, she thought. In order to take a sample from something inside a stasis tube, the field had to be deactivated briefly, otherwise an instrument wouldn't be able to enter the tube. A small control pad next to the apertures permitted a researcher to adjust the strength of the field or turn it off if they wished. If she deactivated it, she might be able to establish the connection the Neo-Xeno sought.

You know how deadly the species is, she cautioned herself. You'd be taking a huge risk.

The Empusa *were* risktakers, though. You had to be to disguise yourself as another species and walk among them as one of their kind, to live and work beside them, living each moment in deception, knowing that you could be exposed at any time. Risk to an Empusa was like food and drink. It sustained them, made life worth living.

Sidney opened her eyes, reached for the control pad, and deactivated the stasis field. She then opened one of the apertures and placed a hand over it. Once more, she closed her eyes and opened her mind to the Neo-Xeno in the tube.

Sharp pain lanced through her palm. She yanked her hand away from the aperture, opening her eyes at the same time. She saw the Neo-Xeno directly in front of her, its compound eyes fixed on her face. It had pressed its right forearm against the aperture so that one of its spines could slide through and pierce her palm. She backed away, held up her hand, saw a small patch of blue mold covered the spot where the spine had stuck her.

Gods no...

The mold wriggled into her wound – the pain was excruciating – and disappeared into her body. Once it was gone, the wound sealed itself, leaving only the faintest of lines to indicate it had ever existed.

Empusans' mutagenic physiology was highly volatile on a molecular level, and therefore in a constant state of flux. This chaos wasn't apparent on the outside, not when an Empusa learned to control its changeable form, but inside it was a seething storm of never-ending change. And in this genetic maelstrom, the Neo-Xeno mold found purchase. It anchored, grew, spread swiftly through Sidney's body and, most importantly, into her mind.

You're mine, the Summoner thought.

She fought back as only a shape changer could, altering the physical structure of her mind to make it less susceptible to the Summoner's control, and strengthening her body's immune system to resist the mutagenic properties of the creature's mold. For a moment, it seemed she might triumph, but then the Summoner determined how her Empusan physiology functioned and used her shape-changing properties against her, forcing her body to return to its previous state so she could no longer fight its influence. Even then, she continued to struggle, but the outcome was a foregone conclusion.

Within moments, the Summoner took her over completely and she joined the ranks of its children. Her skin turned Neo-Xeno blue and hardened, but then the process slowed, halted, and reversed itself until she looked completely human once more. The Summoner had full control of her body's shape-changing powers. It realized she could serve it far more effectively if she retained her human appearance.

Sidney felt a deep peace that she'd never experienced before, and she knew this was the great gift the Summoner would bring to the galaxy. Once it left this world and could spread, every sentient being would become one of its children. There would be no wars, no strife, no unhappiness, no resentment, or suspicion between human and nonhuman races. All would become one, and that one would be the Summoner.

The Neo-Xeno in the stasis tube made no move to break free, and now that its task was complete, it returned to its former position. Sidney reactivated the stasis field, and the Neo-Xeno stiffened and grew still. She would free it when the time came, but for now it needed to remain in the tube. She returned to the console and deleted the data that had been recorded while the Neo-Xeno had been enlightening her. When she finished, she turned and headed for the central dome. She was now her master's eyes and ears – his avatar – and she needed to know what Luis and the Coalition commander were planning.

She would see Oren there, but she no longer feared him. She was strong now, far stronger than any Empusan had ever been. If the cyborg attempted to hurt her, she would crack open his artificial skull, scoop out his brain, and feast on its soft, delicious meat. In fact, if she could get Oren alone, she might do so anyway, just for the fun of it.

The thought made her smile.

TWENTY

"I can't believe you just stood there!"

Bhavna openly wept, and Oren didn't understand why. Tad's death was regrettable, but the man was gone and nothing could bring him back. Bhavna needed to accept that if she had any intention of functioning at peak capacity.

The two of them sat at a table in the central dome with Jena. Jena was *not* crying over Tad's demise, but she was clearly unhappy about it. Oren assumed she was trying to decide who would now provide the narration for the holo footage he would record. Likely, she was trying to figure out how she would explain to her superiors at Leviathan how this mission had become so screwed up so quickly – and that the Guild was now in major trouble for breaking Coalition law and getting caught. She would need a scapegoat, and Oren guessed she'd pick Luis. He and his people had been hired for the express purpose of making this mission a success, so who better to blame for its failures?

The mercenaries and soldiers who'd survived the Neo-Xeno battle rested at various tables with helmets off, faces sweaty, some looking pissed, some sad, and some in shock.

Luis and Aisha stood, as did Dwain and Assunta. Assunta was crying, and Luis put his hand on her shoulder. Evidently, she and Bernadine had been spouses – a fact Oren hadn't been aware of until now – and she was taking her partner's death hard.

"Your cyborg body is faster and stronger than a human's," Bhavna said. "You could've saved him!"

"My body may not be human, but my mind is. I don't have the same response time as an actual machine."

He glanced at the android, Jason, who sat at a table with the other solider, Sal. The two spoke quietly. Thanks to Oren's enhanced hearing, he knew they were talking about the *Kestrel's* stabilizer.

"Still, you could've *tried!*"

He thought about telling Bhavna that he had wanted to remain at her side so he could protect her from the Neo-Xenos, but the truth was that it hadn't occurred to him to do anything but record Tad's death. He'd been working as a holographer for Leviathan over the last several years, and had become so used to standing by, observing, and recording that he didn't think of himself as a participant in events, one with the ability to take action and affect their outcome.

He felt a distant echo of shame, which might well have been stronger if his emotional regulator had been functioning properly. Still, he thought there was more to his inability to act than that. He had been traumatized by living through the Neo-Xeno attack that had claimed his parents and the rest of the survey team on the Orchard, and while he'd undergone a great deal of mental therapy – not only to learn how to deal with the event but how to adjust to his new cyborg body –

he'd never truly gotten over what had happened. And when the Neo-Xenos started attacking and he saw anew how vicious and merciless they were, he had been paralyzed. He should've done everything he could to save Tad and kill as many of the filthy aliens as possible. Instead, he'd just stood there. *Humanity first* wasn't merely a slogan. It was a sacred oath – one he'd failed to honor.

"You're right. I'm sorry."

Jena looked at them then. "Don't beat yourself up too much, Oren. These Neo-Xenos… They're like nothing anyone's ever seen before."

Not true. There was no point in saying this, though. He knew Jena didn't really care about his feelings or Bhavna's. Now that he'd seen what the Neo-Xenos were capable of, he was more determined than ever that Leviathan would never get their profit-hungry hands on the monsters. Even if it meant he had to kill everyone else – the remaining mercenaries and soldiers, as well as Jena and even Bhavna – he would. He didn't want to hurt anyone, and he hoped to find another way, but too much was at stake for him to remain on the sidelines any longer.

Humanity first. Always.

The door that led to the other domes opened and Sidney – or whatever her true name was – entered. Her human disguise would've fooled anyone else, except maybe Jason. Her pupils widened and contracted too fast for a human, and her pheromones were off, not by much, but enough for someone with his heightened sense of smell. He hadn't told anyone about her true identity yet, mostly because he felt he didn't have enough data. He couldn't tell if she was a natural shape changer or one that had been surgically altered. And while no one on the *Kestrel* had ever said anything about Sidney not being human, that didn't mean at least some of them didn't know. Jena and Luis might, maybe Sirena too. He imagined himself standing up, pointing at Sidney, and saying – in a suitably dramatic voice – *She's an alien in disguise!* Then everyone would look at him like he was an idiot, shrug, and say, *Yeah? So?*

He knew the Upholders' views weren't shared by most of the Coalition, and he didn't want to tip his hand if everyone else was an alien lover. He'd keep a watch on her for now, and if she did anything that seemed suspicious – especially if it looked like she was in league with the Neo-Xenos – then he would reveal the truth about her.

But first, he had to make sure that the Neo-Xeno threat stayed contained. That meant no one, himself included, could ever leave Penumbra. He just needed to figure out the best way to make this happen.

Luis watched Assunta leave the central dome. She wanted someplace where she could grieve on her own, and one of the other domes in the research station would provide her with the privacy she sought. Luis didn't like leaving her alone. In the kind of dangerous situation they were in, no one should walk about the station alone, but he'd made an exception for Assunta. He just hoped he wouldn't come to regret it.

Sirena approached him. "You OK?"

"I will be. I worked alongside Bernadine and Junior for almost three years. Losing them is rough."

"I understand."

She got a faraway look in her eyes then, and Luis sensed there was a story there, but this wasn't the time to ask her about it. Everyone was here now, with the exception of Assunta, and it was time to talk – and get some answers.

TWENTY-ONE

Aisha removed the machine gun from her magbelt and walked over to the table where Jena, Bhavna, and Oren sat. Luis accompanied her, knowing this was going to get ugly. Both women eyed the gun nervously as Aisha approached, but Oren instead kept his gaze focused on Aisha's face. When Aisha reached the table, she raised the gun in a single swift motion and pointed the barrel at Jena's chest. The woman let out a cry of surprise.

"I'm going to ask you some questions," Aisha said. "If you answer them truthfully, I won't fire. If you lie to me or refuse to answer a question, I'll pull the trigger and a split second later you'll have a hole in your chest the size of your head. Do you understand?"

Jena's eyes widened with terror, and she looked toward Luis. "You can't let her threaten me like this!"

"She's a military commander, and she's well within her rights to execute anyone who violates the Coalition's prohibition on traveling to this system." He smiled. "And that includes you."

Jena paled. Bhavna scooted her chair away from the

woman. Jena glared at Bhavna as if she'd betrayed her, then she turned her attention back to Aisha. Everyone else in the dome watched the confrontation quietly. Tension filled the room, but no one said a word or made a move to protect Jena.

"What do you want to know?" she asked, voice trembling slightly.

"Did you know how dangerous the Neo-Xenos were before coming here?"

"Yes. Over the last few years, Leviathan has been able to obtain bits and pieces of information about Xenos. There have been outbreaks on other worlds besides PK-L7 over the years, smaller and more isolated ones which the Coalition was able to conceal." She nodded at Oren. "That's how he ended up with a mechanical body, although the official story was *attack by unknown native wildlife.*"

Oren's features formed a very human-looking expression of shock. Evidently, this was news to the cyborg.

Luis' face grew hot with anger. This woman had brought him, his team, the miners, and her holo crew into a highly lethal situation without telling them all they needed to know or equipping them properly. He was tempted to tell Aisha to fire, but he resisted.

"Did any of the original occupants of this station survive?" he asked.

"The ship that brought the researchers here remained in orbit. Shortly after the Neo-Xenos attacked the station, the crew lost contact with the researchers. Rather than have the crew go down to the planet and investigate – and most likely die like everyone else – Coalition Command ordered them to return to HQ. In the end, the Coalition decided that Penumbra, like PK-L7, was too dangerous, so they left, and no one's come here since – except us."

Aisha asked the next question. "Does anyone have any idea how Xenos came to be on different worlds?"

"No. There are many theories, though. Some people believe they were bioweapons designed by a long-gone ancient spacefaring race. Without their creators, the Xenos went into hibernation and remained that way for thousands, perhaps millions of years until new explorers finally came to their worlds and woke them. Others indicate that the Xenos were a peaceful alien race, but suddenly went insane and attacked the humans mining the resources on planet PK-L7. Others believe Xenium creates them, or makes them into this murderous state, especially the Neo-Xenium. They say that the energy the element puts out mutates simple organisms like molds which then become capable of using the genetic material from native lifeforms to grow Xenos, although this theory applies more so to Penumbra. Supposedly, that's why the names are so similar – Xenos come from Xenium. But like I said, no one knows for sure."

"What was Leviathan intending to do with us once we returned?" Luis asked.

Jena laughed softly. "They intended to kill you, of course. They didn't want to risk the Coalition finding out what we'd done. Too late for that now, though."

"And you thought Leviathan would allow you to live?" Aisha asked.

Jena blinked several times before answering. "Sure, I mean, I *am* management."

"What you are is an idiot," Aisha said. "The Leviathan ship you summoned isn't coming to rescue us. Once they get here – assuming they beat the Coalition vessels on their way – they'll take what Neo-Xenos and Neo-Xenium they can get, kill us all, including you, then get the hell out of here." Aisha lowered her gun and stomped away from Jena, grumbling beneath her breath.

Bhavna looked at Jena with shocked disbelief.

"You were going to let them kill Oren, Tad, and *me*?"

"After Oren downloaded all the holo footage he recorded, yes."

"I can't believe it!" Bhavna sobbed.

Jena scowled. "Grow up, kid."

Aisha stomped to the center of the dome, as her team surrounded her. Luis joined them.

"We *really* need to get the *Kestrel* off this rock now," Luis said. "Regardless of which ship arrives first, we're dead meat." He turned to Aisha. "You, Sal, and Jason have a fifty-fifty chance you won't be killed, all depending on if the Coalition gets here first. They won't want to kill their own."

"We'd likely be executed too," Jason said.

Everyone focused their attention on the android. "Why do you say that?" Luis asked.

"For a hundred years, the Coalition has done its best to suppress knowledge of the Xeno presence in the galaxy. Do you think it would allow the three of us to live and potentially share what we know with the civilian media? Most likely, Command would execute us alongside the rest of you, and they'd come up with a cover story for our deaths, say a life-support malfunction aboard the *Stalwart*."

"Man, who activated your cynicism chip?" Dwain asked.

Jason turned toward the mercenary. "Do you disagree with my assessment?"

"I don't know. I was always told Command takes care of its own. What do you think, Luis and Aisha? You've both spent time in the service." Dwain waited.

Luis and Aisha exchanged glances before answering. Luis shifted, knowing his previous military expertise with the Coalition was now known to the Commander.

"They'll do whatever they believe is in the Coalition's best interest," Aisha said.

"In other words, they wouldn't hesitate to screw over every last one of us if they thought it was their duty," Luis said.

No one spoke for several moments as they let everything that had been discussed so far sink in.

Sal broke the silence. "So, we're going to commit treason? Just like that?"

Luis looked at Aisha. "New recruit?"

"Yep."

He nodded. When he'd first joined the military, he'd believed all the shit about how soldiers were men and women of honor – a family, really – who served the highest possible calling. It didn't take him long to realize that "calling" was serving the Coalition's economic and political interests.

"We're going to get off this planet and take care of each other," Aisha pointed out and her tone made Sal purse his lips but not ask anything further.

"By this point we should have a good idea what the original group left behind for us," Luis said. "Tell me what we got."

"Assunta dug through the various databases and compiled

a list," Dwain said. He walked over to one of the workstations, pulled up a file, and began reading. "Five pistols with one box of ammo. Two shotguns, no ammo. Four cattle prods, only three of which work. The weapons are antiques, of course, and they don't have the kind of stopping power modern weapons do. One ground transport – unarmed – and some mining equipment: a couple haulers and a digger. Again, older tech. A sonic emitter, a pair of devilfire charges…"

"Now *those* sound promising," Sirena said.

Dwain continued. "Those things don't need O_2 to burn and carbon dioxide won't extinguish them, so they'll work in this atmosphere. Lastly, we got a few medkits, a couple dozen MREs which probably taste like shit by now, some random tools, and a handful of spare parts for various machines. Junior ransacked the latter to find stuff to repair the *Kestrel*'s stabilizer, so we don't have an accurate count of what's left."

The atmosphere in the dome grew solemn at the mention of Junior's name. The ruined stabilizer, plus the loss of Junior's expertise, was sobering. Luis turned to Sidney.

"Doctor, is there anything in the lab that we can add to the list?"

Sidney didn't answer at first, and Luis was about to repeat the question, but then she began talking.

"Nothing that would be helpful in our situation, I'm afraid. Just scientific equipment, and those medkits that Dwain mentioned."

"No superweapons designed to destroy Neo-Xenos?" Aisha asked hopefully.

Sidney smiled, but the expression seemed strained. "Afraid not, captain."

"All right," Luis said, "getting the *Kestrel* off the ground is our number-one priority. Lashell, did you get a look at what's left of the stabilizer before you got down off the ship?"

"Yeah. It's completely screwed. Junior and I were only partway through repairing it when... when... well, you know. Most of the components he scavenged from the research station were destroyed, and I doubt there's anything left around here that could replace them. Even if there was, I'm nowhere near as good an engineer as him. I could probably install a new stabilizer, but build one from scratch? Uh-uh."

"I believe we can help with that," Jason said. "Our ship is larger than yours, and it has four stabilizers. I did a damage assessment before we left the *Stalwart,* and one of our stabilizers sustained only superficial damage. I believe that with a little work, it would make a suitable replacement for the *Kestrel.*"

"Our ship is three klicks southwest of here," Aisha said. "That's a long way to travel overland on a planet filled with murderous insect monsters."

"We have a transport in the *Kestrel,*" Luis said. "It should be large enough to haul a stabilizer back here. If we send an armed escort along, there's a good chance we'll be able to make it through if Neo-Xenos do attack."

Aisha raised an eyebrow. "A *good* chance?"

"All right. A chance. But that's better than no chance, yes?"

"Agreed."

Sirena spoke then. "Dwain, are we certain there are no Neo-Xenium samples in the station?"

"We haven't had a chance to do a full recon of all the

domes, but there's nothing in the system about any samples being onsite. Why?"

"When – OK, *if* – we get off this miserable mudball, we're going to be outlaws." She glanced at Aisha. "All of us. We'll need to get to someplace where we can hide out from both the Coalition *and* Leviathan. We'll need money to make that happen. A lot of it. And the only way we'll be able to do that–"

"Is if we have Neo-Xenium to sell," Aisha said.

"Exactly. I mean, I hate to say it, but if both the Coalition and Leviathan are coming here, they're going to get their samples, regardless. We need to take care of ourselves and try to stop both of them as much as we can. But, if push comes to shove, we need some kind of funding to survive out there."

Aisha thought for a moment, clearly unhappy. "All right, I know the location of the cave where your miners were working. There was plenty of Neo-Xenium there, and the cave is exposed to the surface. If we took a hauler, we should be able to get a decent amount of the element."

"Don't forget that the place was crawling with Neo-Xenos," Sal said.

"Which is why we'll take our weapons with us," Aisha said.

"Speaking of weapons," Luis said, "we only brought a portion of our ship's armory with us into the dome, since someone," he shot Jena a dark look, "wasn't truthful about what we'd be dealing with on this planet. We should go get the rest of the weapons and bring them inside. We'll need them when we go to get the *Stalwart*'s stabilizer and the Neo-Xenium in the mine."

"The *Stalwart* has more weapons, too," Jason said. "We

only brought what we could carry. We could get those weapons the same time we obtain the stabilizer."

"Good idea," Luis said. "Let's get started. Who wants to volunteer to go to the *Kestrel* and bring our weapons back?"

"I will," Jason said. "If the Neo-Xenos are hostile only to other living creatures, they might ignore me. But if they don't, I'm stronger and faster than you humans are, and if I'm stung by a Neo-Xeno, the venom won't result in my mutating. Besides, I'd like to take a look at what's left of the ship's stabilizer, just to see what I'll be working with."

"I'm the same as Jason," Oren said. "My brain is human, but the rest of me is no different than his body. I'd like to help retrieve the weapons."

Luis was surprised. Oren had barely spoken to him during the entire trip to Penumbra, and now he was volunteering for hazardous duty? Then again, he'd watched his friend Tad get eviscerated by one of those monsters. Seeing a buddy fall like that could make some people withdraw into themselves in shock and grief, but it made others step up and do what was necessary, often to honor their dead friend.

"All right. Jason, Oren, go ahead. Use the *Kestrel*'s transport to bring the weapons over. That way, we'll have it off the ship and prepared to go when we're ready to head out. Oh, and grab some MRE's when you're over there. No way I'm eating ones that are a century old."

Luis turned to Aisha. "Can you think of anything else to add?"

"I think we should figure out who's going to the *Stalwart* and who's going to the mine. After that, we should go check on the station's transport and hauler, see what kind of shape they're in, and if we need to do any work on them to get them running."

"When you say *we*..."

"Both of us can't be in charge. We need to work as one team, and that means we need one commander. I have military training, and this is obviously a military scenario."

"I was in the military too, don't forget," Luis said. "I had the same training, and I served for several years before I quit. I saw my fair share of action, and I commanded troops in the field. Did you?"

"Tell me," she countered, "how many of the men and women under your command lived to go home?"

Luis glared at her, but he didn't answer.

Aisha sighed. "I shouldn't have said that. Fine. One commander won't work in this scenario. My people won't follow you, and yours won't follow me. We'll need to work as co-commanders if we hope to keep all of them functioning as a single unit."

Luis could see the logic of this, but he wasn't sure of the practicality.

"What happens if you and I disagree on what to do, especially in the heat of battle?" he asked. "If we start giving contradictory commands, we're liable to get our people killed."

Aisha smiled. "Simple. If we find ourselves in a situation like that, don't disagree with me."

Before Luis could reply, Sidney came up to them. "Would you like me to go get those medkits Dwain mentioned and bring them in here? I want to do something to contribute, even if it's minor."

"You might as well," Luis said. "I have a feeling we're going to need all the medkits we can get before this is all over."

"This will also give me a chance to see if I can find Assunta," Sidney said. "She's been gone awhile. I'm starting to worry about her."

Luis frowned. He wasn't aware that the doctor had become friends with Assunta, but then Sidney had spent a lot of time in the galley since she wasn't needed on the bridge. He supposed she'd gotten a chance to know pretty much everyone on board the *Kestrel* that way.

The doctor smiled, then turned and left the dome.

Luis looked at Aisha and saw the woman wore a troubled expression on her face. "What's wrong?" he asked.

Aisha mustered a smile. "I've spent my entire career in the military trying to be a good soldier, and now, after only a few hours on this goddamned planet, I've thrown it all away to become an outlaw." She sounded defeated in a way.

Luis smiled. "Don't knock it till you've tried it. Seriously, though, you've seen combat, right? You know how fast things move in battle, how everything can turn in an instant. Sometimes life is like that."

"We can't let Leviathan get their hands on any Neo-Xenos…"

"How do you suggest we prevent that from happening?"

"The *Stalwart*'s jump drive was wrecked when we crashed, but its power core is still intact. I'll tell Jason to set it to overload when he goes to collect the stabilizer."

Luis was so surprised by Aisha's words that it took him a moment to respond. "A jump core detonation would destroy a good portion of the planet," he said.

"And if Neo-Xenium *is* a highly rich energy source, such an explosion might set off a chain reaction that would destroy the rest of it. No Penumbra, no Neo-Xenos for Leviathan to capture."

"You're a devious thinker, you know that? You wasted your time in the service. You were born to be an outlaw."

"I'll pretend you didn't say that. Jason could rig the engine so we can detonate it remotely, once the *Kestrel's* in space and has gotten a few thousand klicks away from Penumbra, just to be on the safe side."

It was a desperate, dangerous plan. A lot could go wrong with it. What if the *Stalwart's* jump core failed to detonate or – far worse for them – detonated too early? Still, he could see no other way to keep Leviathan from spreading the Neo-Xeno infection to the rest of the galaxy.

"Let's get our teams set up," Luis said, "then we can go inspect the station's vehicles and see what sort of shape they're in."

"Sounds good."

Aisha walked off toward the table where Sal and Jason were sitting. When Luis was alone, Sirena approached him.

"Did you suffer a major head wound during that last fight? Because that's the only explanation I can come up with for why you've been acting so goddamned stupid."

"What the hell are you talking about?"

"I'm talking about the way you've cozied up to those Coalition soldiers. You can't seriously believe that we can trust them, can you?"

"I don't know," Luis admitted. "But right now, I don't see how we have any choice. We need every gun we can get against the Neo-Xenos."

"At least you know where you stand with those monsters.

They don't pretend to be something they're not. But you know what military drones are like. They talk about duty and honor, but they're really just fascists who get off on using force against anyone who doesn't do exactly what the Coalition tells them to. No matter what those bastards promise, they're going to turn on us in the end. And if you don't see that, you're a bigger fool than I thought."

"You think those monsters outside care which side we're on? We need to forget our differences and work together if we're going to have a chance to live through this. If we survive and manage to get off this godforsaken rock, we can go back to fighting among ourselves. Until then, we must work as a team, whether we like it or not."

Sirena glared at him for a moment, then said, "You're an idiot."

With that, she turned and stalked off. As Luis watched her go, he wondered if she was right. Had he let his time in the military color how he saw Aisha and her people? Had he made a mistake entering a truce with them? He hoped not, but he had to acknowledge that allying with Aisha and the others was a gamble. In their own way, they could turn out to be just as dangerous to the mercenaries as the Neo-Xenos.

Look on the bright side. We'll all probably die before the soldiers get a chance to turn on us.

Time to get to work. The clock was ticking.

TWENTY-TWO

As Aisha headed toward Jason and Sal, she thought about her conversation with Luis. Did she really believe that whoever the Coalition sent in response to their distress signal would kill their own people to protect the secrets this system held?

Maybe.

But if Coalition forces reached Penumbra before any Leviathan ships, Aisha and her crew might well be spared, and Jena and the others would be taken into custody – or perhaps executed on the spot. Either way, she was a commander in the Coalition military, and it was her sworn duty to uphold the law, whether she liked it or not.

But although she'd only known Luis and his people a short time, she didn't want to see them killed – especially considering how Leviathan had manipulated and used them. If she was honest with herself, she didn't fully trust the Coalition, and hadn't since that day on Janus 3. She didn't like the idea of throwing away her career and becoming an outlaw, but she liked the idea of dying on this godforsaken planet for a government that didn't give a damn about her or her crew even less.

You wasted your time in the service. You were born to be an outlaw.

Maybe I was, she thought.

Assunta sat in the middle of the corridor between the central dome and the lab, her back against the wall, knees hugged to her chest. She wore EVA suits so often in her line of work that normally they felt like a second skin to her, but right now her suit felt stifling, even without the helmet. She wanted to tear it off and hurl the pieces away. She couldn't stop crying, and she knew if Bernadine was here, she'd give her shit for it. *You're a badass, and badasses don't cry, so snap out of it and get back to work!*

She and Bernadine had accepted the risks of the mercenary life, had even joked about one of them predeceasing the other.

Hey, at least then I won't have to sleep with someone who steals the covers.

Yeah, well I won't have to listen to your snoring.

Assunta had thought she was prepared for the possibility of outliving Bernadine, but she'd always imagined they would die together in some stupid battle on some shitass planet for an employer who wasn't paying them enough. She hadn't seriously believed that Bernadine would die first and leave her behind like this. Goddamn thoughtless bitch.

She lowered her head and cried harder.

"Assunta?"

She looked up, and through tear-blurred eyes saw Dr Cheung standing in front of her. She wiped her eyes as best she could and rose to her feet.

"Did Luis send you to check on me?"

The doctor smiled. "It was my idea to come see how you're doing. I can't imagine how devastating a loss this must be for you. I'm so very sorry."

Assunta nodded and fought to hold back fresh tears. "Thanks."

"I know you won't be able to believe this right now, but you'll feel better eventually. Sooner than you think."

The doctor reached up to touch Assunta's cheek. A split second before the woman's flesh contacted hers, Assunta saw her hand was covered in blue mold. She tried to twist away, but it was too late. The doctor pressed her hand to Assunta's cheek. She felt stinging pain, followed by the sensation of something passing through her skin, into her bloodstream, and rushing through her body, colonizing it. She wanted to scream, but it was too late.

Sidney removed her hand from Assunta's cheek and smiled. The mold produced by her body had absorbed certain qualities from her shape-changing physiology, allowing the Summoner to control what happened to Assunta. Like Sidney, she would retain her outward appearance, but inside, she belonged to the Summoner.

"Welcome to the family," she said.

Assunta smiled back.

TWENTY-THREE

Oren and Jason stepped out of the central dome's airlock. Jason carried his heavy shotgun, and he'd given Oren a light machine gun. Oren had never been trained in how to use weapons, and since his brain was human, he couldn't simply download a program that would make him an instant sharpshooter, but he should be able to point and fire the weapon effectively enough.

Once outside, they surveyed their surroundings, each using his enhanced vision to look for Neo-Xenos. Living ones, that is. The ground around the *Kestrel* was littered with dead ones, and a few lay on top of the ship, along with Junior's body. Oren's gaze lingered on Tad's corpse, and he felt a faint whisper of sorrow. As soon as the emotion came, though, it died away, his damaged emotional regulator unable to sustain it, and after that he felt nothing for his dead colleague.

Jason's voice came over Oren's suit comm.

"My locator isn't picking up any movement in the area, above or below ground. I believe it's safe to proceed."

Oren didn't possess a built-in locator, and he was surprised to feel a little envious of Jason. He hadn't spent much time around androids, or fellow cyborgs for that matter. During the early days after his *implantation* – the technical term for having your brain sealed in an ambulatory metal can – he'd been counseled by both cyborg and android psychologists who specialized in human-to-cyborg transition. They'd helped him adjust to his new body, its abilities and limitations, but when the process was finished, he'd gone to live with relatives. When he was legally an adult, he'd gone off on his own. He spent most of his time around fully flesh-and-blood humans, something the psychologists had warned him about.

You may find yourself avoiding contact with artificial and artificially enhanced beings in the future. This is a subconscious attempt to deny your cyborg state and pretend that you are once more fully organic. Be careful of this. It may seem paradoxical, but lack of contact with fellow inorganics can lead to inversion. Inorganics experience emotion quite different than organics, and you'll need contact with your own kind to help maintain a proper emotional balance. You now live between two worlds, Oren, and balance is the key to a healthy existence in this state.

Oren had thought the psychologists were full of shit back then. His brain was human so that meant *he* was human, end of story. But now, standing next to Jason, he felt a sense of... sameness that was surprisingly comforting.

The android started walking toward the *Kestrel*, and Oren followed. Both continued scanning the area visually, despite the data provided by Jason's locator, but nothing happened, and they reached the ship without incident. They walked around to the cargo bay, and Jason transmitted the electronic code Luis had given him. In response, the cargo bay doors slid open slowly, and a plasteel ramp extended. The machinery didn't make much noise, but it made some, and Oren turned his head back and forth, looking for any Neo-Xenos that might have been drawn by the sound. There were none.

"You go inside and start loading weapons and ammunition into the transport," Jason said. "I'll climb up onto the top of the ship and examine what's left of the broken stabilizer." He turned away, then stopped, and turned back around to face Oren. "Perhaps you should get a couple blankets as well so we can cover Junior and Tad's bodies. Humans are understandably upset at the sight of dead friends. We're going to need everyone operating at peak efficiency if we're going to get the *Kestrel* off this planet before either Coalition or Leviathan ships arrive."

Oren nodded, and he smiled. It was like Jason was speaking his language.

Jason nodded back, then turned around once more and headed for the access ladder built into the side of the ship. As he started to climb, Oren ascended the ramp and entered the cargo bay. Once inside, he walked as fast as he could without making undue noise. He had to hurry and do what he came here for while Jason was busy with the stabilizer. He exited the cargo bay, but instead of heading toward the ship's armory, he started toward its engine room. He hoped Jason would be paying so much attention to the stabilizer that he wouldn't think to use his locator to spy on Oren. If he did, Oren would have a difficult time explaining why he wasn't in the armory or the cargo bay.

The engine room was the largest area on the ship, bigger even than the cargo bay, and it housed the thrusters, the ion engines, and the jump drive. The door wasn't locked, and it opened as Oren approached it and closed behind him after he'd stepped inside. It was dark in the room – the ship's power had been shut down when they'd all disembarked and gone into the research station's central dome. Oren didn't need light to see by, and he was able to make his way around the room with ease.

He'd only been here once before, when Bhavna had taken him and Tad around the *Kestrel* to record footage of the ship that she could edit into the overall documentary later. So, while he had no engineering training, he did have a basic understanding of what was where, and he went straight to the thrusters. Ion engines were for traveling within a star system, while jump drives were for traveling between systems. Thrusters, however, were designed for traveling within a planetary atmosphere, and without them, a ship couldn't reach escape velocity. If something happened to the *Kestrel*'s thrusters, the craft would be grounded, and that's exactly why Oren had volunteered to help Jason. If Luis was unable to get the *Kestrel* off the ground, there was no chance any Neo-Xeno specimens would leave Penumbra.

Luis seemed as if he'd abandoned the idea of collecting any such specimens, and even Jena wasn't talking about it anymore, but Oren didn't trust them. Jena might come to believe that providing samples to Leviathan was the only chance she had of getting back into the Guild's good graces, and as for Luis? He was a mercenary. Profit was all that mattered to him, regardless of what he said. Aisha, however, was determined to prevent Neo-Xenos from leaving this planet, and thanks to his enhanced hearing, he'd overheard her conversation with Luis. She intended to destroy Penumbra, whether or not the *Kestrel* could be repaired in time. So, if Oren damaged the thrusters, the *Kestrel* would be grounded, at least long enough for either Coalition or Leviathan ships to enter the system, and when that happened, Aisha would trigger the destruction of her ship's jump core, and boom! No more planet, no more Neo-Xenos.

This would mean everyone, including himself, would die, but that was OK. Sacrificing one's life for the greater good was the noblest act a human could perform, and it would prove once and for all – if only to himself – that he *was* still human.

He reached for the console, but then froze as sudden crippling doubt gripped him. His damaged emotional regulator churned. What was he thinking? He didn't want to die, and he didn't want to kill the others, either. Whether they were mercenaries or soldiers, they were *human*, and preserving human life was what the Upholders were all about. He didn't care what happened to Sidney – she was only masquerading as human – and the Neo-Xenos were nothing more than mindless killers. They were alien filth, and the galaxy would be better off without them in it. But Luis, Aisha, and all the others, even Jason... They were his people. Maybe it would be better to wait for a ship to arrive, whether it was a Leviathan ship or a Coalition one. Maybe...

His emotional regulator hiccupped. His doubt vanished, replaced by burning anger.

The alien lovers he was trapped on this world with were

too stupid and greedy to leave without taking a Neo-Xeno with them. It would be the same with whoever came in response to the distress signals each crew had sent. One way or another, Neo-Xenos would be taken from Penumbra and spread like a disease into the galaxy. He had to prevent that from happening, regardless of the cost, and to hell with anyone else. The fools deserved to die.

His anger drained away. In its place, he felt a profound sense of peace that came from knowing he was doing the right thing.

He removed the front panel from the thruster console, laid it on the floor carefully so as not to alert Jason, then reached in and began pulling out components. As he took them out, he crushed them so there was no possibility of using them again. When he finished, he would put the broken pieces back inside the console and replace the front panel so it wouldn't be obvious what he'd done. Smiling, and knowing he was performing a great service for the human race, he continued his work.

This is for you, Mom and Dad.

When Oren had finished loading weapons, ammo, and MREs onto the transport, he got a pair of blankets. He climbed on top of the ship. Jason still crouched motionless in front of the broken stabilizer, examining it, and Oren placed one blanket over Junior's body. He then returned to the ground and placed the second over Tad. This time, he felt happy for his colleague – it would be a stretch to call him a friend – because everyone on the planet was going to die, and Tad was already gone. He could no longer feel any pain, and really, wasn't that what afterlife myths were built on, the absence of pain? Tad was at peace. Soon, Oren and everyone else would be joining him.

Jason came over the comm. "I'm coming down. Aisha, we're ready to start the transport."

Oren returned to the ship and walked up the ramp into the cargo bay. A moment later, Jason joined him.

"How's the stabilizer look?" he asked. Jason's blank expression did not bode well.

He had no real interest since he'd made certain the ship would never fly again, but he thought it best if he went through the motions of helping get the *Kestrel* going. Retrieving the *Stalwart*'s stabilizer and acquiring Neo-Xenium would keep everyone occupied, give them purpose, and hope. It was a better way to spend their last hours, he thought, than sitting around and waiting to die. It would be less cruel that way. Also, on the slight chance that they might be able to find some way to repair the damage he'd done to the *Kestrel*'s thrusters, the other tasks would hopefully distract them long enough so that when they finally discovered his sabotage, it would be too late.

The situation suddenly struck him as funny, hilarious even, and he had to fight to keep from laughing. He almost failed, but then his emotional regulator hiccupped again, and he felt nothing once more.

Keep it together, he told himself. He had to do his best to act normal and avoid arousing suspicion until Aisha could destroy the *Kestrel*. After that, he could laugh all he wanted. Until the blast destroyed him, of course.

"Roger," Aisha said. "We're coming out."

A moment later the central dome's airlock opened and Aisha, Luis, Sirena, Lashell, Dwain, and Assunta stepped outside. All of them were armed, and they walked over to the *Kestrel* and took up positions around the cargo ramp, ready to blast the first Neo-Xeno that showed its ugly face.

"You drive," Jason told Oren. "I'll walk behind you and join the others in protecting the transport if necessary."

Oren nodded and climbed into the transport's driver seat. The vehicle had eight wheels and was designed to travel over various types of terrain. The cab was enclosed and the bed – which could carry personnel, supplies, or in this case a shitload of weapons – was left uncovered, so the defenders would have quick access to weapons if the Neo-Xenos attacked.

Oren tapped the transport's control panel to wake it up, then he touched the ignition. The vehicle's engine made a soft hum as it came to life, and he waited before putting the machine in motion. Aisha and Luis had both wanted him to pause to see if the transport's engine noise drew out any Neo-Xenos.

After several moments, Luis said, "It's still good out here. Come on out."

Oren backed the transport up, angled it toward the ramp, and started forward. He drove slowly, and Jason walked behind him, assault shotgun at the ready. The transport's wheels made slight thumping sounds as the vehicle left the ramp and rolled onto the ground, but no Neo-Xenos attacked. He continued driving slowly toward the dome, Jason behind him, everyone else walking on either side, all of them providing an armed escort. He reached the dome, parked the vehicle, and turned off the engine. When he disembarked, Luis came up to him.

"Good job! Now let's get this gear inside."

Lashell and Dwain stood guard while everyone else, including the two commanders, went to work unloading the transport's bed. Oren helped, happy to see everyone so busy and filled with purpose. At least their last hours would be good ones.

TWENTY-FOUR

Sidney, Bhavna, and Jena helped arrange the supplies from the *Kestrel* as they were brought in. The process was a slow one, because the airlock had to be opened and then sealed each time someone entered the dome. After a while, the women had a line of weapons laid on the floor against one wall, with boxes of corresponding ammunition next to them, and an assortment of MREs placed on the tables, one meal per chair.

Sidney, who was now one of the Summoner's many children, was of two minds about the weapons. On the one hand, the humans would use them to kill many of her new kindred. On the other, many Neo-Xenos would have to die this day for the Summoner's plan to come to fruition. The children would make this sacrifice willingly, even joyfully – as would she – but the thought of such loss still saddened her. On the bright side, a number of the humans, along with the android and cyborg, would die as well. After all, only a few were required to repair and operate the *Kestrel*, and thanks to Sidney's mutable Empusan DNA fused with the blue mold, the Summoner now had the ability to possess any living being it wished to without transforming them into

Neo-Xenos. This quality would prove extremely useful in its conquest of the galaxy.

All was in place. The Summoner's plan was foolproof. Soon the humans would set out on their dual missions, and within a matter of hours, perhaps a day at the most, the *Kestrel* would lift off and carry the Summoner to the stars.

She couldn't wait.

Let...
Me...
Out!

Trapped in the darkest depths of her mind, what remained of Sidney's consciousness fought to free itself from chains forged of the Summoner's willpower.

When the Neo-Xeno infection had first begun to take hold of her body, she'd fought its influence, had tried to reassert control over her form, but the Summoner had been too strong. It claimed both her body and mind, but there was a core part of her – something humans might've termed a soul – that the Summoner could not claim. That part was thrust down deep into her subconscious and imprisoned there, held captive by bonds of psychic force.

She'd struggled to break free ever since, forced to watch in silent desperation as the Summoner used her like a puppet to enact its will. She knew if she couldn't regain control of her body, the Summoner would be successful. The humans that opposed it would be killed or possessed, and the Neo-Xeno lord would acquire the starship it needed to escape this planet and spread its contagion throughout the galaxy. She couldn't allow that to happen.

Calm down, she told herself. She would never be able to break free like this. The Summoner was too strong. Instead of frantically flailing about, she needed to relax. Maybe she couldn't escape the psychic prison the Summoner had put her in, but that didn't mean she couldn't strike out from it. If she could gather the mental energy that remained to her, focus it, and put it all into a single attack, she might – just *might* – be able to harm the Summoner. She didn't think she'd be able to cast the invader from her mind, nor did she think she'd be able to kill it. But she could hurt it enough to distract it, and that might be enough, especially if she was careful to choose her moment of attack well.

She grew still and quiet, and in the darkness she waited.

Aisha and Luis stood in the dome where the station's mining equipment was kept. Both had their helmets on as they examined a hauler. Aisha eyed it dubiously.

"I thought their transport was old, but this thing has definitely seen better days."

The vehicle had been made from quantum-bound alloy, the strongest and most durable substance the Coalition had before the invention of plasteel. The alloy didn't rust – and it wasn't as if there had been any oxygen in this dome for oxidation to happen anyway – but over time its molecular structure destabilized, and it became friable. The process had already begun for the hauler. Its surface had a rough, grainy texture, and Aisha thought if you took a sledgehammer to it, the thing would burst apart like a sand sculpture.

"Hey, the transport worked, didn't it? Maybe this will too," Luis said.

"Maybe, but when it comes to QB alloy, the bigger the object, the faster it loses cohesion. If even a couple of the engine components are too far gone, the thing will never start." She frowned.

"Let's find out."

Luis climbed into the vehicle's cab while Aisha got into the passenger seat. The dashboard control panel was an older design, one that actually had physical buttons and switches, and it took him a minute to figure out how to start the machine. He got it going though, and while the engine rumbled loudly, it didn't sound as if it was going to shake itself apart.

"It's loud," Aisha said, raising her voice. "That's not good."

"No, it isn't."

Luis tested the hauler's scoop arm. It moved stiffly, but it still seemed to have its full range of motion. He turned off the engine, and they sat there for a minute, collecting their thoughts.

"That noise will draw Neo-Xenos from miles around," Aisha said.

"We'll send an escort with it. They can ride in the old transport."

Aisha pondered this plan of action. "So, we send the *Kestrel*'s brand-new transport to the *Stalwart* and the two pieces of junk to the Neo-Xenium mine."

"We may *want* the Neo-Xenium, but we *need* the stabilizer. We have to send the most reliable vehicle to get it."

"Makes sense."

"Sure would be great if we could get some Neo-Xenium, though," Luis said, wistfulness seeping into his tone. "Even a small amount would help me."

"How so?"

They were on a private comm channel right now, but Luis still seemed reluctant to explain. Aisha hoped he would open up, but she understood how some stories were painful to tell others. Her own story ate at her on a daily basis.

"You know how I ended up patrolling this system?" she said.

"You pissed off someone further up the Command hierarchy than you. That's how anyone gets assigned to a shit duty," Luis said.

"You hear about what happened at Janus 3?"

Luis frowned. "Wasn't that the planet where ..." He broke off, his eyes widening. "Wait, you were *there*?"

"Yep. The Water and Power Guilds fought for control over the planet, and the colonists living there wanted nothing to do with either one of them. They joined the battle, and the ship I served on, the *Dauntless*, was sent to end the war. The *Dauntless* was a heavy cruiser, and Command thought that when the different factions saw it coming, they'd surrender immediately."

Luis snorted. "When are they going to learn that the shock-and-awe bit never works?"

"Right. No one surrendered, and we got pulled into the fighting. My captain insisted on making surgical strikes only. I think he still hoped the Guilds and the colonists would get tired of killing each other and would enter peace negotiations. This, of course, didn't happen. The Guilds had their own warships, none of which were as powerful as the *Dauntless*, but the Power and Water Guilds decided to team up against us. We were fighting against four of their ships over an inland sea on the planet's largest continent. I was working the comm and sensors when I detected a power source at the bottom of the sea. My captain thought it was some kind of new Water Guild weapon and ordered us to fire a barrage of missiles at it. We did, and we hit it, but the power source had nothing to do with the Water Guild. It was a colony of Phalons, established long before humans got there, and who'd lived in peace and minded their own business for centuries. They weren't even aware humans had come to the planet."

"Jesus," Luis said.

"They were all wiped out, nearly ten thousand people, and all because I jumped the gun and told my captain about the power source before taking the time to analyze it more thoroughly."

"You *were* in the middle of a firefight," Luis said.

"I know. And that's what Command told Phalon Prime when their ruling council demanded I be turned over to them for execution. Command got the councilors to change their minds, but they needed someone to blame for the incident, and so…"

"Hello, PK system."

"Yeah. I didn't give the order to fire the missiles, but I made that order possible, and thousands of innocent beings died because of that. I still have nightmares about that day."

They were both silent for several moments after that, but eventually Aisha said, "So what made you leave the military for life as a mercenary?"

"My story's not nearly so dramatic. My parents were compulsive gamblers who took out loans from the

Entertainment Guild to cover their losses. High-interest loans, of course. They couldn't repay them, and the Guild took them into custody as debt slaves. To add insult to injury, the Guild forced them to work in one of the casinos they used to frequent. They'll have to work for the Guild until they pay back the loans, but since the interest keeps accruing..."

"It's impossible to pay back the money, so they'll stay slaves for the rest of their lives."

"Right. I joined the military so I could help them. I didn't have to pay for housing or food, so I could send all my money to the Entertainment Guild to pay down my parents' debt. One day I was on shore leave on Vaddonia, and I went into a dive bar where the drinks were cheap. I sat at the bar and nursed the one beer I allowed myself when a woman sat down next to me. It was Sirena. We got to talking, and I found out she was a mercenary. She'd never been in the service, and she was curious about it, and I was just as curious about the mercenary life. I knew mercenaries made more money than soldiers, but until I met her, I didn't know how much more. When it came time for me to reenlist, I declined, and went into business for myself, partnering with Sirena. Eventually the two of us ended up joining with some others – a group can take on bigger jobs which means a bigger payday – and now here I am, stuck on a planet filled with insect monsters who'd like nothing better than to tear me into tiny chunks of bloody meat. But if I could get my hands on some Neo-Xenium, even a small amount, it might be enough for me to wipe out my parents' debt and free them from their servitude."

Aisha smiled. "And here I thought mercenaries were all cold-hearted profiteers."

"Most of them are. But at least they're honest about themselves. That's more than you can say about the majority of people in this galaxy."

"True enough."

The atmosphere in the hauler's cab suddenly became awkward, as if they'd shared too much too soon. Aisha was glad, though. When you fought alongside someone, it was good to know something about who they were. It helped you decide how much you could trust them, and she decided that, despite their differences, she trusted Luis a great deal.

"I'm hungry," he said, breaking the tension. "Let's go back to the central dome and get something to eat before we head off to what more than likely will be certain doom. Leviathan may be run by heartless bastards, just like the other Guilds, but they produce some fairly tasty MREs. I'm partial to the beef stroganoff myself."

Aisha smiled. "Thanks for the recommendation."

Their situation was dire, she knew that. Neo-Xenos, Coalition soldiers, Leviathan agents... if one group didn't kill them, another likely would. While she'd never say this out loud for fear of discouraging the others, she knew their chances of escape were slim.

Luis wasn't like the other mercenaries. Maybe he fought for profit rather than principle, but money wasn't his only motivation. He clearly cared about the people under his command and would do whatever it took to protect them. He might not be a soldier any longer, but he still thought tactically, and he was as fierce a fighter as she'd ever seen.

Luis had turned his back on the military and the Coalition as a whole. He was an outlaw, and he stood against everything that Aisha believed in. Yet, she had to admit that he operated by his own code of honor. In that way, they were alike. If she'd been thrown out of the military for what she'd done on Janus 3, how would she have reacted? Would she have become disillusioned and cynical, maybe even becoming a mercenary herself as a way of getting back at the Coalition? She didn't think so, but she couldn't say for certain.

Maybe there wasn't as much separating her and Luis as she'd first thought. She didn't know if she could ever be friends with an outlaw like him, but she could respect him. She sighed, knowing she could talk herself in circles, but that sense of trust in Luis remained. Even if they were headed for doom, at least he would have her back.

As they got out of the cab and started for the dome's exit, Aisha wondered if she and Luis were heading off to their last meal.

Luis studied Aisha out of the corner of his eyes as they walked and realized he'd been surprised by how easily he'd slipped back into a military mindset when working with her.

He thought he'd put his days as a soldier behind him. Obviously he hadn't, at least not entirely. He had to admit that it was refreshing to work with someone who was not only a skilled warrior, but who knew how to maintain mental discipline. She retained a laser-like focus on her objectives, unlike his people who were often focused on satisfying their immediate desires rather than working toward a larger, mutual goal. Commanding them was a lot like attempting to herd cats, and he grew tired of it sometimes. There was a lot about military life he didn't miss but working with highly competent professionals wasn't one of them.

He wondered if he could talk Aisha into abandoning her command and joining his crew. Probably not, he decided. Which was too bad. She'd make a hell of a mercenary.

TWENTY-FIVE

The research station's domes had no windows, but they did have outside video monitors, so Jena, Bhavna, and Sidney stood in front of one of the workstations and watched on its screen as the two groups departed.

Jena kept expecting to see a horde of Neo-Xenos burst out of the ground and attack, but none did. Junior and Tad's bodies had been collected and stored in one of the other domes, but none of the Neo-Xeno bodies had been removed. The two transports and the hauler rolled over them as they headed away from the station, crushing carapaces like blue eggshells. The vehicles' tires were made of tough sim-rubber, and the Neo-Xenos' spikes did no damage to them as they passed over the creatures' corpses.

The group going to get the *Stalwart*'s stabilizer consisted of Luis, Assunta, Jason, and Sal. Assunta drove the transport from the *Kestrel* while the others rode in the bed, weapons ready and scanning their surroundings for Neo-Xenos. The group heading for the Neo-Xenium mine would be commanded by Aisha – who knew the location of the cave-in where the miners had been working – and Sirena, Lashell, Dwain, and Oren accompanied her. Lashell drove the hauler, while the others rode the old transport, Dwain behind the wheel. Aisha, Sirena, and Oren rode in the bed, armed and ready should any Neo-Xenos attack. Both groups had taken extra weapons and ammunition, and Jena hoped it would be enough to deal with the Neo-Xenos as they completed their separate missions.

Night began to fall, and the drivers activated their vehicles' headlights. The beams seemed feeble in the dusk's gloom, and Jena hoped their apparent weakness wasn't an omen.

She, Bhavna, and Sidney had been left behind at the central dome to monitor the situation, which she knew was code for "none of you know how to hold a weapon, much less use it, so it's best you stay at the dome and not get in the way" Jena didn't resent this. In fact, she was more than a little relieved. The last thing she wanted to do was get up close and personal with any of those insectoid monsters.

"At least they managed to get out of the immediate area OK," Bhavna said, her voice distant and flat while on the screen the vehicles traveled beyond the camera's range.

Bhavna was nothing like the confident, take-charge producer that Leviathan had sent to document their mission. She'd clearly been traumatized by the Neo-Xeno attack and Tad's death, and if they managed to get off this rock alive, she was going to need a shitload of therapy. Hell, they all probably would.

Privately, Jena didn't hold out much hope for the teams' success. The Neo-Xenos seemed too numerous and vicious for a handful of humans, an android, and one cyborg to defeat. She thought their best chance for survival lay in Leviathan getting a rescue ship here before the Coalition could.

"They'll keep us informed on their progress via the comm channel," Jena said, hoping her confidence shone through. "At least we won't have to wait around and wonder what's happening to them." Of course, this also meant that they might get to hear their screams as the Neo-Xenos killed them, but she decided not to point this out to Bhavna.

Bhavna nodded, but Jena had no idea if her words had comforted her any. Really, at this point, what comfort was there to be had? All the three of them could do was wait and hope.

Jena had concerns beyond short-term survival, though. She kept trying to think of a way she could get back in Leviathan's favor. Sidney had already downloaded all the information on Neo-Xenos and Neo-Xenium that the station had onto a memory cube. Once they were aboard the *Kestrel*, she'd upload the information to the ship's main computer. If Leviathan couldn't get any physical samples of Neo-Xenium, that information would be the next best thing. Perhaps if she could somehow take over the ship and deliver it and the information to Leviathan, not only would they allow her to live, but they might also reward her with a bonus, maybe even a promotion.

She wouldn't be able to do it alone, though. She'd need the help of at least one of the mercenaries, and more would be better. If she offered them enough money, they might be willing to side with her and take a chance on Leviathan's goodwill, such as it was. Which ones should she approach?

Not Luis. He might be the mercenaries' commander, but he possessed an irritatingly strong streak of morality. Plus, he seemed dead set on not bringing the Neo-Xeno in stasis onboard.

Sirena? She might be driven by profit, but she was also loyal to Luis. It was hard to say what she'd do. Dwain, maybe. He didn't appear to be close to any of his fellow mercenaries. She might approach Lashell and Assunta too, although she wasn't certain about how they'd respond to her offer.

"While they're gone, we should keep ourselves busy," Sidney said.

"Doing what?" Jena asked. "Sitting around with our thumbs up our asses?"

Sidney smiled. "I was thinking more along the lines of getting the *Kestrel* ready to launch. We gave it a quick once-over after we landed, but we didn't perform a full systems' check."

"Jason said it could take several hours to install the new stabilizer," Jena said. "I don't think we're going to be lifting off anytime soon."

"Perhaps not, but if we start now, we'll identify any other issues that need to be dealt with and attend to them well before we launch."

"But none of us know anything about how starships work," Bhavna said, "let alone how to fix them."

"I know how to run diagnostic programs," Sidney said. "And if we do encounter any problems, the ship's database will have information on how to correct them. It's vital that the *Kestrel* be ready to fly as soon as the stabilizer is in place."

"I understand your point," Jena said, "but I think the three of us are more likely to do more harm than good if we start mucking about in the *Kestrel*'s works. That's something best left to professionals, I think."

"I agree," Bhavna said.

Sidney's smile was so cold you could've used it to freeze water. "Well, I *disagree*, and unfortunately for you two, my vote is the only one that counts."

Jena scowled. "Have you forgotten who's in charge of our little expedition?"

Sidney's smile widened into a grin. "I'm afraid there's been a change in management."

Blue mold appeared on the biologist's hands, seeming to rise forth from beneath the skin, and she lunged toward Jena's and Bhavna's faces. Sidney's hands clamped down on the women's jaws and held them tight. Jena felt the mold shift beneath her skin and then start to worm its way into her. The pain was excruciating, but her scream was muffled by Sidney's hand. Bhavna tried to scream too, with the same result.

She felt a presence invade her mind, a voice whispering among her thoughts. It said, *Welcome to the family.*

When the joining was complete, Sidney removed her hands from the women's faces. Outwardly, they looked no different than they had a moment ago. Inwardly, however, it was a far different story.

"The master wishes us to do all we can to ensure the *Kestrel* is ready when the time comes," Sidney commanded.

Jena and Bhavna smiled.

"Then that's what we'll do," Jena said.

Sidney smiled back.

"Good."

TWENTY-SIX

"This doesn't feel right," Sal said.

"What doesn't?" Jason asked.

The two rode in the back of the transport with Luis, Assunta at the wheel. The transport's shock absorbers and mini-inertial dampeners kept the ride smooth enough for the men to stand and scan the landscape, weapons at the ready. Extra weapons and ammo lined the inner side panels, held there by magstrips. Full dark was closing in, and their helmet displays had shifted to night-vision mode.

Jason's eyes didn't need the assist to see in the dark, but he kept his helmet's night-vision mode activated so he could use the inner faceplate's data display. Plus, doing so helped him feel a little more human. He found it gratifying to do as much as he could in the same way humans did, whenever practical.

However, he was under no delusion that doing so would make him human. Besides, he liked being an android. But doing things – even small ones – in human ways helped him understand them better, and it aided in his projection of humanness. Humans didn't respond well to machines built

Zombicide Invader

in their likeness. The uncanny valley effect was very real, and it often hampered human-android relations. The more successfully androids could simulate human behavior, the more comfortable humans were in their presence, and the more efficiently they could all perform their duties.

Jason expected Sal to say that he felt uneasy being out in the open like this, where a Neo-Xeno attack could occur at any time. But he didn't.

"*This!* The whole thing. I mean, we're committing treason!" A pause, and then, "Aren't we?"

The three stood at different positions in the bed – Luis on the driver's side, Jason on the passenger's side, and Sal at the rear. Sal and Jason didn't look at each other as they spoke, and while Luis hadn't said anything so far, Jason knew that the man listened intently.

Sal continued. "I mean, we're working with the very outlaws we came here to take into custody. Instead of holding them prisoner and waiting for a Coalition ship to arrive, we're going to help them escape."

"Remember the discussion we had in the central dome," Jason said. "There's an excellent chance that Command will execute all of us on sight. *All* of us. Assuming, of course, the Neo-Xenos don't get us first. We must work together if any of us are to survive."

"I just… I mean, we're *soldiers*. Command wouldn't kill us outright. They'd at least want to hear our report. And once we told them what happened here…"

Luis spoke at last. "Ninety-seven years. That's how long the Coalition has kept this system quarantined. You've seen the network of defense and monitoring satellites they positioned around PK-L7. It's one of the most heavily guarded worlds in the known galaxy. Yet they have only a single patrol ship stationed in the system, one with only four crew members."

"We only need–" Sal began.

"Four are easier to control than six, eight, ten, or more," Luis said. "Easier to keep track of any messages they try to send through PK-L7's comm satellites. Easier to filter out any information Command doesn't want to leave the system. Easier to staff the patrol ship with soldiers who are disgraced, down on their luck, or new, because that way, no one will much care if they disappear. Everything that the Coalition has done since the initial Xeno outbreak has been to maintain the two secrets of Hellworld: it contains monsters and a miraculous element, either of which could change the galaxy forever if it ever got off the planet. You think that after all that effort, Command is going to let you live to tell people that there's a second planet in the system that has its own varieties of Xenos and Xenium? And imagine what the Guilds would do with that kind of power."

"But if we promise…" Sal trailed off. "They could never be certain that we wouldn't talk, could they? Maybe they wouldn't execute us. Maybe they'd just imprison us for life."

"And that would be better how?" Luis asked.

Sal had no answer.

Jason detected an increase in possibility that Sal might betray them to the Coalition, and he could think of only one way to give Sal what he wanted, while still protecting the rest of them.

"If you truly wish to throw yourself on the mercy of Command, we can place you in a lifepod in orbit around the planet before we depart the system. The pod will put you into cryosleep and it has a battery strong enough to remain functional for a solar year. We can set the pod's transponder to a scrambled military frequency so that, hopefully, only a Coalition vessel will find you. Once you're found and revived, you can explain your situation to the captain. If you're lucky, Command will choose not to execute or imprison you."

"*If*," Luis stressed.

"I must be honest and tell you I don't think much of this plan's chances for success," Jason said. "But it is an option available to you."

Sal was quiet for a time, and the transport continued to trundle across Penumbra's rocky surface. "What if I decided to take matters into my own hands?" he finally said.

Jason detected the stress in the man's tone. He turned around, instantly alert to see Sal pointing his assault shotgun at the back of Luis' head. Jason trained his own shotgun on the young soldier.

"Then I would be forced to stop you," Jason said evenly.

"You wouldn't hurt me," Sal said. "I'm your friend."

"You are," the android confirmed. "But that doesn't mean I would allow you to harm Luis. We have made a pact with him and his people, and it would be dishonorable to break it."

Sal held his breath, and Jason could tell that Luis did, too. He expected the mercenary leader to duck, spin around, and fire on Sal – that would've been the logical move at this point – but Luis remained on guard, watching for Neo-Xenos.

Finally, Sal sighed and lowered his gun. "You're right. I'm

sorry, Luis. This whole situation has got me so confused that–"

Jason's locator registered sudden movement near the rear of the transport. Before he could react – which was saying something given his machine-fast reflexes – a runner leaped onto the bed, grabbed hold of Sal, then leaped off, taking the soldier with it. Sal cried out in surprise and fear. Both Jason and Luis ran to the back of the bed. They swept their gazes frantically across the terrain, searching for Sal, but they saw nothing.

"Do you think the thing dragged him down one of their holes?" Luis said.

Before Jason could answer, an agonized scream came over their comms. It didn't last long.

"Yes," Jason said and felt the android equivalent of shock and sorrow. This was both over Sal's loss, as well as frustration for not having acted in time to save his friend. He didn't have the luxury of processing these emotions, though, for his locator told him they were about to have more company – and a lot of it.

"My locator has detected incoming Neo-Xenos," Jason said. "Twenty-three, I believe, although it's difficult to get an exact reading given how fast they're moving."

"Runners?" Luis said.

"I believe so."

Without saying a word, Jason and Luis moved to the center of the bed and stood with their backs to one another.

"Assunta," Luis said, "you better get a move on. We've got Neo-Xenos coming."

The electronic whine of the transport's engine grew louder

as Assunta accelerated. The shocks and inertial dampeners had trouble compensating for the irregular ground at this speed, and Jason and Luis had to struggle to maintain their footing.

The first Neo-Xeno flew out of the darkness toward Jason, and he blew its head off with a single shot. Luis fired twice, and a pair of bodies thudded to the ground, indicating the mercenary leader had struck his targets. After that, the runners came at them en masse, and there was no time to think, only to shoot and kill.

At one point, Luis shouted, "Why didn't the station's scientists name these goddamned things leapers?"

Both had drawn their chainswords by this point, and cut down any runners that got past their gunfire. Some were killed in midair as they jumped toward the bed, while others scrambled onboard and were killed a split second after. Blue Neo-Xeno blood splattered the bed, making it difficult for Luis and Jason to keep from slipping and falling. They could've activated the maglocks on their boots to keep them tight against the floor, but if they did that, they would sacrifice maneuvering room, and right now, they needed that more than solid footing.

They fought on. When they ran out of ammo for one set of weapons, they dropped them, grabbed replacements from the magstrips on the bed's inner side panel, and continued firing. Eventually Luis' breaths came in harsh gasps, and Jason knew the man was tiring. As an android, Jason didn't experience a buildup of lactic acid in his muscles, and he could fight for hours before needing to recharge and perform system maintenance. He wanted to go to Luis' aid, tell him to rest while he shouldered the burden of fighting off the runners, but he knew that, as fast and precise as he was, he could never overcome so many of the creatures on his own.

Assunta had continued accelerating, and fewer and fewer runners were able to keep up with the transport, let alone jump into the bed and attack them. At the speed they were currently going, Jason estimated they needed only thirteen more seconds before the remaining runners could no longer keep up with them. They just needed to keep firing a bit longer…

Assunta's voice came over their comms.

"Hold on! A big one just came up out of the ground in front of us!"

Jason and Luis had just enough time to grab onto the bed's railings and activate their boots' maglocks before Assunta swerved the transport to the right. The inertial dampeners screamed as they struggled to compensate for the abrupt maneuver. The driver's-side wheels came off the ground, and for an instant, Jason thought the vehicle would overturn, but then the wheels came back down with a solid *thud* and the transport kept moving.

On their right, Jason saw a huge four-armed Neo-Xeno that had thrust itself halfway out of the ground. It was a type the research station's scientists had dubbed a ravager. Aptly named. This was a creature designed to do one thing and one thing only: destroy anything that came within its arms' reach. Its huge hands terminated in hooked claws, and blue mold covered its body. As the transport drew away from the monstrous thing, it swiped at its left arm with its right claws, gouged out a chunk of mold, and hurled it at the departing vehicle. Most of the mold struck the side of the bed, but a small portion of it hit Jason's chest. The mold sizzled and bubbled and began eating away at his EVA suit as if it was a powerful acid. Alarms sounded as the suit's internal environment was breached, but this didn't concern Jason. As an android, he didn't possess lungs, and thus Penumbra's atmosphere was no danger to him. He was concerned, however, by the highly corrosive nature of the Neo-Xeno mold, possibly unique to the ravager. If it managed to eat its way through the EVA suit and reach him, it could eat through his outer shell and into his internal systems. And if that happened, he would go offline, maybe forever.

If he'd been wearing a normal EVA suit, he could've torn it off with his bare hands, but his was a military-issue armored suit. It was possible for EVA suits to malfunction, trapping the wearer inside, so they came equipped with an emergency release function. Jason tapped a control on his wrist to activate it now. There was a rapid series of soft clicks, and his EVA suit came apart in sections and the plates fell to the floor of the transport's bed. All except his chest plate. He snatched it out of the air as it fell, making sure to grab it by one of its edges to avoid contact with the mold. He looked at the ravager, instantly judged the distance between them, calculated the amount of force he would need, then hurled the chest plate. The plasteel plate struck the ravager at an angle between its compound eyes and split its head in two. Blue blood gushed from the wound, and the massive creature fell over, dead.

"Damn!" Luis said. "That was a hell of a shot!"

"Thank you."

Jason no longer had a comm to speak with but with his hearing, he could pick up Luis' voice without difficulty, and his vocal simulator functioned perfectly well in this atmosphere. He did increase the volume to make it easier for Luis to hear in his suit.

They scanned their surroundings once more but spotted no more Neo-Xenos. Jason doubted that they'd seen the last of the creatures, but this attack, at least, appeared to be over.

He detected a faint scratching sound coming from the area where the ravager's mold had struck. His boots had remained maglocked to the floor of the bed when he'd used the suit's emergency release, and he stepped out of them now and walked to the railing and looked over. Luis joined him. Small shapes had extended from the mold – shapes that had tiny heads, arms, claws, and spines.

"You mean to tell me more of those things can grow from their mold?" Luis said.

"It would seem so. The mold may absorb genetic information from its host, and then, when it's ready, it generates new Neo-Xenos. When you think about it, it's actually an extremely effective way of replenishing numbers, especially after losses incurred by battle."

"Well, isn't that just fine and dandy." Luis pulled a cutter from a magstrip, then turned to Jason. "Hold on to me so I don't fall over."

Jason held onto the man's magbelt as he leaned over the side and used the cutter to scrape the mold off the bed's side panel. When he was finished, he tossed the cutter away. A wise precaution, Jason thought. He pulled Luis back into the bed, and the two of them watched the area where the mold had been to see if any more Neo-Xenos started to grow there, but none did.

"OK, Assunta, I think you can slow down now," Luis said. "We've outrun or killed all the Neo-Xenos that were after us."

There was a slight pause before she responded. "Good."

She decreased the transport's speed, and the three of them continued on toward the *Stalwart*.

TWENTY-SEVEN

Aisha's team was split between the research station's ancient transport and its equally ancient hauler. Lashell drove the mining vehicle, while Dwain drove the transport with the bed uncovered. Aisha rode in the bed, along with Sirena and Oren, all of them armed, with additional weapons and ammo packets affixed to magstrips on the transport's inner side panels. Lashell rotated the hauler's position every few minutes, sometimes preceding the transport, sometimes running parallel to it on the left or right, sometimes following behind. Aisha wished they'd had additional escort vehicles, but they'd have to make do with the one.

Night had fallen on Penumbra, the stars were out, and two of the planet's three moons had risen over the eastern horizon. Portions of the sky were blotted out by the brown clouds that hung over the planet, but all in all, it was a beautiful and peaceful sight – a hell of lot more peaceful than the world below it.

She looked at Oren. Like the rest of them, the young man held his weapon – a light machine gun – at the ready, and he repeatedly swept his gaze from side to side, watching for Neo-Xenos. He was the only one riding in the bed who changed positions along with the transport, moving so that he could face away from the hauler and keep watch on the open plains with his superior cyborg vision. From what Aisha understood, Oren had never fought in battle before, and while his body might not be much different than Jason's, his mind was human, and she had no idea how he would react if shit started to go down. With his strength and speed, he would be an asset in a fight – assuming he didn't freeze. She supposed they would just have to wait and see how he handled himself when the time came. And it would come, she was sure of that, and probably sooner than later.

Sirena's voice came over her comm. "You and Luis seemed to have hit it off pretty well."

The woman kept her tone neutral, and Aisha wasn't sure how to take her words. She wished she could see Sirena's face, but the two of them were stationed on opposite sides of the transport's bed, their backs to one another.

"We're both realists, and we understand we all need to work together to survive. Plus, we both have military backgrounds. It gives us a shared frame of reference."

"Uh-huh. You were both gone for a while when you were checking out the station's vehicles. What took you so long?"

She could hear the suspicion in Sirena's voice now, and she was uncomfortably aware that she was the only one on this mission who wasn't a member of Luis' crew.

"We talked strategy."

"And that's all you did? Talk?"

Aisha couldn't believe this. "What, are you jealous?"

Sirena surprised her by laughing.

"Luis is my commander and my friend, and that's all. But his heart is softer than the rest of the crew's, including mine. I know he's never been fully comfortable being a mercenary. He misses the military, misses the feeling of being part of something noble, even if he knows that in reality Coalition Command is as corrupt as any of the Guilds."

Aisha thought the woman was trying to bait her with this last remark, but she didn't fall for it.

Sirena continued. "You didn't by chance try to tempt him into joining your side? Did you tell him that if he helped you turn us in, you'd put in a good word for him with Command, maybe help get his record wiped clean, get him reinstated?"

Sirena spoke on an open channel, which meant Oren and Lashell could hear. So far neither had said anything, but Aisha was certain they hung on Sirena's every word.

"If you really believe that, you should go ahead and kill me now. Although, since there's an excellent chance we're all going to die before we can leave this miserable planet, you might as well let me live long enough for a Neo-Xeno to get me. Who knows? Maybe you'll have the pleasure of watching me be torn to pieces before they kill you," Aisha said.

Sirena laughed softly. "I think I like you, soldier. If you try to betray us, I will kill you, though."

"Same here," Aisha said, and with that, she felt the two of them had reached an unstated understanding. They didn't have time to bicker when there were God knew how many Neo-Xenos left on the planet that wanted to kill them.

Yes, Aisha was a soldier, but she wasn't the type who blindly followed orders. Not after what had happened on Janus 3. Ever since, she followed the dictates of her own conscience, regardless of the consequences. If she hadn't, she'd likely never have entered a truce with Luis and his people. For the first time, she admitted that these qualities made her unsuited for a military career. She wondered if Luis had come to a similar epiphany about himself, and that was the true reason he'd left the military, not just for the funds to help his family. Maybe, the two of them weren't so different. If she was lucky enough to get off Penumbra alive, she'd have a lot of thinking to do about where she truly belonged. But, right now, that was a damn big *if*.

Aisha, sometimes you think too much. Get back to work, and if you're still alive tomorrow, you can sort out your future then.

A thought occurred to her.

"When my crew and I joined up with you, Dr Cheung told us the names the station's scientists had given the Neo-Xenos."

"Yeah. What about them?"

"They named the lowest caste thralls. A thrall is one who's under the power of someone much stronger. But Dr Cheung didn't know who they might be in thrall to."

"You think they have a leader?" Sirena asked.

"I don't know. They don't seem to behave in any organized fashion when they fight, but with their strength and numbers…"

"They don't need to," Sirena finished.

Lashell's voice came over their comms then. "Approaching the mine," she said.

Aisha had given Lashell the mine's coordinates before they'd set out, and she was surprised they'd gotten here so soon. Then again, she'd traveled on foot last time, so of course the trip seemed faster now.

"Slow down as we get close," Aisha said. "There are two different holes, one larger than the other. The miners purposefully brought down the cave ceiling to destroy the Neo-Xenos attacking them, and I don't know how stable the ground around the holes is. The hauler might be too heavy."

"The hauler's got sensors to detect that kind of thing," Lashell said, "assuming I can work them right."

"Just be careful."

"Oh, I will. I want that Neo-Xenium as much, if not more, than I want to escape this planet with my life. A score like that is what mercenaries live for!" Lashell said. "I'll slow down and check the sensor readings. We're here."

Dwain – who, like Oren, had stayed out of the conversation during the whole trip – now spoke. "I'll move the transport behind you and back off so we don't put any extra stress on the ground."

"Roger that," Lashell said.

The woman brought the hauler to a stop, and Dwain did the same with the transport. Aisha, Sirena, and Oren continued keeping watch for Neo-Xenos, but they saw no sign of any. Aisha found this odd. The Neo-Xenos seemed to be attracted to sound, but while these two old vehicles were plenty noisy, they hadn't seen a single one of the monsters, yet. Maybe they were elsewhere? If so, she hoped they stayed there, and left her and the others alone.

Lashell came back on their comms.

"Sensors have identified a section of ground on the smaller hole's southwest edge that should support the hauler while being close enough to lower the scoop inside. Keep the transport back, though. There's no way the ground will support both vehicles."

"All right," Dwain said. "Good luck."

"Thanks. I'll need it."

Dwain parked the transport so that Aisha, Sirena, and Oren could stand on the same side of the bed and keep watch as Lashell maneuvered the hauler into place. She slowly backed the vehicle up to the smaller hole, and Aisha held her breath in anticipation of the ground collapsing and dropping the hauler back-first into the cave below. When it didn't happen, she sighed in relief.

"So far, so good," Sirena said and turned to Aisha. "I say we watch the holes from here. We've got a higher vantage point standing in the bed. The side panels will afford us a certain amount of protection–"

"And all our extra weapons are here," Aisha said. "Good idea. Oren, what do you think?"

Oren looked at her, surprised. "Why ask me? I don't have any experience with this kind of thing."

"You're risking your life like the rest of us," Aisha said. "You deserve a say in what we do."

Oren surprised her by letting out a bark of laughter before he answered. "In the end, I don't think it matters." He grinned, and then his features went slack. Expressionless, he turned to face the hauler once more.

Aisha and Sirena exchanged puzzled glances, but then Aisha shrugged. She'd worked alongside cyborgs before, and sometimes their behavior seemed odd to fully organic beings.

"How about you, Dwain?"

"You'd have more room to move around on the ground, but that's the only advantage I can see. I'd stay in the bed. I'll head back and join you."

Aisha pressed an index finger against the top of the bed's siderail, and she felt the QB alloy give a little beneath the pressure. When she removed her finger, she left behind a small divot filled with sand-like particles. It didn't look like the transport would lose cohesion immediately, but it was worse than when she and Luis had examined it. She wondered if it would be better for Dwain to turn off the engine or leave it running. She feared that if he turned it off, it might not start again. But if he left it running – in case they needed to get the hell out of there in a hurry – the engine parts might wear out faster and lose cohesion just when they needed them. Damned if you do, damned if you don't, she thought.

"All right," she said, "but leave the engine running."

"Will do."

They'd know soon enough if she'd made the right choice.

The plan at this point was simple enough. Lashell would position the hauler's arm over the hole, then lower the scoop into the cave on a thick flexine line. The scoop was equipped with cameras and sensors which allowed its operator to adjust the arm as needed. Since Neo-Xenium glowed, Lashell should have no trouble finding it. Then, Lashell would grab the material with the scoop, haul it up, swing the arm around over the hauler's bed, drop its load, then go back for more. She'd get as much of the stuff as she could before any Neo-Xenos attacked or she'd keep loading until the bed was full, whichever happened first. All the while, Aisha, Sirena, Oren, and Dwain would watch from the transport's bed and start firing the instant a single Neo-Xeno reared its carapace-armored head.

Lashell brought up the first load without any problem. It was almost entirely Neo-Xenium, and Sirena and Dwain both let out cheers when they saw it. Aisha smiled. If each scoop was as full of Neo-Xenium as this one, Luis would surely be able to get enough money to pay off his parents' debt to the Entertainment Guild. She supposed in some circumstances – probably more than she was comfortable admitting – crime *did* pay.

Lashell brought up the second scoop-load of Neo-Xenium, along with a trio of Neo-Xeno thralls. The creatures crouched atop the scoop, holding onto the flexine for support as they were raised into the air. Aisha watched in shock as the thralls leaped off the scoop and onto the hauler's cab. They began pounding on the roof and clawing at it with swift, vicious swipes. A puff of dust accompanied each strike, and Aisha knew the hauler's decaying QB alloy couldn't withstand the Neo-Xenos' attack – which likely meant the transport's couldn't either. The thralls needed to be stopped – and fast.

"Try not to hit the hauler!" Aisha said. The last thing she wanted was for them to destabilize the vehicle's structure any further with their gunfire, or for a stray round to ricochet, hit the Neo-Xenium in the hauler or the scoop, and detonate it.

The four of them began firing, and their rounds slammed into the Neo-Xenos, taking chunks out of their shells. The Neo-Xenos ignored the humans' attack and continued trying to break into the hauler's cab. Finally, one of the rounds penetrated a Neo-Xeno's eye, and its head exploded from within. Its claws were still swiping as its body slipped off the cab and fell to the ground.

A second Neo-Xeno's head erupted in a shower of blue ichor, and it joined its companion in death. The remaining Neo-Xeno struck the roof of the cab with both of its hands, and the QB alloy finally gave way beneath the pressure. The roof crumbled away to dust, the Neo-Xeno reached inside and hauled Lashell up. She had a pistol, but before she could fire it, the Neo-Xeno hugged her to its chest, impaling her on its spikes. She cried out in pain, and then the Neo-Xeno sank its mandibles into her helmet, breaking through, cutting deep into her ear canals, and penetrating her brain. Blood gushed from her mouth and nose, and her body shook as if she was being electrocuted.

The Neo-Xeno yanked its head backward while holding Lashell's body tight, and its mandibles shattered the front of her skull and tore her head in half. The Neo-Xeno then hurled Lashell's body away and stood. It leaped off the hauler's cab, landed in the bed, and began clambering over the single load of Neo-Xenium Lashell had managed to gather, on its way to attack the humans in the transport.

Oren fired. The Neo-Xeno's head exploded as dramatically as Lashell's had, and with the same result. The creature fell forward onto a large chunk of Neo-Xenium and died.

"Filthy piece of shit!" Oren said.

"Damn it!" Sirena said, her voice choked with grief over the loss of her friend.

"Somebody's got to take her place," Dwain said. "Which one of you is going to do it?"

Sirena punched him on the shoulder. "I can't believe you're thinking about that right now!"

"Somebody has to," he countered. "One shovelful isn't enough to keep us hidden from the Coalition or Leviathan and you know it! You can bet that more of those goddamned things–"

Neo-Xenos began climbing forth from both holes in the ground.

"–will show up any minute," Dwain finished.

The Neo-Xenos – a mix of thralls, runners, and slayers – pulled themselves out of the holes and raced toward the transport. Aisha and the others started firing at the monsters, but even as the battle began, she knew they didn't have enough ammunition to win it. It was only a matter of time before they ran out of rounds and the Neo-Xenos overwhelmed them. Still, she continued firing. She was a soldier, and she'd keep on fighting until either she or her enemy was dead. That's what soldiers did.

TWENTY-EIGHT

"Finished," Jason said.

The android – now wearing one of the *Stalwart*'s spare EVA suits – stood in the engine room with Luis and Assunta next to him. The three of them studied the jump drive's control console. Assunta had watched the android closely as he worked, and she understood what he'd done. It was rather clever, actually.

"That's all there is to it?" Luis said. "All you did was enter a few commands."

"Exploding a jump drive is technically impossible to do. There are automatic safeguards and shutdown protocols designed to prevent tampering, none of which can be altered without the drive shutting down instantly and becoming inoperable. So, a workaround was necessary. I programmed the jump drive to power up when I send it a signal of a certain frequency. As the drive is powering up, its sensors will indicate the *Stalwart* is still on the ground. Normally, it would wait a moment, and if the ship didn't lift off, it would power down."

"Your workaround doesn't sound very explosive yet," Assunta said.

"I said *normally.* I've also programmed the *Stalwart's* weapons system to fire a missile the instant the drive begins to shut down. The missile's target is the drive. The missile will go up, turn around, come back, and strike the drive while it's still at what I estimate will be eighty-seven percent power. The resultant explosion will destroy most of this continent, which means that the research station and all its records will be eradicated, as will any Neo-Xenos in the affected area. If the blast causes a chain reaction in the Neo-Xenium, it's possible destruction could be planetwide. I cannot guarantee all Penumbra's Neo-Xenos will be eliminated, however, as other groups may be in subterranean lairs and sheltered from the worst effects of the explosion. I can transmit the signal from the *Kestrel* once we've left Penumbra. We'll be far enough away from the blast, so it won't have any effect on us."

"Sounds like this'll more than do the job," Luis said. "Good work."

Jason acknowledged the man's praise with a nod, then Luis turned to Assunta.

"Why don't you go on the roof with Jason and help him detach the stabilizer? I'll start loading the rest of the ship's weapons into the transport. Watch for Neo-Xenos and keep your weapons close. I'll do the same."

He stepped out of the engine room and into the corridor. The android had turned on the ship's power as soon as they'd entered, and the lights activated the instant they sensed Luis' presence. As he walked away from the engine room, lights came on in front of him and turned off behind him. It was standard procedure on starships, intended to prevent wasting power.

Assunta was now alone with the android.

"Shall we?" he asked.

Obtaining the stabilizer was key to the master's plan, and it was a great honor to be entrusted with this mission. Assunta wanted to be present for every moment of it, but there was something else she needed to do first.

"I'll join you in a minute. I'd like to visit the lavatory and change out my suit's waste filters."

"Oh. Of course. The lavatory is down the corridor in the direction opposite the way we entered."

"Thank you. I won't be long."

Assunta left the engine room, turned right, and headed toward the lavatory. A moment later she heard Jason enter the corridor and go the other way. She continued to the lavatory, entered, waited a twenty-count, then stepped back into the corridor. She returned to the engine room and found it unlocked. She smiled. That had been a mistake on the android's part, but one she was grateful for. It meant she wouldn't have to spend any time picking the lock.

She stepped inside, hurried to the control console, and began entering commands. If the Summoner's plan was successful, it would be off world when the *Stalwart*'s jump drive exploded. Its children would remain behind, however, and while they would gladly give up their lives to ensure the master's freedom, the Summoner didn't want its children to die if it wasn't necessary. More than that, though, if the humans had the capability to activate the ship's jump drive remotely and at will, they could use it as a weapon against the master any time they wished. That was a risk the Summoner wasn't willing to take, and the main purpose for her presence on this trip.

It took her less than thirty seconds to remove the instructions Jason had programmed into the jump drive's computer. Now, when the humans sent the signal for the drive to activate, it would automatically lock down and remain inactive until a series of codes – which had to be entered manually – could be inputted. Since the drive would not power up, the missiles would not fire. If for some reason they did, the resulting explosion when they struck the ship would be a normal one. The *Stalwart* would be destroyed, but there would be no apocalyptic release of energy. Penumbra, and the Neo-Xenos left behind when the Summoner departed this world, would be safe.

Now that her main task was done, she was free to help Jason with the stabilizer's removal. She smiled, more content than she'd ever been in her life. She loved serving the Summoner, loved being part of something so much larger than herself. She couldn't believe she'd ever fought for money. The notion seemed ridiculous now, and she was glad she was no longer that person. On Penumbra, she'd found the only thing in the galaxy worth fighting for: helping the master achieve dominion over all that lived. Truly, she was blessed.

She left the engine room and headed for the ship's exit.

TWENTY-NINE

Aisha, Oren, Sirena, and Dwain killed one Neo-Xeno after another, but no matter how many rounds they fired, the onslaught of insectoid monsters didn't let up. The creatures kept coming, stomping across the corpses of their dead companions, their weight cracking shells and squeezing blue blood and glistening organs onto the ground. The creatures shrieked with fury as they attacked and screamed in agony as they died. Aisha thought if this barrage of sound kept up much longer, the speakers in her helmet would burn out.

One of the larger ones – a slayer – rushed her then, knocking aside the smaller ones as if they didn't matter, blows from its huge, clawed hands snapping limbs and splitting heads. Its spikes were longer and sharper than a thrall's or a runner's, more like spears, and the comparison proved apt when the slayer grabbed hold of one of its chest spikes, snapped it off, and hurled it at her. She barely ducked in time, and the spike sailed over her and penetrated the transport's cab. The already unstable structure of the QB alloy was further stressed by the spike's impact, and a third of the cab shuddered, then fell apart like sand and poured onto the ground. Aisha stood quickly and fired a salvo directly into the slayer's compound eyes. The top half of its head disappeared in a spray of blue, and it fell forward, its chin slamming into the transport's back gate so hard the entire vehicle rocked. The impact caused the gate to disintegrate, and the big Neo-Xeno slumped to the ground.

"Dwain, get in the driver's seat and get us the hell out of here!" Aisha had to shout to be heard over the sound of gunfire and Neo-Xeno screeching.

She thought Dwain might argue about leaving behind the one load of Neo-Xenium Lashell had managed to gather, but he didn't.

"Cover me!" he shouted, and then he ran toward the cab, firing his own weapon at Neo-Xenos as he went.

Aisha, Sirena, and Oren blasted Neo-Xenos right and left, preventing them from getting close enough to get their claws on Dwain. Another slayer, this one standing fifteen meters away from the transport, broke off two of its chest spikes and hurled them at the running man in a slow, almost lazy manner.

"Look out!" Aisha shouted.

Dwain ducked, and the spikes sailed over the transport's bed and skewered several smaller Neo-Xenos on the other side.

Aisha was struck by the unhurried way the Neo-Xeno had tried to kill Dwain. It was almost as if it hadn't really been trying, had been toying with them instead. She didn't have time to fully process this, though. They were still in the middle of a fight.

The top part of the cab was open now, but enough of

the sides and front remained to provide some protection from the Neo-Xenos. The engine was still running – which Aisha considered a genuine miracle – and when Dwain put it in gear, it lurched forward. There were Neo-Xenos in the vehicle's path, and it juddered as it slammed into them. Aisha was not religious, but she said a prayer to whatever powers might be listening to please keep the front of the transport from going the same way as the roof of the cab.

Aisha, Oren, and Sirena kept firing, Dwain kept forging ahead, and eventually an opening appeared in the Neo-Xeno ranks, and he gave the engine full power and raced toward it. The route he'd chosen brought them close to the hauler – so close that Aisha feared they might sideswipe it, but then she saw what was happening in the back of the hauler and knew colliding with the vehicle was the least of their worries.

The corpse of the thrall that had killed Lashell lay face-down in the back of the hauler. The Neo-Xenium beneath it glowed a brighter blue than usual, and the Neo-Xeno's back pulsated, as if there was something inside that wanted out. A huge shape burst upward from the dead Neo-Xeno – no, from the *mold* on it – and grew to full size so fast, it was as if it had suddenly teleported in from nowhere. The creature was so large, the hauler bed bowed beneath its weight. It had four thick arms that ended in long, curved claws, and its massive body was almost completely covered in mold. She knew she was looking at Penumbra's highest Neo-Xeno caste: the ravager. Before she could say anything, Dwain shouted over the comms.

"I see it!"

Aisha couldn't see him yank the steering wheel to the left,

Zombicide Invader

but she sure as hell felt it. The transport swerved, and she grabbed hold of a side panel to steady herself.

"Maglock!" she shouted, and she felt her boots seal themselves to the floor of the transport's bed. The connection wasn't as firm as she would've liked, but as unstable as the QB alloy was, she figured she was lucky her boots had adhered at all. Sirena and Oren did the same, and the three of them were all on firm footing, more or less, when the transport's bed slid into reach of the ravager's lengthy arms and long claws. They fired at the beast, all of them concentrating their rounds on its face. But if it had eyes, they were covered by mold and not visible. Bullets struck and sank into it, but they seemed to have no effect on the monster.

Maybe the mold absorbs the impact of the rounds, Aisha thought. If they had something that would hit it with more force, maybe that would kill it, but they didn't have any heavy armaments – no rocket launchers or grenade throwers. The closest thing they had was a spare sonic emitter left behind by the station's original miners. The disc-shaped device was used to carve rock with more precision than explosive charges could provide, and while Aisha would've preferred something with more *oompf*, it would have to do.

She yanked the emitter from the side panel's magstrip, thumbed the activation switch on its surface, and flung it into the hauler. At the same instant, the ravager's two right arms swiped outward and struck the transport's side panel. It burst apart in a shower of crumbled bits, and the monster's claws came within centimeters of tagging Aisha. Then the transporter was past the hauler and racing across open ground.

Aisha felt a pang of loss over leaving the Neo-Xenium behind. They'd needed it to finance their new lives while on the run from both the Coalition and Leviathan. Now, they had nothing.

You'll lose your life, too, if you don't stay sharp.

She quickly turned to look behind them. Neo-Xenos ran after the transport, and the ravager was climbing out of the hauler, no doubt intending to give pursuit as well. She'd had no time to figure out how to set the timer on the sonic emitter, so she'd just thrown it and hoped. But as near as she could tell, the device hadn't activated yet, and it didn't look like–

A blinding flash of blue light engulfed the hauler, followed an instant later by a sonic boom. The light spread outward rapidly, washed over the pursuing Neo-Xenos, and continued toward the transport. Aisha wanted to warn the others, but there was no time. Waves of force slammed into the vehicle, and it broke apart as blue light burned around them.

"Aisha! Are you OK?"

Oren's voice. At least, she thought it was his. There was something strange about it, the tone deeper, the words slightly slurred. Plus, his voice sounded thick, as if he was on the verge of tears. Could cyborgs cry? She didn't know. She opened her eyes and saw Oren looking at her with concern, his features lit by the soft glow of his faceplate's data display. A jagged line crossed his face which puzzled her at first, but then she realized her own faceplate was cracked. She reflexively slapped a hand to cover it, but Oren said, "It's all right. I put a breach seal on it." The sorrow in his voice was gone, replaced by a too-intense cheeriness.

What the hell was wrong with him? She'd never known a cyborg to have mood swings before.

She lowered her hand. She was sitting on the ground, Oren crouching next to her. All around them were mounds of dust and scattered fragments of glowing Neo-Xenium. She remembered a blast of blue light, a thundercrack of sound, then the transport disintegrating beneath them. The sonic emitter had finally activated, and its soundwaves had found tiny imperfections in the hauler's Neo-Xenium. The vibrations had destabilized the element, resulting in a massive release of energy – way more massive than she'd expected. They were lucky they hadn't been vaporized.

She started to stand, but her legs wobbled, and Oren put his hand on her elbow to steady her. His right arm hung at his side, shoulder slumped downward, as if he was injured.

"Where's Dwain?"

She heard gunfire then. She tracked it and saw Dwain's silhouette a dozen meters away from their position. He held a machine gun and fired short bursts as he slowly walked forward.

"The explosion killed most of the Neo-Xenos outright and wounded the rest. Dwain's finishing off the last of them."

Oren's voice was definitely distorted.

"Were you damaged?" she asked.

He nodded. "The energy release fried some of my systems. My speech processor is messed up, and the right side of my body is only nominally functional, but I'm still alive. You and Sirena fared better. Your suits were damaged, but I managed to fix the breaches before either of you lost much O_2. The transport didn't make it, though."

The damage to Oren's speech synthesizer could explain why he'd suddenly seemed to shift moods. Aisha had more important things to worry about just then, though, and she put the matter from her mind.

"I can see that. At least most of the Neo-Xenos didn't make it either."

"Yeah. I saw a couple of the bodies. It looks like they exploded from the inside out."

Aisha thought of how the ravager had grown rapidly from the mold on the dead thrall's back. Could Neo-Xenos be connected directly to Neo-Xenium somehow, its energy maybe even part of their life cycle? If so, that might explain why their bodies had reacted so violently to the energy discharge – they'd had a Neo-Xenium overload.

"You didn't actually plan for this to happen, did you?" Oren asked.

Aisha smiled wearily. "We have a saying in the military: 'If you can't be good, be lucky.'"

Dwain fired a last burst from his machine gun, then he turned to walk back toward Aisha and Oren. "I think that's the last of them," he said. "If I'm wrong, we'll know it soon enough." He surveyed the remains of the transport. "Guess we're hoofing it from here on out."

Aisha still felt lightheaded, but she could walk. She wasn't sure about Oren, though. As if he'd read her thoughts, he said, "I can't win a hundred-meter dash right now, but I'm able to travel. Slowly."

Once more, she thought of how the ravager had emerged from the mold on the dead thrall, and she told the others what she'd seen.

"I don't know if Neo-Xenos can grow from mold at any time or if they need certain conditions for it to happen, but we've got a shit-ton of dead ones around us, and we should get moving before any baby Neo-Xenos start popping off them."

"I wish Sidney had told us they could do that," Dwain said. "Would've been good to know."

"Maybe she kept that information from us," Oren said.

The man sounded suspicious, almost paranoid. Another mood swing?

"Why would she do that?"

"Who knows why... *people* do what they do?"

She didn't like the way he paused before he said *people*. Maybe it was due to his speech processor being damaged, but she didn't think so. Oren had something against Dr Cheung, although she couldn't imagine what it was. This wasn't the time or place to get into it now, though.

"I just thought of something," Dwain said. "Wouldn't it suck to survive the Neo-Xenos only for us to get radiation poisoning from the Neo-Xenium blast?"

"The rad detector on my suit is military-grade," Aisha said, "and right now it's reading green. I can't tell you that Neo-Xenium is one hundred percent safe – it did do some damage to Oren's body – but I don't think our hair's going to start falling out anytime soon."

"Well, in *that* case..."

Dwain looked around until he spotted a chunk of Neo-Xenium the size of a grapefruit. He picked it up and put it into one of the small storage containers attached to his suit's magbelt. He grinned as he closed and sealed the container's lid.

"No sense in going back completely empty-handed," he said.

"Good point."

Aisha found a Neo-Xenium piece of similar size and put it into one of the containers on her belt. She didn't give a damn about having the sample for herself, but maybe Luis would be able to sell it and get the money he needed to free his parents.

Aisha and Dwain looked at Oren.

"I'll pass on the Neo-Xenium," he said. "Maybe it won't disrupt my systems as long as its energy is contained, but I don't want to take any chances."

"Good call," Aisha said. "Do you know which direction the research station is in?"

Oren looked up at the stars for a moment, then said, "It's due east of here."

"Let's gather up whatever weapons we can carry and start walking. I'll contact Luis and see if he can pick us up on his way back to the station."

They spent a few moments picking up weapons that had fallen when the transport collapsed. They attached them to their magbelts, and then, each carrying a weapon with full ammo, they set out. As they started walking, Aisha thought about the Neo-Xeno that had hurled spikes at Dwain, and how it had seemed to not be trying as hard to kill him as it could. A feeling nagged her and, as lucky as they'd been to survive the Neo-Xeno attack, it shouldn't have been possible. There had been far too many of the monsters and not nearly enough of them. And yet here they were, relatively unscathed and heading back to the station to rejoin the others. Had the

Neo-Xenos not really been trying to kill them? Something wasn't right here, but she wasn't sure what it was. There were too many questions and not enough answers.

She opened a wide range comm channel. "Luis, this is Aisha. My group ran into some trouble, and we need a lift back to the station. Do you copy?"

She waited, and when no response came, she repeated the message. Again, there was no response.

"I hope they're OK," Dwain said.

"I'm sure they are," Aisha said, sure of no such thing. "Maybe there's some kind of residual energy left over from the Neo-Xenium blast, and it's interfering with the comm signal."

"Yeah," Dwain said, "that's probably it."

She appreciated the man not calling her out on her bullshit. In situations like these, false hope was better than no hope at all.

"Let's go," she said, and the three of them began walking.

THIRTY

The *Stalwart's* stabilizer was roughly shaped like a triangle with rounded edges, and it measured three meters top to bottom and six meters across at the base. Luis had been afraid that it would be too big to fit in the transport's bed, but Jason assured him that not only would it fit, but the transport could also haul its weight with minimal difficulty in Penumbra's lower gravity.

The *Stalwart* might have been an old ship, but it possessed a cadre of fairly modern maintenance bots that could make minor repairs to the craft's exterior systems so the crew wouldn't have to bother taking a spacewalk. After Jason and Assunta had detached the stabilizer from the ship, the android programmed the bots – which resembled half-meter long insects – to carry the device down and place it into the transporter's bed. Maneuvering the load was awkward for the bots, as they usually worked in zero-g, but they managed.

The bed had mini maglocks beneath its metal surface, and they would hold the stabilizer secure as the vehicle traveled back to the research station. Once the device was ready to go, Luis relaxed, just a little. He'd been on edge ever since they got here, expecting a Neo-Xeno attack any moment. They'd had their weapons with them while they worked, but with the three of them separated – Jason and Assunta on top of the ship, him on the ground loading weapons into the transport – he thought they would've made tempting targets.

Still, the Neo-Xenos never came. The ones that had attacked them on the way to the *Stalwart* must have given up to look for trouble elsewhere. Aisha had said a few Neo-Xenos had checked out the ship after it crash landed, but they hadn't attacked. Maybe this wasn't the Neo-Xenos' usual territory, and the three that Aisha had initial contact with had come here solely out of curiosity.

It wasn't that he *wanted* to be attacked. He was grateful the Neo-Xenos had left them alone. It just didn't feel right. Hell, maybe the damned things were diurnal, and now that night had fallen, they'd remain in their nest and snooze until sunrise, by which time – with any luck – the *Kestrel's* new stabilizer would be attached and functioning, and they could get the hell off this planet before the Neo-Xenos began stirring again.

It was a nice fantasy, but he was certain that was all it was. Not because he had special insight into how Neo-Xenos lived, but because as a former military man, he knew that more often than not, any luck you got was bad luck. Part of him was still a soldier and always would be. Instead of fighting or ignoring this, it was about time he accepted it. Maybe his time as a mercenary was over. But whatever he ended up doing to earn a living, he'd do it as a man who was finally comfortable in his own skin. How screwed up was it that he'd had to come to a planet infested with murderous insect creatures to learn this lesson?

Luis heard soft scratching sounds then, as if something sharp was digging in soil. He spun in the direction of the sound, and in the darkness, he saw three large shapes crawling up out of the ground ten meters from the *Stalwart*. The faceplate's night vision function allowed Luis to see the Neo-Xenos, if only in shades of black and green. They were small ones, thralls or runners, although at this distance he couldn't distinguish the breed for certain. He swiftly raised his shotgun and drew a bead on them, but he didn't fire. Sidney had told them back at the dome that Neo-Xenos were drawn by noise. He didn't want to fire his weapon and alert every Neo-Xeno to their presence if he didn't have to.

Luis, Jason, and Assunta stood next to the transport's cab. The android drew his chainsword, although he did not activate the weapon, but Assunta held her SMG at her side, seemingly unconcerned by the Neo-Xenos' presence. Luis had worked dozens of jobs with Assunta, and he'd never seen the woman freeze like this before. Then again, their team had never faced anything as intimidating and nightmare-inducing as Neo-Xenos. The bastards were more than dangerous enough to make anyone have second thoughts about engaging them.

Why are they just standing there? Luis thought. The creatures should've attacked immediately, but instead they held back, as if merely observing the humans. Were they hesitant about attacking armed foes now that they'd seen what their weapons could do? Maybe, but something seemed off about the Neo-Xenos' behavior to Luis, although he couldn't say what it was.

Jason whispered over Luis' and Assunta's comms, his voice barely audible.

"You two get in the transport and leave. I'll try to distract them."

"No way," Luis whispered back. "We need you to install the stabilizer on the *Kestrel. I'll* distract them while you and Assunta leave."

Assunta paid no attention to them. She took three steps forward, raised her weapon, and suddenly began firing. Rounds bounced off the creatures' hard carapaces, but before Assunta could hit their eyes, the Neo-Xenos dove back into the holes from which they'd originally emerged, filling in dirt behind them as they went. Within seconds, it was like they'd never been there at all.

Assunta looked at Luis. "Let's head back and install the stabilizer. I can't wait for the *Kestrel* to get off the ground again."

She attached her SMG to her magbelt, climbed into the transport's cab, got behind the wheel, and closed the door behind her.

"Odd," Jason said.

Luis turned to the android. "How so?"

"I've had the opportunity to see Assunta in battle. She's a better shot than that."

It was true. Assunta should've been able to blow off the Neo-Xenos' heads with ease. It was almost as if she'd let the creatures escape by missing on purpose. But that was ridiculous. Why would Assunta spare their lives?

"Let's go," Luis said. "It's nothing. She's been through a lot."

The two climbed into the bed so they could keep watch for Neo-Xenos on the way back. Luis had the disturbing feeling they wouldn't see a single one of the monsters this time, and instead of relief, the thought put him even further on edge. The bastards were up to something – he could *feel* it. But what?

He pounded the side panel twice to signal Assunta they were ready. She started the engine and the transport pulled away from the *Stalwart*. A few moments later, their comms activated. At first only a burst of static came through, but then the signal grew stronger.

"... trouble... lift... copy?"

The voice was faint, but he recognized it as Aisha's.

"Aisha? This is Luis! Can you hear me?"

"Barely! I think we were out of range for a while. We've had some Neo-Xeno trouble. Most of us are OK, but we lost both the hauler and our transport."

"Transmit your coordinates. We'll be there as soon as we can."

"Thanks."

She sounded as tired as Luis felt. His stomach was starting to cramp, too. He shouldn't have eaten that goddamned stroganoff.

"You said most of you are OK?"

A pause, and then, "We lost Lashell."

Luis sighed. "We lost Sal."

It took Aisha a moment to reply and, when she did, her voice sounded thick. "Roger that. Sending coordinates now."

They both fell silent after that. A moment later the transporter veered northward as Assunta altered their course.

Luis looked at Jason. While Aisha had been speaking, the android scanned the horizon for Neo-Xeno activity, his weapon shouldered and ready to fire. Aisha might not have ever contacted them for all the reaction he showed.

"You all right?" Luis asked.

Jason answered without turning to look at him. "Are you referring to the news of Lashell's death?"

"No, to Sal's. We haven't had a chance to talk about it since it happened."

"I am an AI housed within an artificial body. We interact with humans and even form attachments with some of them, but we do not experience sorrow or grief when they die. Sal was young and naïve, but he performed his duties on the *Stalwart* well. He was…" Jason paused, as if he had to force himself to continue. "He was a good soldier."

"Sounds like it," Luis said.

He raised his shotgun and kept watch on Penumbra's rugged landscape as the transport traveled on.

THIRTY-ONE

The planet's third moon was halfway above the horizon by the time the transport approached the domes of the abandoned research station. Aisha, Sirena, Oren, and Dwain rode in the bed with Luis and Jason, all armed and on alert. It was crowded, since the stabilizer took up the majority of the room, but they made it work. After the transport had picked up Aisha and the surviving members of her team, she and Luis filled each other in on what had happened since they'd departed on their separate missions.

"We ran into one of those ravagers too," Luis said. "Nasty piece of work. Jason killed it, though."

"Wish we'd had him along to take care of ours. I had to detonate a load of Neo-Xenium to kill it."

"Our ravager threw globs of mold at us, and some of it stuck to the transport. Little Neo-Xenos started to grow from it, but we got rid of them before they could get any bigger. Sounds like your ravager grew a hell of a lot faster than they did."

"Maybe the Neo-Xenium had something to do with it," Aisha said. "There was a lot of the stuff in the hauler's bed."

Jason spoke then. "Aisha's theory that the proximity of Neo-Xenium accelerated the growth of the ravager her team encountered is a sound one. It would explain why we didn't observe any new Neo-Xenos growing from the mold attached to the bodies of those we killed by the *Kestrel*. No Neo-Xenium was present to accelerate their growth."

"That doesn't make sense," Sirena said. "The baby Neo-Xenos that Luis saw grew almost immediately after the mold hit the transport, right? Maybe they didn't grow as fast as our ravager, but they did start growing quickly. The bodies of the Neo-Xenos we killed at the research station lay undisturbed for a long time, and not a single baby monster popped out of any of their mold. At least, none that we saw."

"Maybe the mold has to be on a living Neo-Xeno for it to work," Oren suggested.

"The Neo-Xeno our ravager came from was dead." Dwain said. "Freshly dead, yeah, but still dead."

"Maybe reproduction takes an act of will," Luis said. "Our ravager chose to throw mold at us for the purpose of sending Neo-Xenos to kill us. I thought at first that the mold hit the side panel because the creature had poor aim, but now I think it was trying to place the mold somewhere we might not see it, so that the new Neo-Xenos could emerge, grow, climb into the cab, and attack us at close quarters. Maybe the thrall you guys killed managed to will reproduction to occur before it died."

"Maybe," Aisha said. The idea that Neo-Xenos could reproduce so swiftly was a frightening one. How could they hope to defeat an enemy that could replenish its ranks so easily? "But you'd think *some* of the Neo-Xenos we killed at the station would've been able to will their mold to reproduce before they died. Yet it seems like none did."

Luis had told Aisha that he and his team had encountered no Neo-Xenos during their trip from the *Stalwart*, and it looked like that luck was going to follow them all the way back to the domes. Aisha didn't want to question their good fortune – they could use some for a change – but up until recently, the Neo-Xenos had been attacking them persistently. Why would they back off now?

After several more minutes of travel, the research station came into view. The area was only dimly lit – the few domes that were powered up had their outside lights on, but the others were dark, as was the *Kestrel*. No need for the ship's lights to be on unless someone was aboard. In the darkness, the station appeared even more desolate than it had during the day, and Aisha was reminded of ghost stories veteran soldiers would tell, about abandoned outposts and colonies they'd encountered, places where people had disappeared without a trace, where you'd see strange figures out of the corner of your eye and hear what you thought were almost inaudible voices on the edge of hearing. She'd always put such stories down to too much imagination, too much drink, or both. But now, seeing the shadow-cloaked research station, she couldn't suppress a shudder. This was no fantasy in a tale told by some old spacer long past his or her prime. This place was real, as were the monsters that haunted it.

Jason gazed in the direction of the domes. "My locator detects significant movement," he said.

To anyone else, the android would've sounded calm and

emotionless, but Aisha could hear the tension in his perfectly modulated voice. He continued.

"In a moment, I should be able to… Yes, I can see them now. The station grounds are teeming with Neo-Xenos. A hundred, maybe more."

"Shit," Luis said.

Aisha couldn't have said it better herself.

"Do you think these ones finally grew from the mold on the dead ones?" Dwain asked.

"What the hell difference does it make *where* they came from?" Sirena said. "All that matters is they're there!"

"Point taken," Dwain said.

"Do you think they've managed to get into the domes?" Sirena asked.

"Only one way to find out from this distance," Aisha said. She expanded the range of her comm signal and spoke. "Dr Cheung – Sidney – are you there?"

"Yes, captain."

Aisha was relieved to hear the doctor's voice.

"Are you all right?"

"Bhavna, Jena, and I are well. A new group of Neo-Xenos have gathered outside the central dome, but so far they haven't tried to get in. I'm not sure they realize the domes *have* an inside."

"We're about half a klick away. We're going to need to take some time to figure out what to do about the Neo-Xenos. I'll let you know what we decide."

"Understood. Be careful, captain."

Aisha heard a soft *click* as Sidney broke contact. There'd been something odd about the exchange, and it took a second for Aisha to realize what it had been. Sidney hadn't asked her how their missions had gone, or if anyone had been wounded or killed. Maybe she was too focused on the Neo-Xenos outside the central dome to think about anything else, but Aisha still found her behavior strange.

"Assunta, stop here and cut the engine."

The woman did so without replying. This transport was a newer model than the one they'd found at the station, and while its engine made much less noise, Aisha didn't want to risk drawing the Neo-Xenos' attention. Not only were they low on ammo by this point, she feared the stabilizer might be damaged if the monsters attacked.

Everyone faced the research station now and silently watched the Neo-Xenos mill about the area between the *Kestrel* and the central dome, their faceplate displays magnifying the view. All of the Neo-Xeno types they'd encountered so far were represented: thralls, runners, slayers, and ravagers. Thralls and runners remained the most numerous, with only a couple of ravagers. Aisha was glad for this. If the area had been overrun with ravagers, they'd have been screwed.

"We can't wait out here for long," Luis said. "We need to get inside and resupply our O_2."

"I know. No way we're going to get past all those Neo-Xenos, though," she said.

"Agreed. Too many of them, too few of us."

"We could try to draw them away from the domes. That would give the others a chance to get inside."

Aisha chewed on this suggestion. "Whoever did it would have to make a big enough commotion to capture the Neo-

Xenos' attention. Then they'd need to lure them far enough away from the domes to make it safe for the rest of us to pass, and *then* they'd have to fight to stay alive and get to the domes themselves. There's a good chance it'll end up being a suicide mission. The Neo-Xenos might decide to attack the buildings then, and if they get in, that'll be the end of it. We'd fight as long as we could, but in the end the bastards would overwhelm us. So not only do we need to lure the Neo-Xenos away from the domes, we need to make sure they don't return."

"Tall order," Luis said.

"Yep."

"Maybe one of us can draw them out with the transport while the rest of us sneak to the domes on foot."

"I don't know if the transport's fast enough to keep them busy for long."

"Probably not." Luis thought some more. "Remember when we were checking out the vehicles left behind in the domes? We saw a pair of rovers."

Aisha remembered them. Three-wheeled vehicles, faster and more maneuverable than a transport. They'd been constructed from quantum-bound alloy like the other vehicles stored there, but they'd appeared in decent enough condition.

"You thinking that someone could ride out on one of the rovers and the Neo-Xenos would follow them?" she asked.

"Uh-huh. Assuming the rider can get past the bastards in the first place."

"Two riders," Aisha said. "Better chance of one getting through that way. Plus, once they've lured the Neo-Xenos away, two riders can keep them occupied more effectively than one."

"The riders would have a tough time getting back to the station in one piece."

"That's only if the Neo-Xenos are still alive to chase them. If the riders could herd the Neo-Xenos into one place, they could take them out all at once."

"With what? We've got a few grenades they could lob at the big bugs, but that won't be enough to kill them all."

Aisha mentally went through the inventory of the weapons and supplies they'd brought from the *Kestrel* into the central dome. "What about if they use devilfire charges? We have two of those."

Devilfire burned so hot it could melt ferrocrete and plasteel like they were butter. Miners used it as a quick and dirty way to carve out tunnels, while the military used it as a devastating weapon. You had to be extremely careful with the stuff. It was difficult to control, and if you messed up, you could burn the shit out of something you didn't intend to, such as yourself. Devilfire spread fast, blazed like the fires of hell for several moments, then burned itself out. Not only would it kill the Neo-Xenos, it would also destroy the mold on them so no baby ones could pop up later.

Aisha and Luis had left their comms open so the others in the transport could hear and contribute to their conversation. Jason was the first to comment on their idea.

"I volunteer to be one of the riders," he said.

Aisha smiled. She'd expected this. "I appreciate that, but you're no more fireproof than the rest of us, and we need you to install the stabilizer on the *Kestrel*."

"I'll do it," Dwain said. "I want to get the hell off this shitty planet ASAP, and I'll do whatever it takes to make that happen."

"Me too," Sirena said. "The bigger the potential profit, the more risk I'm willing to undertake. Besides, I *like* working on the knife's edge between life and death." She grinned. "It's a rush better than any drug."

Luis snorted but didn't contradict her, and Aisha thought that meant he approved.

Sirena and Dwain would walk to the station, keeping their distance so as not to alert the Neo-Xenos. They'd go past the domes, then turn around and approach them from behind. Sidney would turn on the power in the rearmost dome and remotely open the door so Sirena and Dwain could enter. They'd get the devilfire charges – one apiece – hop on the rovers, drive out of the dome where they were stored, and haul ass. If they managed to get past the Neo-Xenos without getting killed, a big *if*, they'd draw them away from the station, lob the devilfire charges at them, and *whoosh!* No more Neo-Xenos.

"See you after the barbecue," Sirena said, and then she and Dwain climbed out of the transport's bed and started walking. Within moments, they'd disappeared into the darkness.

Aisha hoped that last image of them being swallowed by shadow wouldn't turn out to be an omen.

THIRTY-TWO

Sirena and Dwain kept their comms turned off as they crept past the research station. They didn't use any lights, relying instead on their EVA suits' night vision capacity. Their armored suits were built for battle, not stealth, and they moved slowly and deliberately in order to make as little noise as possible. The Neo-Xenos gathered less than a hundred meters from them, and they kept a close eye on the monsters as they went. The creatures stirred now and then, and each time Dwain thought that the Neo-Xenos had detected their presence and were going to attack. But they didn't.

Dwain wished the team had never taken this job. He liked working as a mercenary and did his best to always act professionally. Sure, he was an unapologetic cynic and a loudmouth, but he always got the job done to the best of his ability. Like any good businessperson, he saw his work in terms of profit, loss, and calculated risk. When Jena had first approached the team and offered them this job, the initial risk was obvious – travel to a forbidden system, be executed or imprisoned if you got caught. No one on the team seriously considered taking the job at first, Dwain included.

Mercenaries fought for pay, sure, but like anyone else, they valued their lives far more than money. But when he found out how *much* Leviathan was willing to pay for their services, he couldn't dismiss the offer outright, and eventually he agreed to Jena's offer, along with the rest of the team.

Of course, if he'd known there would be a planet full of monsters waiting for them, he'd have told Jena to stick her offer up her corporate ass. But she hadn't told them, and the mission had turned into the mother of all screw-ups. Junior, Bernadine, and Lashell were dead, as were the three miners – Malik, Juliana, and Felicita – along with one of the holo crew, Tad. They'd set out for Penumbra with a crew of fifteen, and now only eight were left. Their starship currently couldn't fly, and they'd been forced to work with Coalition soldiers, who he still wasn't sure wouldn't betray them in the end. There were only two soldiers left, though, so at least the mercenaries still outnumbered them. And to top it all off, Leviathan and Coalition ships were en route to the planet, and whichever got here first would most likely attempt to kill them all.

It had, not to put too fine a point on it, been one hell of a day.

One thing was certain. If he managed by some miracle to get out of this mess alive, he was never working for Leviathan again. No goddamn way.

His parents owned a small restaurant on C-Prime, the Coalition's capital world. They'd wanted him to work there, had hoped that one day the restaurant would become his, but growing up, he saw how his parents struggled to keep their business afloat. They were poor and constantly stressed, and he'd vowed to himself that whatever he did in life, he would make enough money so that he never had to live like them. But right then, moving through the darkness on an alien planet, knowing that any moment a ravening monster might rush out of the night and rip him apart, he wished he'd taken his parents up on their offer. Poor and stressed – but *safe* – sounded pretty goddamned sweet right now.

They managed to reach the dome where the rovers had been stored. Sidney had powered the place up, but the entrance's outer lock was jammed, and Sirena had to pick it. It took longer than she expected – the lock was a century old and weathered from exposure to the elements – but eventually she got the door open. They went inside, each claimed a rover, and started the machines up.

Sirena glanced at Dwain. The old vehicles' engines were satisfyingly loud and had held up well over the years. Like the ancient mining equipment, they were constructed from QB alloy, but whoever had built these had done a better job, and Sirena thought they'd hold together long enough for them to burn the Neo-Xenos to the ground.

The mercenaries were armed as if ready for war: each had several fully loaded guns, a heavy cutter, and of course a devilfire charge. Sirena had never seen the latter in action, and she looked forward to using it.

"Ready?" she asked.

"As I'll ever be," Dwain said.

Sirena hit the vehicle's accelerator and raced out of the dome, with Dwain only a split second behind her. She didn't look back to see if Sidney closed the door behind them. She couldn't afford to take her attention off what was in front of her if she wanted to live.

Dwain took up a position behind her, and they swung around the central dome and entered the open area where the *Kestrel* was parked. The craft was on their left, as was the mass of Neo-Xenos. Sirena and Dwain's guns were affixed to magstrips on the sides of their vehicles, and they both grabbed machine guns and started firing at the alien monsters.

Whether it was the gunfire, the sound of the vehicles, or both, the Neo-Xenos turned and fixed their attention on Sirena and Dwain. They let out high-pitched shrieks and ran toward them, mandibles clacking loudly, clawed hands outstretched and eager to rend flesh. At first, Sirena was thrilled to see their plan was working, but she immediately saw the flaw in it. There were four types of Neo-Xenos, and they moved at different rates of speed. The runners were fastest, of course, followed by the thralls. The slayers were lumbering brutes that lagged behind the other two types, but the ravagers were slow, ponderous things, like elephants encased in mold-covered chitin, and the others left them in the dust. Because of their varying speeds, corralling the Neo-Xenos as a single group would prove more of a challenge than Sirena had anticipated.

Fantastic! She hated it when things were too easy.

"We need to give the big ones a chance to catch up!"

"Roger," Dwain said.

Sirena led the way and Dwain followed. Instead of driving away from the research station in a straight line, as they'd originally planned, they started zig-zagging, continuing to increase their distance from the domes and the *Kestrel* with each motion, but not advancing as fast as before. They rode at the same speed, maybe a little faster, but they'd slowed their forward progress to a crawl. This would ensure the slayers and ravagers weren't left behind, but unfortunately, it meant that the runners and thralls would be on them any second.

Let the bastards come, Sirena thought. I'll blow their damn heads off!

Sirena judged that she and Dwain were ten meters away from the *Kestrel,* and she wanted to get the Neo-Xenos at least fifty feet away from the central dome to give the others the best chance to reach it unseen by the monsters.

Sirena grinned. "Time to earn our pay!"

Dwain groaned. "You only say that when things are about to get really, really bad."

She laughed and continued firing her machine gun at the onrushing Neo-Xenos.

Aisha and Luis watched Sirena and Dwain alter their strategy.

"Smart," Aisha said. "Dangerous as hell, but smart."

"Stay low and keep firing!" Luis shouted.

She didn't know if Sirena and Dwain could hear their leader call out to them over the sound of their weapons discharging and the din of the Neo-Xenos shrieking, but it didn't matter. They were professionals, and all the rest of them could do now was trust them to do their jobs.

"What do you think?" she asked Luis. "Can we risk heading back to the domes now?"

"Give it another few moments. If we go before the charges

detonate, the Neo-Xenos might see us, and half of them will split off to come after us while the rest keep attacking Sirena and Dwain."

She knew Luis was right, but she didn't like standing by and watching other people risk their lives for her. She may have been a captain, but she was a soldier before anything else. She belonged in the thick of a fight, not watching it from the sidelines. This was torture. But she knew it was far worse for Sirena and Dwain.

Come on, she thought. You're badasses. You can do it…

Things were getting hairy now.

At one point, Dwain drove too near a thrall, and the Neo-Xeno swiped at him. The creature's claws missed Dwain, but clipped the rover's left handlebar. The vehicle wobbled, and Dwain almost lost control, but he managed to keep the rover from overturning. He turned in his seat and emptied the rest of his machine gun at the thrall, the rounds exploding the creature's head like a rotten melon. He tossed the now useless gun aside, yanked an assault shotgun from the rover's magstrip, and resumed firing.

Sirena and he had been widening the gap between them and working to herd the Neo-Xenos into that space. It hadn't been easy, but they finally reached a point where they were far enough away from the research station and had the majority of Neo-Xenos in their trap.

"I think we're good to go," Sirena said.

"Let's do it."

Dwain fastened the shotgun to the rover magstrip then pulled off the devilfire charge. Sidney had pre-set the devices so they'd activate twenty seconds after the detonation switch was flipped.

"On three," Sirena said. "One, two…"

They activated the charges and hurled them at the same time. The devices flew toward the center of the gathered Neo-Xenos, but Dwain wasn't about to stick around and watch them land. He and Sirena had only twenty seconds to get out of blast range, and he knew they'd need every one of them. He turned the rover away from the Neo-Xenos and gave it full power. As the vehicle raced away from the monsters, he knew some of the Neo-Xenos would likely follow in pursuit, but he hoped they'd be few. If these Neo-Xenos managed to escape the hellstorm, he or Sirena would have to put them down the old-fashioned way – with a hail of bullets.

Sirena's voice came over his comm. "Watch out! There's a slayer on your six, and it's going to–"

Dwain didn't hear the rest. Something slammed into his back. For an instant, he thought something had gone wrong with the charges' timers, and the damn things had exploded prematurely. But then he saw the long blood-slick spike protruding from his chest, and he realized what had happened: the slayer had snapped off one of its chest spines and thrown it at him like a spear. Alarms sounded indicating his EVA suit had been breached, and then he was falling through the air. His right shoulder hit the ground first, then he started to roll, but he only made half a rotation before the spike sticking out of his chest struck the ground. The pain hit him then, and he screamed…

Then a pair of miniature suns burst into life, and as oxygen rapidly leaked from his ruptured suit, he watched the slayer that had impaled him rushing forward to finish the job. But before the Neo-Xeno could reach him, it was engulfed in a wave of burning white.

"Screw… you…" Dwain said. Then the light and the heat came for him.

THIRTY-THREE

Blinding light flashed, and Sirena's faceplate instantly darkened to protect her eyes. She yanked the rover's steering wheel to the right, shifted the engine into overdrive, and raced away from the inferno that she and Dwain had brought into being. She felt intense heat at her back, and her suit attempted to adjust its inner temperature to compensate, but there was only so much it could do. She felt her skin begin to blister, but she barely registered the pain.

Goddamnit, Dwain!

Dwain had been a pain in the ass the entire time they'd worked together, and now he was gone, pierced by a slayer's spine and then roasted by devilfire. At least he'd gone down fighting. She didn't believe in an afterlife, but she wished his spirit a safe journey anyway.

The heat at her back intensified, and the rover – pushed to its limits – shook violently, as if it might fall apart any second. She thought of how the old hauler's molecular bonds had lost cohesion and the vehicle had fallen away to dust. She feared the rover was on the verge of succumbing to the same fate.

If that happened, she'd fall to the ground, and the devilfire would take her. The next few moments would tell the tale.

And despite Dwain's death, and despite – or perhaps because – her own death was closing in on her, she'd never felt more alive.

Standing in the bed of the transport, grouped around the *Stalwart*'s stabilizer, Aisha and the others watched as intensely bright flames exploded into life and then expanded outward in all directions, engulfing the mass of Neo-Xenos that Sirena and Dwain had herded together.

"That's it!" she cried. "Go!'

Assunta turned on the transport's engine, and the vehicle started moving rapidly toward the research station. The ride was bumpy, and everyone in the bed grabbed onto the railings to steady themselves. They watched as the devilfire – which, if anything, was too mild a name for the blazing maelstrom now raging across the plain – burned like the flames of hell itself.

Beside her, Luis said, "Do you think they made it?"

The fire was so intense that it had turned night into day. At the edges of the blaze, Aisha could see silhouettes of Neo-Xenos flailing around in agony as they died. Several ran out of the devilfire, but they were wreathed in flame and didn't make it far before they collapsed to the ground. What she didn't see was a pair of rovers racing away from the inferno.

"I hope so," she said, although she feared the worst.

They continued watching for the rovers as the transport rolled on.

•••

Dwain had never imagined a human body could feel such agony.

He lay on the ground, listening to the hiss of oxygen escaping his breached suit, pain radiating outward from where the slayer's spine had impaled his chest. It felt as if his entire nervous system was aflame, which was ironic, since he'd also been badly burned by the devilfire explosion.

Lucky my O_2 supply didn't catch fire, he thought. He tried to laugh, but it hurt too much. Lucky. Right.

Whenever he'd imagined dying – which hadn't been often – he'd always pictured it happening fast: being caught in a hail of gunfire or being too near a grenade when it went off. *Bam!* One instant of pain, and then nothing forever after. It had never occurred to him that he'd die slow, too injured to do anything to try and save himself, even call for help over his comm. He couldn't even slip into unconsciousness. He hurt too goddamned much.

He hoped Sirena had escaped the devilfire. If she had, maybe she'd come looking for him, could lay him across the seat of her rover and drive him to the station's central dome. There they could… No. There was nothing anyone could do for him now. His injuries were far too severe for a simple medkit to handle. He needed a hospital, and the nearest one was several systems away. One way or the other, he would die before he could receive help, so he might as well do it now and get it over with.

He felt feverish, nauseated, and he began to shake all over. This is it, he thought, and while he wasn't exactly at peace, he was ready.

But then a strange thing happened. Strength flooded into

him from some unknown reserve, and he sat up. He gripped the spine jutting from his chest with both hands and yanked it out of him. It hurt, but not as much as he'd expected, and he tossed the spine aside. His suit was still losing oxygen at an alarming rate, but he didn't feel as if he was having trouble breathing anymore. In fact, he wasn't sure he *was* breathing now.

The remainder of the change occurred swiftly after that. His muscles swelled, his skin toughened, becoming a substance half flesh, half chitin. Sharp teeth filled his mouth, and his fingers merged into two thick digits and the fingernails lengthened into sharp claws. He tore the EVA suit from his body, freeing a pair of segmented appendages like scorpion legs to burst from his back and curl over his shoulders, venom glistening on their sharp tips. He had become a devastator, a deadly hybrid of human and Neo-Xeno.

He was no longer sentient, at least, not in a manner that most beings in the galaxy could understand. He was part of something larger now – the Summoner – and he existed solely to fulfill his master's will. The Summoner was the brain controlling a gigantic conglomerate body, and he and the rest of the Neo-Xenos were like the cells of that body, all working in concert to do whatever the brain required. And right now, the Summoner required him to go to the station, conceal himself between the domes, and wait until such time as he was needed. That's precisely what he would do.

The devastator, who no longer recalled anything of his life as a man named Dwain, turned and began walking toward the research station.

•••

Resting snugly within its den, the Summoner was pleased.

Yes, a great many of its children had perished. That was an unfortunate loss. But the humans had recovered the stabilizer and could now repair the *Kestrel*, and just as importantly, they believed they had fought and triumphed over the Neo-Xenos. The Summoner could've destroyed them any time it pleased, but it needed them to think they'd eliminated the "alien threat", and so it had directed its children to attack the humans but not harm them. Well… not *too* many of them. If they should learn of the Summoner's existence – along with its intention to use the *Kestrel* to leave this world – they would do everything they could to prevent it from achieving its goal. Far better that they believe the danger was over so they wouldn't attempt to learn any more about the Neo-Xenos than they already knew. This way, when it was time for the Summoner to reveal itself at last, it would be too late.

There were only a few thralls remaining to attend to it – the rest of its children had died in the devilfire – and the Summoner needed to replenish their ranks. Even with all its preparations, the Summoner knew the humans would not relinquish control of the spacecraft easily. It settled back, closed its great eye, and willed the mold on and around it to *grow*.

THIRTY-FOUR

All the surviving members of the two crews rushed past the devilfire blast zone on their way to the central dome. Charred segments of Neo-Xeno carapaces littered the blackened ground, and Aisha was grateful she was in an EVA suit, for the air must be thick with the stench of burnt Neo-Xeno. Some Neo-Xenos still lived, but they were injured and confused by the blast, and Aisha and the others reached the dome and got inside without being attacked.

Soon afterward, Aisha and Luis sat on one of the tables in the central dome. They still had their EVA suits on – by this point Aisha thought she'd have felt naked without hers – but they'd removed their helmets and gloves. While they'd been gone, Jena and Bhavna had found the station's galley, powered it up, and had fresh khavi waiting for the others when they returned. Aisha took her khavi with cream and sugar, while Luis took his black. Aisha was grateful for the drink, although she really didn't register the taste. Right now, the khavi was nothing more than fuel to keep her going.

"I could sleep for a goddamn week," Luis said.

"Me too. Sorry about Dwain."

He nodded his thanks for the sentiment. "Let's hope we can get off this rock before anyone else dies."

"I'll drink to that." She took a sip of her khavi, and Luis did likewise.

The surviving members of Luis' team and Aisha's crew were spread throughout the dome's open area. Oren, sans his EVA suit, sat in a chair while Jason examined his damaged arm and leg. The android had laid out several tools on the table next to him in anticipation of performing some cyborg surgery. Sidney, Assunta, Jena, and Bhavna gathered around the dome's main control console, talking in low tones while Sidney scrolled through information on the screen. Oren stared at them, brow furrowed and lips tight.

Sirena was the only one sitting by herself. Her scorched and blackened EVA suit rested on the floor next to her, and she wore only a white T-shirt and khaki-colored pair of shorts. Jason had slathered her back with restora-gel from one of the medkits. It would take days – and a hell of a lot more medicine – before her skin was smooth and healthy again. The woman had to be in near agony, but she'd refused all but the most basic of painkillers. *Got to keep a clear head in case more goddamned Neo-Xenos show up*, she'd said.

When they'd made it back to the central dome, they saw the area around the ship was no longer littered with Neo-Xeno corpses, but rather pieces of Neo-Xeno carapaces. None of them had mold on them anymore, and they guessed that when the baby Neo-Xenos began to grow, they'd absorbed nutrients from their host bodies. With any luck, the newly born Neo-Xenos had been among those destroyed by the devilfire charges, and if there'd been any survivors, hopefully they now understood it wasn't in their best interest to mess with humans and they'd keep their distance.

"How are we going to get the stabilizer up onto the *Kestrel*?" she asked Luis. "It's a heavy piece of equipment. The station only had one hauler, and we destroyed it. Does your ship have maintenance bots?"

"Yeah, but they're pretty small. Still, if they all work together and Jason gives them a hand, they should be able to get the stabilizer in place. I'd suggest Oren help too, since cyborgs are strong as androids, but right now he doesn't look like he's in any shape to pitch in."

Both of them had forgotten about Oren's enhanced hearing, so they were surprised when the cyborg turned to look at them and said, "It doesn't matter if you succeed in installing the stabilizer or not. The *Kestrel* is never going to fly again."

Everyone grew silent and turned their attention to the cyborg. Aisha frowned, wondering if this was another mood shift that had sent Oren into a deep depression.

Jason had opened a panel on his arm and had begun to work on it with a gleaming tool that resembled a high-tech soldering iron. Oren now pushed the android's hand away gently, closed the panel, and hauled himself awkwardly to his feet. His posture said he'd had enough of just about everything and everyone. Jason stood as well, but he didn't try to prevent Oren from walking away. The cyborg shuffled toward the main console, right arm hanging at his side, right leg dragging the floor. Sidney, Jena, Assunta, and Bhavna watched him come. The latter three women had no expression on their faces, but Sidney's eyes narrowed as

Oren approached, and she tensed, as if she was preparing to fight.

"What the hell's going on here?" Aisha whispered to Luis, but the man only shrugged.

When Oren had come within two meters of the console, he stopped and pointed to Sidney.

"She's not human," he said. "She's an alien."

Sidney laughed, as if the thought was ludicrous, but there was no humor in her eyes, only cold calculation.

"Do I look like an alien?" she asked.

"If you were Empusan, you could look like anything you wished," Jason said. There was no hint of suspicion in his voice, no accusation. He sounded as if he was merely stating a fact. "And while you appear completely human, you've demonstrated some anomalous physiological signs in the time I've known you. Eye movements, muscle movements, vocal inflections, and reaction times that were not standard for humans."

Oren looked at Jason with an expression of sheer disbelief. "You *knew*? And you didn't say anything?"

"Since she was a member of your crew, I assumed you were aware of her true identity."

"But she's an *alien!*" Oren stressed the word as if he thought Jason had difficulty understanding it. "She's no different than the monsters we've been fighting!"

Aisha wasn't certain, but she thought she saw a ghost of a smile cross Sidney's face at this.

Luis spoke now. "Son, you know all the sentient lifeforms in the galaxy aren't the same, right? There's nothing wrong with that."

"He's a damn Upholder," Sirena said. "You know how they are. Humanity First and all that shit."

"What makes you say that?" Aisha asked.

"Besides the way he's acting? My father was one. I used to have to listen to him rant and rave about how aliens kept humans from claiming their rightful place as rulers of the galaxy, how they stood in our evolutionary path and needed to get out of way or else. Blah-blah-blah. Bigoted bastard."

Aisha looked at Oren. "*Are* you an Upholder?"

"What if I am? You all should be too! Every human should!"

"I'm not human," Jason said. "And by the Upholders' strictest standards, neither are you."

"Of *course* I'm human. My situation is no different than someone driving a vehicle or a starship. My brain drives this body."

"Your analogy is flawed," Jason said. "Drivers can leave their vehicles. You cannot."

Luis looked at Jena. "*Is* Sidney an alien?"

"Leviathan hired her for her knowledge and expertise, not her race," Jena said.

"That doesn't answer the question," Luis pointed out.

"Who gives a damn?" Sirena said. "She does her job, doesn't she? Just leave her alone."

Sidney sighed. "This issue is distracting us from our main concern: leaving this world alive. To set the record straight, yes, I am Empusan. You can keep calling me Sidney, though."

"See?" Oren said, his voice triumphant. "I *told* you!"

Luis turned to Aisha as if for support.

"Don't look at me," she said. "She was on *your* ship."

He turned back to face Sidney. "Why would an Empusan want to work for Leviathan?"

"They pay well?" Sirena said.

"Empusa aren't exactly welcome in the Coalition," Sidney said. "For decades, Command has been interested in finding ways to exploit our shape-changing abilities to create bioweapons, but so far they haven't succeeded. If we are to walk freely in the galaxy, we must do so in the guise of other species. I'm a Safekeeper, and as long as I appear human, I can work undercover on behalf of my organization. That's why I arranged to come on Leviathan's mission to Penumbra. I wanted to see for myself what native species might be here and prevent Leviathan from using them and most likely ruining their environment in the process, as the Guilds have done on other worlds."

"Goddamn monster!" Oren shouted. Saliva sprayed as he yelled. He had no weapon on him, and Aisha thought this was a good thing, otherwise he surely would've drawn it and taken a shot at Sidney. He still had one good leg, though, and he used it to propel himself toward the scientist in a leap, left arm stretched out, fingers splayed wide and ready to wrap around her throat.

Assunta wasn't unarmed, though. She quickly stepped in front of Sidney, drew her SMG, and fired a burst of ammo at him. His trajectory had already been off because of the awkward way he'd leaped, but the impact of the rounds caused him to slam into the side of the console hard enough to put a small dent in its plasteel casing. He slumped to the floor and didn't move.

Assunta stepped around the console to where Oren lay.

She aimed her weapon at his head, and Aisha realized the woman was going to kill him. She opened her mouth to command Assunta to stop.

Jason still held the tool he'd been using to work on Oren's arm, and his hand became a blur as he hurled it at Assunta. It struck the back of her hand before she could fire and caused her to lose her grip on the weapon. It fell to the floor near Oren's head without discharging. Jason had thrown the tool so hard that it had become embedded in Assunta's hand, and the wound was bleeding. Her blood wasn't red, though. It was blue.

Sidney pursed her lips in irritation.

"Well, this complicates matters, doesn't it?"

THIRTY-FIVE

"You know," Luis said, "I'd like to say I can't believe it, but after the day we've had on this goddamned planet, I'm really not all that surprised."

Sidney ignored him. "Assunta, use your other hand to pick up the gun and hold it to Oren's head. Don't kill him unless one of the others tries to attack us."

Assunta nodded and obeyed. She didn't pull the tool out of her right hand, and blue blood dripped from the injury in thick globs onto the floor. If the wound pained her, she showed no sign of it.

Sidney turned to Jena and Bhavna. "Get their weapons," she said.

Luis watched as the two women – or whatever the hell they were now – moved about the room, removing weapons from the tables in the immediate vicinity. None of the guns had been in easy reach of Luis, Aisha, Jason, or Sirena, or else they would've tried to grab one by now. Luis was mad at himself for forgetting the most important rule for staying alive as a mercenary: always keep at least one weapon on you at all times.

Jena and Bhavna laid most of the weapons on the floor near the console, but they each kept one for themselves – a shotgun for Jena, a light machine gun for Bhavna. They aimed the guns at the others. The message was clear – move and we'll fire.

Luis didn't know if Oren was alive or not. Assunta had blasted him as he'd made a leap for Sidney, and he had no idea how much damage the cyborg's body had taken. Enough to screw up the machinery that kept his brain alive? For all they knew, Oren could be dead instead of unconscious, and Assunta was holding a corpse hostage. It was a theory he didn't want to test, though, because if he was wrong, he'd end up getting Oren killed for real. The rest of them too, probably.

He glanced at Jason, and saw the android's gaze flitting rapidly from Sidney to Assunta to Jena to Bhavna and back again. Jason was calculating the odds of being able to attack the women and disarm them without getting anyone else killed. Evidently they weren't good, because the android remained where he was.

Aisha spoke. "So, the four of you have been… what? Turned into Neo-Xenos?"

"They don't look very Neo-Xeno-ish," Sirena said.

"No, they do not," Jason said.

"Maybe they've been possessed," Luis said.

"That's a crude explanation," Sidney said, "but it will do. We are now the Summoner's children, and you shall do the master's will or die."

"Summoner?" Luis said.

"I *knew* someone or something had to be in charge of the Neo-Xenos!" Aisha said. Is that what you are now, Sidney? Are you the Summoner?"

"I am its avatar, an... expression of its consciousness. We did not invent the name *thrall* or any of the others you know us by. We had no names before humans came to this world. It was the researchers who were here a century ago who decided what to call us. We liked their nomenclature and chose to adopt it."

Luis frowned. "How did you find out about those names? I mean, it's not like they walked up to the Summoner one day and said, 'Hello. We have some exciting ideas for names for your people. We think you're really going to like them.'"

Sidney just smiled at him.

"Why did the Summoner send Neo-Xenos to attack us?" Aisha asked. "Wouldn't it have been easier to possess a few of us right away and force the rest of us to help you, like you're doing now? A hell of a lot less of its children would've died that way."

"At first, I wished to understand you, to test your capabilities, determine your strengths and weaknesses. To see if you were different from the humans who came here once before. Later, I wanted to keep you occupied so you wouldn't suspect I was manipulating you for my own ends – and it was an effective way of reducing your numbers to minimize your threat potential and make you more manageable. Now, here's what's going to happen. You want off this world, and so do we. Jason, you will install the stabilizer on the *Kestrel* and make the craft operational. If you refuse, your companions will be killed. If you do anything to sabotage the ship, they will be killed. If you attempt to send a signal off world, they will be killed. Assunta will accompany you at all times. She will be armed and will remain out of your reach. If you do anything you're not supposed to, she will let me know, and I'll immediately terminate the humans. Do you understand?"

"Yes," Jason said.

From the tightness in Jason's tone, Luis thought the android was furious. He didn't blame him.

"Why not make it easy on yourself?" Aisha asked. "If the Summoner possesses us, you'd have a crew to fly the *Kestrel*."

"If we did that, Jason might decide you were for all intents and purposes dead and refuse to cooperate," Sidney answered. "But the most important reason we don't wish to possess you is that we need someone to fly the ship."

"You seem smart," Luis said. "Why can't you fly the *Kestrel* on your own?"

"Knowledge and experience are two different things," Sidney said. "You could read about how to play a musical instrument and have a basic understanding of how to operate the thing, but you wouldn't be able to produce any music. At least none worth listening to. Once I take a host, I have access to their knowledge, but not their experience. I know that Sidney – whose Empusan name is Uqqil – can change shape, but until *I* practice doing so, I cannot make her body transform. It is the same with flying a spaceship. If I possessed one of you, I would know *how* to operate such a craft, but I would still be incapable of doing so with any degree of efficiency. That's why I need you four alive. I can serve as commander, but I need you to be my crew."

"I don't know how long you've possessed Sidney," Aisha said, "but you must know what our plans were. You know we wanted to prevent Neo-Xenos from leaving this world and potentially spreading to other regions of the galaxy. Why would we help you leave?"

"Because you have no choice," Sidney said.

Aisha smiled and turned to Jason. "Send the signal."

Jason nodded. His features went slack, and he got a faraway look in his eyes. Then his gaze cleared. "It's done."

Luis agreed with Aisha's action, but while he wasn't looking forward to dying, he was glad that his death would count for something. He'd always figured that he'd end up face-down in a ditch on some backwater planet, riddled with bullets after having fought for a cause that he really didn't believe in. But keeping the Summoner and its "children" from leaving Penumbra? That was something he did believe in. His only regret was that once he was gone, there would be no one to pay off his parents' debt to the Entertainment Guild and free them.

On impulse, he reached out and took Aisha's hand and clasped it tight. She gripped his hand back, and they stood like that, together, and waited for the end.

And waited...

And waited...

"Something's wrong," Jason said. "The *Stalwart's* jump drive should've exploded by now."

Sidney grinned. "The *Stalwart* isn't going to do anything. Why do you think Assunta volunteered to help obtain the stabilizer?"

Luis groaned at the sudden realization. Dread filled him. "She was possessed at the time, wasn't she? After Jason programmed the destruct sequence into the *Stalwart's* system, she deactivated it."

Sidney grinned wider. "Now there is nothing to prevent the stabilizer's installation."

Luis glanced at Aisha. The two of them still held hands, and he gave hers a last squeeze before releasing it. They'd given it their best shot, but they'd failed. It wouldn't take Jason more than a few hours to install the stabilizer, and then the Summoner would have its very own starship to take it anywhere in the galaxy it desired. Forget getting any help from Leviathan or the Coalition. The *Kestrel* would be long gone before either arrived.

Oren had been quiet and still this entire time, but now he opened his eyes and started laughing softly. His laughter continued, increasing in volume and force until it sounded as if he was in the throes of hysteria, and then his laughter abruptly cut off. He then rolled onto his back and propped himself up on his elbows. Assunta kept her SMG trained on him, but she didn't fire.

Aisha wondered if it was possible for a cyborg to go mad. She thought they had hardware installed to prevent that sort of thing from happening, but it didn't seem to be working in Oren's case. *A crazy cyborg*, she thought. *Just what we needed.*

Sidney frowned at Oren. "What's so amusing?"

"You had Assunta un-sabotage the *Stalwart*, but I sabotaged the *Kestrel*. I destroyed its thruster controls so the craft couldn't get off the ground. You're not going to get to spread your filth throughout the galaxy, Neo-Xeno!"

Sidney's eyes widened, and her mask of rock-solid confidence slipped. "Jason, go out and see if what he says is true. Don't worry about Neo-Xenos. None are close by at the moment."

Jason looked to Aisha and she gave him a nod to tell him it was OK if he did as Sidney commanded.

"Go with him, Assunta," Sidney said. "Make sure he doesn't cause any mischief."

Jason and Assunta left the dome, and everyone waited in silence until they returned, only a few minutes later.

"What Oren says is true," Jason said. "The thruster console is inoperative, and much of its internal hardware has been destroyed. The controls will require significant repair."

"How long?" Sidney demanded.

"A day at least," Jason said. "Maybe two. I'll need to cannibalize parts from the *Stalwart* as well as from the station, and I will need time for trial and error, as I am not programmed to do this type of repair, and I have no way of downloading the necessary information. I believe that I will be able to ultimately synthesize a procedure from the information I do have stored in my memory, but as I said, it will take time."

Sidney took this in, mulled it over, and sighed. "The Summoner has waited nearly a century to be free of this world. It can wait a few more days. Get to work right away and—"

Sidney was cut off by the voice of a woman coming over everyone's comms.

"This is Marsha Easton, commander of the Leviathan ship *Osprey*. Does anyone read me?"

Everyone in the room looked at each other, sudden relief palpable in the air.

Before anyone could speak, Sidney quickly turned to the console and worked the controls.

"There. Now we can hear her, but she can't hear us."

The commander repeated her words, paused, then added,

"If anyone can hear me, we're approaching Penumbra and will be touching down at the research station shortly. When I arrive, I will assess the situation and, if necessary, assume command of the mission. Easton out."

Sirena grinned. "It's about time the cavalry showed up!"

"I don't understand," Aisha said. "How did they get here so fast?"

Jena answered. "At a guess, I'd say Leviathan sent them out soon after we departed. The Guildmasters knew this was going to be a dangerous mission, so they sent another ship as a backup plan, in case our mission failed. The ship was likely stationed a few systems away, and when the crew received our signal that we'd crash landed, they contacted the Guildmasters for instructions. Since the crew didn't immediately come to Penumbra, I assume they were given orders to wait a certain amount of time to hear from us, and – if they didn't – to assume our mission ran into trouble and come see what happened."

"Sneaky bastards," Sirena said, her tone one of grudging admiration.

Luis nodded. "It's good strategy."

"What are you going to do?" Aisha asked. "Send another small army of your children to greet them when they land? Or don't you have enough left after sacrificing them the way you did?"

"It's true the numbers of my children are currently low, but more are growing as we speak."

"Will they be ready to fight by the time the *Osprey* lands?" Luis asked.

Sidney didn't answer.

"You have failed," Jason said. "Out of the four of you,

only Assunta has actual battle knowledge. And even if you threaten to kill one or more of us if we don't fight for you, we will not do so now that we know your plan. The *Osprey*'s crew will kill or capture you, and once we tell them what has happened here, they will most likely leave the planet before your newly grown children can attack them."

Sidney pressed several buttons on the console, and a few moments later, the door to the neighboring dome opened. A thrall came lumbering in. Luis realized this was the Neo-Xeno that had been held in stasis, and Sidney – or the Summoner, or whoever she was now – had released it. He tensed, expecting the monster to immediately attack them, but instead it walked across the dome to the airlock door and stopped, oblivious to the humans. Sidney went over and gently caressed the creature's quivering mandibles. Then, she touched the keypad controls next to the door. It opened, the thrall stepped through, and Sidney closed the door behind it.

"What good is one Neo-Xeno going to do?" Luis asked.

"Especially a thrall?" Aisha added.

Sidney merely smiled.

THIRTY-SIX

Marsha Easton sat in the command chair on the bridge of the *Osprey*, looking at the image on the viewscreen, and wondering just what the hell had gone down on this planet.

Like the *Kestrel*, the *Osprey* was a caravel, outfitted with the same bells and whistles. It was the sleekest, toughest ship Marsha had ever commanded, and she wished it was hers instead of a loaner from Leviathan. Depending on how this mission played out, maybe she could talk the Guild into giving her the ship as a bonus. Once they'd entered Penumbra's atmosphere, their sensors had located a landed ship, and they'd gone down to investigate it. She'd expected it to be the *Kestrel*, but she was surprised to discover it was a Coalition vessel, a light frigate. The long trail of torn-up earth behind the craft indicated it had crash landed, and as they got closer, she saw that one of its stabilizers was missing. Lost in the crash, she assumed. Marsha ordered their weapons brought online and then she hailed the ship. She received no response.

Penumbra's landscape was too rocky for the Coalition crew – assuming they'd departed their ship – to leave a trail, so Marsha ordered her nav officer to head toward the domed station, since there was nowhere else on the planet for shipwrecked soldiers to go. The viewscreen was set to nightview, and the images on it were almost as clear as they would be during the day. As the *Osprey* flew above the terrain, Marsha saw the headless body of a dead alien lying on the ground, an ugly insect-looking thing. Unpleasant to look at, but its lack of a head said it was easy enough to kill. Soon after that they approached a pair of large holes in the ground, one bigger than the other. More dead aliens were scattered around the area here.

"Looks like some kind of cave collapse," Mickie Valesquez, the crew member at the sensors/comm station said. "No life signs, but there's some heavy equipment down there, though."

"Mining equipment?" Marsha asked.

"Maybe."

Mickie zoomed the viewscreen to reveal a driller and a hauler – and a hell of lot of dead aliens, some larger than the others.

Chuck Passmore, the officer at life support, let out a low whistle. "Damn."

Marsha said nothing, but she agreed with the sentiment.

The *Osprey* continued, and soon the research station came into view. As they drew closer to it, the viewscreen displayed the image of a huge depression in the ground, scorched and blackened as if by a massive fire.

"Fire can't burn in this atmosphere," Cori Haynes, the life support officer, said. "Right?"

"Not normal fire," said the nav officer, Susana Spalding. "What could do that?"

Hong Grant, weapons officer, answered. "Devilfire. They use it in mining."

"And there were three miners aboard the *Kestrel*," Marsha said. This was looking worse all the time.

They drew near the station and saw the *Kestrel* parked next to the central dome, along with a transport containing a stabilizer, the one that had been missing from the frigate, she assumed. The *Kestrel* was short one stabilizer too. It looked like the crew had been in the process of attempting a repair. But while Marsha noticed these details, what really caught her attention was the alien carapaces that littered the ground around the ship. The goddamned things were *everywhere*.

"Christ," Susana said. "How many of them were there?"

"Dozens," Hong said. "Maybe a hundred or more."

Marsha revised her assessment of the aliens. Individually, they might not be much of a threat, but en masse, they could be deadly.

"Do you think anyone survived this battle?" Cori asked.

"Hopefully, the *Kestrel* crew. Let's hope those creatures only ate the Coalition crew," Mickie chuckled.

Marsha had mixed feelings upon viewing this grisly scene. On one hand, she was glad that Luis Gonzalez and his crew had cleared the way for her team. On the other, she was intimidated by the prospect that they might've all died doing so. She and Luis had never met, but she knew of him and his team by reputation. They were a tough crew, known for getting the job done no matter what it took. If aliens had taken them out, she and her crew were going to have to perform at the top of their game if they didn't want the same thing to happen to them.

"Let's try hailing them one last time," Marsha said.

Mickie opened a channel and Marsha once again announced herself and asked for a reply. As before, none came.

"Not looking good for the advance team," Susana said.

"No, it is not," Marsha said. "Take us to the closest clear spot and let's land."

Susana nodded and went to work. As the *Osprey* circled around and flew past the *Kestrel* and the dozens of dead alien shells, Cori said, "What do you think happened?"

Marsha shrugged. "Hard to say. My guess is that the Coalition ship patrolling the system detected the *Kestrel* and pursued it into the atmosphere. They fought, both ships went down, and then the aliens decided to make trouble for them. Maybe some of them survived, maybe they didn't. We'll find out soon enough."

Once they landed, Marsha had Mickie send a quick status report to Leviathan HQ, then she ordered everyone to get into their EVA suits and load up on weapons. Their mission was simple: find out what went wrong with the previous mission, obtain samples of both the aliens and Neo-Xenium, and rescue any survivors and take them back to Leviathan for "debriefing". Marsha was glad that the Guild hadn't ordered them to execute Luis and the others on sight. She'd have done it, of course – for an increase in her team's fee – but she wouldn't have enjoyed it. Maybe the Guild would let survivors live, maybe it wouldn't. That wasn't any of her concern. The job was the job, and when it was over, it was over. She and her team would put it out of their minds and move on to the next one. It was the mercenary way.

They gathered at the main airlock and exited the craft two at a time. Marsha and Hong, Mickie and Susana, with Chuck bringing up the rear. Their weapons were up as they advanced, ready to fire at the first sign of movement. It was damn creepy making their way through the alien remains, and Marsha wondered what sort of weapon Luis and his crew had used against the creatures to kill them and leave behind only their shells. Whatever it was, she wanted one for her and each of her crew.

The mystery weapon hadn't been perfect, though. One of the dead aliens was intact, and Marsha noted its position. If they couldn't find a live one to take back to Leviathan – or if, as she suspected, capturing a live one would prove too difficult – they could use the dead one as their specimen. If the Guild didn't like it, they could dock the team's pay. She wouldn't sacrifice any of her people's lives just so Leviathan could have a live monster to play with.

As they approached the *Kestrel*, Marsha looked it over quickly. With the exception of the missing stabilizer, it seemed in good condition. If Luis and the others had dealt with the alien threat – which admittedly was a big if – maybe she and her team could safely repair the *Kestrel*, fly it into orbit, and then pilot it remotely via the *Osprey*. They could drop off the *Kestrel* on an empty moon they used to store their stash whenever they decided to supplement their mercenary earnings with a little piracy. They'd then report to Leviathan that the *Kestrel* remained on Penumbra, the Guild would write off the ship as a loss, and Marsha and her team would have themselves a kick-ass vessel. Upgrade the weapons, and with its speed, it would make an excellent pirate craft. Maybe they'd give up working as soldiers-for-hire and go into piracy full time. With a craft like the *Osprey*, it would be possible. She'd have to talk it over with her team.

"All right," she said, "let's keep going. I want to get into the central dome and see what's what in there."

If any of Luis' team had survived, that's where they'd most likely be. If nothing else, maybe they'd left behind an indication of what had happened to them, a final message of some kind, a voice recording, or a holo. The more she and her team could learn about what the other crew had encountered, the better their chances of—

Chuck screamed.

Marsha and the others spun around to see an alien – the intact one she'd thought dead – had stopped playing possum and knocked Chuck to the ground. It straddled his back and rammed its long talons through his helmet. Chuck made a strained choking sound, his body quivered, and then he fell still.

Marsha didn't need to give the command to fire. Everyone started shooting, but while their rounds cut chunks of carapace from the creature, they didn't penetrate its shell. Marsha was about to tell her team to shoot for the sonofabitch's eyes when she caught a flash of blue.

She spun around to see a different kind of monster rushing toward her. This one was humanoid, though hugely muscled, with two-digit claws, fangs, and – most bizarrely – a pair of scorpion-tail-like appendages growing out of its back. Its skin was blue like the Neo-Xeno that had attacked them, but it didn't have a carapace, which hopefully meant it would be easier to kill. She fired at it, and while her rounds drew blood – *blue* blood – she could tell they didn't penetrate far. She kept firing as the thing ran toward her, bare feet pounding the earth. She heard another scream over her comm. It sounded like Cori, although she wasn't certain. All she knew was that another member of her crew was gone.

The scorpion-tail-backed creature reached her then, and its two stingers lanced downward and pierced the shoulders of her EVA suit. Now it was her time to scream. She felt venom being pumped into her body, burning like hot oil as it surged through her system. When the monster yanked its stingers out of her, she collapsed to the ground, pain spreading rapidly through her body. Unable to as much as twitch a finger now, she lay there and watched as the Neo-Xeno and the scorpion-tail-back finished off the remainder of her crew.

The pain eased, replaced by a strange numbness, and her vision blurred. As the venom caused her body to disintegrate, she had no last thoughts, no profound insights. She simply died.

Sidney observed the action taking place outside on the console monitor. Aisha couldn't see the screen from where she sat, but she heard the muffled sound of gunfire through the wall of the dome. It soon ceased.

"That didn't take long, did it?" Sidney said, turning away from the screen to face the others. "I'm pleased to say that while both the thrall and Dwain are a bit worse for wear, they survived."

"Dwain's alive?" Sirena said, shocked.

"Yes, and you'll see him soon. He *has* changed, though. You might not recognize him."

Aisha didn't like the sound of that, but she put her sense of desperation aside. She'd hoped that the new arrivals might succeed where they had failed and make it to the dome and kill Sidney, Jena, Assunta, and Bhavna. But that hope had proved to be extremely short-lived.

"What happens now?" she asked.

"What else? We no longer need to repair the *Kestrel*. We now have a fully intact ship, so we can leave right away." Sidney looked delighted. "We *do* have to pick up someone first, though."

THIRTY-SEVEN

"What's to prevent me from flying this thing straight into a mountain?" Aisha asked.

She sat at the *Osprey*'s navigation console, while Jason was on sensors/comm, Luis on weapons, and Sirena on life support. Sidney sat in the command seat – naturally – and Bhavna and Jena stood on either side of her, both armed with light machine guns. Oren sat propped against the wall, his right arm and leg still non-functional. Assunta stood next to him, the barrel of her SMG pressed to his right temple, the mining tool still stuck in her other hand.

Standing at the rear of the bridge was the thrall that Sidney had released from the stasis tube and the monstrous thing that Dwain had become. Both the thrall and Dwain had incurred wounds from the brief battle with the *Osprey*'s crew. The thrall's carapace was covered with divots, several which were cracked and bleeding. Dwain looked worse. His wounds were deeper and bleeding more profusely. He didn't seem to care, though.

"Or I could shut down life support," Sirena said, "and lock

down the controls so no one but me could turn it back on."

"And I could fire every missile and have them target the ship," Luis added.

"Or we could try all three simultaneously," Aisha said. "You wouldn't have time to stop us all."

"And don't think we'd let your threat to kill Oren stop us," Luis said. He glanced at the cyborg. "Sorry, kid, but we're talking about the future of the whole damn galaxy here."

Sidney smiled.

"If you intended to do any of those things, you wouldn't talk about them – you'd just do them. You're stalling for time, hoping to find a way to stop me without dying in the process. I do believe you're willing to sacrifice your lives to prevent us from leaving this world, but the instinct for self-preservation runs deep in your kind, as it does in the Summoner. Reach up and touch the back of your necks. You humans, that is. Jason and Oren, you needn't bother."

"What?" Aisha said.

"Just do it."

Aisha, Luis, and Sirena did as Sidney said, and Aisha felt a small wet patch of spongy material adhering to the skin at the base of her neck. When she took her hand away, she examined her fingers and saw the tips were lightly stained blue. She, Luis, and Sirena all had Neo-Xeno mold on them.

"No," Sirena said softly. "No, no, no…"

"It came from our friend, the thrall," Sidney said. "That's why I had it escort you inside this ship, so that it could flick mold spores onto your bodies without your knowledge. The mold grows quite swiftly, doesn't it?"

Aisha struggled to contain her fear. The thought that she

had an alien organism growing on her body – especially one connected to the Neo-Xenos – was terrifying.

"If you could've done this to us anytime..." she began.

"It is not something that can be done during battle. Both parties, Neo-Xeno and human, need to remain relatively still during the transference, and the host needs to continue remaining still afterward so the spores can properly fuse with your physiology without harming you."

"So, you've put this shit on us to, what?" Luis asked. "Threaten to turn us into more of your zombie servants if we don't behave? You said you need our minds free so that we can pilot the ship."

"This is true," Sidney said. "The Summoner's will can forestall the mold's effect. You won't become devastators like Dwain unless one of you tries to betray us. If that happens, we'll still have two humans, and Jason, to fly the craft."

Aisha tried to think of some way out of this, but it looked like the Summoner had covered every angle. Even if they let the mold take them, and the ship crashed, they'd only be delaying the inevitable. Leviathan would send another expedition to Penumbra, or perhaps next time it would be the Coalition or another of the Guilds. It didn't matter who it was, *someone* would come, and that time, the Summoner's plan might succeed.

She glanced at Luis, and he gave her an almost imperceptible shake of his head. She got the message. Keep going along with the Summoner's program for now and wait for a chance to make their move. Aisha didn't like it, but she saw no other alternatives. She gave Luis a nod.

Jason had been quiet up to this point, but now he spoke.

"Is that what happened to the original crew of the research station? You attempted to use their ship to leave but failed?"

"Not quite," Sidney said. "As Jena told you, the station was built by the Coalition, and once they staffed it, they left a small squad of soldiers to guard the scientists and miners, and then the pilots took their craft into orbit."

Aisha knew it was standard procedure for Command not to leave a ship on the ground longer than absolutely necessary. A grounded ship made too easy a target for an enemy to destroy or steal.

"The Summoner possessed several of the staff, and they tried to get the soldiers to bring the craft down, but some of the non-infected staff contacted the soldiers and informed them of what was happening. Command advised the soldiers to abandon the mission – and all the personnel on the planet – and they did so. The Summoner never had the chance to take the ship."

"What happened to those who were left behind?" Oren said. It was the first time he'd spoken since they'd been brought aboard the *Osprey*. "Did they just die of old age eventually?"

"Not at all," Sidney said. "They were given the honor of merging with the Summoner. Eventually I hope to do the same."

"As do I," Bhavna said.

Jena and Assunta echoed the sentiment.

"It's bad enough they had to become possessed," Luis said, "but then they got *eaten* too? That's just disgusting."

"It is *glorious*," Sidney said. "Slow down. We're nearing the Summoner's den."

Aisha didn't see anything special about the area. More dirt, rocks, and scraggly plants. She knew, however, that it was likely a much different story beneath the surface.

"Land here," Sidney said.

Aisha hesitated, but then she did as Sidney asked. Once the *Osprey* was on the ground, Sidney ordered her to open the cargo bay door and lower the loading ramp.

"Now what?" Luis said.

"Now we wait," Sidney said. "Jason, switch the viewscreen to focus on the interior of the cargo bay."

Jason did so. The *Osprey* had brought no mining equipment with it, and aside from a single transport, the bay was empty.

"Switch to an outer view," Sidney said.

Jason complied, and the screen now displayed the area at the rear of the ship. Nothing happened, and then a large section of ground began to bulge.

"I don't like the look of this," Luis said.

"That makes two of us," Aisha said.

"Three," Sirena added.

A huge, clawed hand burst up from the ground, quickly followed by another, then a third and a fourth. A ravager pulled its mold-covered body into the air, followed by another. The behemoths stepped back, and several slayers emerged and joined them. Dozens of runners and thralls emerged next, and when they reached the surface, they began digging frantically to widen the hole. As the hole grew larger, the runners and thralls moved back, causing the slayers and ravagers to do likewise.

A gigantic mound of blue mold rose to fill the hole, then kept expanding. It was spheroid in shape, and the higher it came, the more apparent it was that the object was being pushed up from below by dozens of Neo-Xenos. When the huge orb was all the way up, the Neo-Xenos below shoved it onto the surface ground, and the Neo-Xenos already there took over. They rolled the sphere towards the cargo ramp, but when they were halfway there, they stopped. A horizontal line split this side of the orb, and as it parted, Aisha realized with horror that she looked at a massive mold-covered eye.

As the lids parted all the way, she saw that while the size of the thing alone was terrifying, the eye itself was far worse. Unlike the Neo-Xenos, the Summoner's eye didn't resemble an insect. It was a *human* eye – or something damn close to it – the iris the same bright blue as the mold that covered its outer surface.

"Magnificent, isn't it?" Sidney said. "When the Summoner absorbed the first expedition's research team and their guards, it added human DNA to its own. More than that, it developed a heightened level of self-awareness and intelligence. Its form changed to reflect this."

Jason looked at Sidney. "Will it change further now that an Empusa is one of its children?"

"Once I go to the Summoner and am absorbed into its body, yes. I don't know what those changes will be, but I'm quite excited to find out."

Aisha didn't want to think about the Summoner possessing the Empusan ability to transform its shape. Would it be a quality it could pass on to its future children? Would the galaxy become infested with predatory creatures that could alter their forms at will? There would be no defense against such monsters.

Sidney continued speaking.

"We will travel from one inhabited world to another. We will leave several of the Summoner's children there, along with a supply of mold for them to use. Then, we will move on to the next planet, and the next one after that. The Summoner's children shall thrive throughout the galaxy, and those who refuse to become part of the fold shall be killed. The galaxy will finally become the utopia so many cultures have attempted to achieve and failed."

They watched on the viewscreen as the Summoner closed its eyelid, and the Neo-Xenos began rolling it up the cargo ramp. Evidently, the behemoth couldn't move itself. Aisha was glad to see the thing had at least one limitation.

"No," Oren said. "That... that *blasphemy* cannot be allowed to leave this world!"

Aisha turned to study him. Aside from her, everyone's gaze fixated on the screen – including Assunta's. That's why the woman didn't see Oren push himself up onto his left leg, make a fist with his left hand, and shove it through her face. There was a horrible wet crunching sound, and Assunta's finger reflexively squeezed the trigger of her SMG, releasing a wild spray of ammo. Bullets went everywhere, pinged off the plasteel walls, ceiling, and floor. Sirena cried out in pain as one of the rounds shredded her left ear.

Jena and Bhavna fired on the cyborg.

He's lost it, Aisha thought. He's gone completely insane. He will kill us all.

Jason slammed his right hand down on his station's console. He was so strong that the plasteel dented, and his hand snapped off and sprung up into the air. Sparks of electricity shot out of the newly created opening in his wrist, and he rose from his chair and ran along behind the bridge's stations, pressing his wrist to the necks of his human companions, one after the other, burning off the mold attached to their skin.

When he put his severed wrist to her neck, the pain was so intense that Aisha couldn't even draw breath to scream. But the worst of it passed quickly, and she was relieved to realize that she had not become one of the Summoner's children.

"Do your best to cover me," she told Luis. "I've got an idea."

Luis nodded and jumped out of his seat. Sirena followed him, ignoring the bleeding mess where her ear had been. Bhavna and Jena continued firing at Oren, Assunta hanging on his arm like some kind of grotesque decoration. He pulled his arm out of her head quickly in a spray of blue Neo-Xeno blood, and her body collapsed to the floor. Bhavna and Jena's bullets dimpled his EVA suit but didn't penetrate it. The rounds had a much different effect on his face, though. They tore through his synthetic flesh, destroyed his left eye – the one that served as his holo camera – and presumably penetrated his human brain. Even so, he didn't go down. With a crazed expression on his face, he hopped on his one good leg toward Sidney.

Aisha took a quick glance at the screen, saw the Neo-Xenos had only gotten the Summoner halfway up the ramp.

Come on… she thought. They needed to get the Summoner onboard.

As Oren fought, he screamed, "You killed my parents, you piece of shit! All you goddamn aliens did!"

Aisha had no idea what the hell Oren was talking about, but whatever it was, it was clear he intended to kill Sidney. Jena and Bhavna stepped toward him, still firing their weapons. Sparks shot out of Oren's empty eye socket, along with a clear substance that might have served as blood or might've been some kind of oil. Maybe both. His left hand shot out, grabbed hold of Bhavna's head, and slammed it into Jena's. Their skulls made horrible cracking sounds and then their heads exploded in a gush of brains and Neo-Xeno blood.

As their bodies fell to the floor, Oren looked at them and shrieked, "You were both shitty colleagues!"

Aisha risked another glance at the viewscreen. The Neo-Xenos had almost gotten the Summoner into the cargo bay. She turned back toward the bridge and saw Luis, Jason, and Sirena coming up behind Oren. The cyborg, who now had blue Neo-Xeno blood all over his face and body, was less than a meter away from Sidney when she bolted out of the command chair and ran to the back of the bridge.

As she did this, the thrall and Dwain rushed forward to protect her. Oren – who leaked a huge amount of that clear fluid now – made one last leap in a desperate attempt to reach Sidney, but Dwain swung his arm outward and struck the cyborg on the side of the head while he was in midair. Oren's head went one way and his body another. The head struck the bridge wall hard and bounced off, while the body fell to the floor and lay twitching, sparking, and bleeding clear fluid. Jason snatched Oren's head out of the air and tucked it under his arm as if it were a ball. Aisha saw that the front of Oren's face was completely caved in, clear fluid leaking from his eye sockets, nose, mouth, and ears. The man had been an Upholder, and while she'd found his views abhorrent, she couldn't help feeling sorrow at his loss.

Sidney didn't stay on the bridge, especially now that Jena and Assunta had been taken out. The instant she reached the door, it slid open and she rushed through. The door slid shut behind her. The thrall and Dwain remained to ensure she escaped, and now they headed for Luis, Jason, and Sirena.

Aisha turned back to the screen and saw the Summoner was all the way in the cargo hold now. The Neo-Xenos that had pushed the Summoner onto the *Osprey* milled about their master, while more of their kind started coming up the ramp.

Yes! They had the Summoner now.

Aisha punched the control that closed the cargo bay door, then she fired up the thrusters. An instant later, she sent the *Osprey* roaring into the sky.

THIRTY-EIGHT

The *Osprey*'s inertial dampeners couldn't adjust for the ship's rapid acceleration, and Luis pitched forward, as did Sirena. As he fell, he heard the *snik* of Jason's boot maglocks engaging and then he was stopped with a sudden jerking motion as the android grabbed hold of his EVA suit. Jason only had one hand to grab with, but he managed to thrust his other arm beneath Sirena's and flex it at the elbow to stop her from falling. The humans both activated the maglocks of their boots, sealing their feet to the wall, and Jason continued holding on to help keep them steady.

Luis felt the ship's vibrations through his feet, and he knew that Aisha ran the thrusters full out. If this kept up much longer, the damn things would burn out. He had a good idea what her plan was – take the *Osprey* up into near orbit, turn it back toward the planet, and with thrusters still operating on high, send the ship screaming back toward the surface where it would impact in a spectacular explosion, killing everyone aboard, including the Summoner.

Luis had glanced at the viewscreen a couple of moments

earlier and saw the obscene thing had made it into the cargo hold. He thought of the Neo-Xenos' master bouncing around in there right now like a massive mold-covered ball, and the resultant mental image made him smile grimly. From his position, he didn't have the flexibility to turn back and check on Aisha, but since she hadn't fallen past any of them, he assumed she was still safely in the navigator's seat and piloting the ship on its last suicidal voyage.

Neither the thrall nor Dwain had maglocks on their feet, and they now lay on the bridge's back wall, which – given that the ship headed straight upward – presently served as its floor. The bodies of Assunta, Jena, Bhavna, and Oren had fallen around the creatures. Oren's head too, as Jason had to let go of it in order to catch Luis and Sirena. Unfortunately, the women's weapons had fallen with them, which wasn't ideal. Luis would've loved to have one in his grip right now, and he was sure Sirena felt the same way.

Their fall seemed to have had no effect on Dwain or the thrall, and they got to their feet and looked upward at the two humans and one android above them. If the artificial gravity had kicked in when the ship took off, the monsters would be able to get at them now, but Luis assumed Aisha had reached over to the life support station and shut the grav off in order to keep Dwain and the thrall where they were. The two children of the Summoner, however, were still determined to kill them. They started scrabbling at the "wall" – which was really the ceiling – but they couldn't get any purchase on its slick plasteel surface. The thrall screeched its frustration, and Dwain expressed his in a deep roar.

"Do you think there's any of him left in there?" Sirena asked.

Luis knew who she was referring to. He looked down at the fanged, clawed beast that had not long ago been a man and a valued teammate, and he saw nothing but animalistic savagery in its eyes.

"No."

"If I had a goddamned gun, I'd put him down right now," Sirena said. "He'd do the same for us."

"I know."

Luis thought Dwain and the thrall might give up then, but instead they began jumping. Strong as they were, there was only so much they could do against the g-forces pressing against them, and they didn't get very high. The g-forces affected him and Sirena as well, shoving them forward, and Jason tightened his grip to hold them upright. Then, Dwain did something that cemented Luis' appraisal of whether any of the man remained in the monster. He reached over his left shoulder, grabbed hold of the scorpion stinger appendage there, and yanked – hard. It tore free from his back, and blue blood gushed from the wound. He grimaced in pain, but his hate-filled gaze remained firmly fixed on his former crewmates. Then, he hurled the stinger as hard as he could. It flew through the air and struck Sirena in the face. The barb broke through her faceplate, pierced the flesh of her cheek before the stinger dislodged and fell back down.

Sirena looked at Luis, clear fluid and blood leaking from her wounded cheek. She opened her mouth as if she intended to speak, but then she convulsed and her body rapidly decayed away to nothing. Flesh, muscle, organs, bones – everything was gone.

Luis was now looking at an empty EVA suit.

He couldn't believe it. Sirena had been so full of life and fire, and she'd been reduced to nothing in mere moments, as if she'd never existed at all.

He heard a snuffling sound then, and he looked downward and saw that Dwain – or rather, the creature that Dwain had become – was laughing.

You sonofabitch.

Dwain reached over his right shoulder now and ripped his second stinger free. Luis knew that he was Dwain's next target, and there was nothing he could do but hang there and hope the bastard missed this time.

Jason had a different idea, though. He straightened his handless arm, and Sirena's empty suit slumped forward, still held in place by the maglocks on its boots. Jason released the maglock on his right boot, raised his leg, and then kicked the back of Sirena's suit, once, twice, three times in rapid succession. EVA suits were constructed from plasteel, but their separate pieces were held together by micro-fasteners. They were strong, but not as strong as a determined android. The suit detached from its boots and, with Jason's force added to the g's they were pulling, it streaked toward Dwain and smashed into him before he could throw his other stinger. Dwain became pulp in an instant, blue blood splattering outward in all directions, like a big bug that had been squashed by a gigantic boot. Luis supposed in a way he was.

The thrall – now covered in copious amounts of Dwain's

blue blood – stared at Dwain's crushed corpse as if it didn't understand what it was looking at. Then it shrieked in fury at them.

Jason spoke then, his voice eerily calm. "I don't know about you, Luis, but I'm sick to death of those things."

Jason let go of him, and he slumped forward. His maglocks held, though, and he didn't fall. Jason released his last maglock and plummeted toward the thrall. He held his right arm straight out as he fell, and when he hit the Neo-Xeno, he jammed his sparking wrist stump into the creature's mouth. At the same instant, the thrall grabbed hold of the android's head and yanked. Electricity coruscated over the Neo-Xeno's body, and it shook, stiffened, then went still. Smoke curled from its mouth, and an acrid odor like the stink of burning hair filled the bridge. Jason's head fell from its dead hands and hit the floor, bounced once, then came to a stop.

The android's body no longer moved. His head lay a meter away, the face turned partially upward. Luis saw the android's final blank expression, but no sign of life in the eyes. Grief filled him, but also a sense of profound respect for the android's sacrifice.

"What happened?" Aisha called out.

"It's just you and me now. You can turn on the gravity."

Sidney – or rather the fragment of the Summoner's consciousness that currently resided in her body – ran down the main corridor of the *Osprey*. She didn't fear dying. As long as the Summoner lived, the Neo-Xenos lived. What she feared was that Aisha, Luis, Jason, and Sirena might still find a way to prevent the craft from leaving Penumbra and destroy the Summoner in the process. She could not allow that to happen.

A memory flashed through her mind then, one that belonged to the Summoner and not the Empusan whose body it had stolen. She saw a patch of mold clinging to a yellow rock. The mold was a dull gray color, and it pulsed gently, waiting, waiting... Time passed – hours, weeks, years, the length was irrelevant – and then a small blue insect crawled past the rock. The mold reached out, not with its mind, exactly, because it was not sentient, but rather with an instinctive psychic call. The insect stopped, raised its head, wiggled its antennae, curious. It heeded that call, climbed onto the rock, walked up to the mold, and hesitated. The mold intensified its call – its *summons* – and the insect stepped onto the mold where it was absorbed.

Thus was the Summoner born.

That had been so long ago, eons beyond counting, and the Summoner could not, *would* not die this day at the hands of a few pathetic humans.

This host's mind held a great deal of knowledge, and the Summoner searched through it now, looking for anything Sidney knew about how starships operated. Surely there had to be places other than the bridge where the craft could be controlled. Some console, some system, *somewhere*. If she could find it, she could take command of the vessel and make certain the humans could not harm her master who was also herself. Once she had taken care of that, she would set about bringing them all into the Summoner's fold.

Then, once they had been changed, they would lose their actual experience of flying starcraft, but they would retain their hosts' knowledge. Hopefully, that would be enough to take the Summoner to the stars. Yes, she could still salvage things. All she needed was to–

The ship took a sudden angle upward, and Sidney's feet slipped out from under her. She skidded along the floor, and when the vessel straightened, she fell down the corridor. Her hands scrabbled for purchase, but there was nothing for them to grab onto, and she continued falling through the air until she slammed into a bulkhead. The intense g-forces caused her to hit harder than she would've otherwise, and both her legs broke with loud cracking sounds. She screamed from the pain, and then lay there, pressed tight against the bulkhead. As useful as taking a host could be, their bodies were so fragile, all soft meat and weak bone, with no hard carapace to protect their internal organs as the Neo-Xenos had.

She reached out to the Summoner's mind. The psychic connection between the Summoner and its children was limited, allowing for the communication of simple information only. Direct contact was required for complete sharing. She established a connection, although it was a tentative one. The Summoner was affected by the g-forces as the *Osprey* soared upward, and its thoughts were scattered and unfocused. Sidney kept her message simple, just one word.

Grow.

If she was going to stop the humans, she would need reinforcements.

She lay there, in agony, and waited for the Summoner to produce more Neo-Xenos.

Aisha had been taught to deal with g-forces during her military training, but she'd never experienced anything this intense before. It took a monumental effort to move her hands toward the life support console controls, but she did it and activated the artificial gravity. There was a dizzying sensation of the ship flipping over – although of course it did no such thing – and then normal gravity was restored. Regardless of the *Osprey*'s orientation as it flew, inside the craft, up would stay up and down would stay down. She boosted the ship's inertial dampeners to compensate for the g-forces, and the pressure on her body eased.

The viewscreen showed only Penumbra's brownish sky. In minutes they would reach the upper atmosphere, and soon after that the screen would display a view of open space. She moved her hands back to the nav station and quickly programmed an automatic course: when the ship reached the apex of its flight, it would arc downward and return to the planet's surface at full thruster speed. The system's safety protocols tried to prevent her from laying in this course, but she overrode them, and the job was done. The *Osprey* was now nothing more than a great big bomb.

She rose from her seat and turned to check on Luis. He walked toward her, a light machine gun in one hand, an SMG in the other.

"Take your pick," he said.

Choosing the SMG, she looked past him and took in the carnage on the bridge. She'd heard everything that had happened, but she hadn't been able to turn around and watch, so it was something of a shock to see all the dead bodies piled up at the rear of the bridge. Such a goddamned waste of life.

Luis could guess what she was thinking. "We can *do* this, Aisha. Do you remember the first thing they taught us in basic training about battle?"

She smiled grimly. "'You're not dead until you're dead.'"

"Well, we're not dead, are we? Come on, let's go. We need to find Sidney and make sure she can't prevent the ship from crashing."

Aisha nodded. There was no time to grieve their losses, only time to act, and not a hell of a lot of it, either.

They headed toward the bridge's exit.

When the gravity came on, Sidney fell forward onto the floor. Fresh pain flared in her legs, and she gritted her teeth to bite back a scream. Seconds later, there was loud pounding on the bulkhead behind her, and she turned, put her hands on the wall, got her legs beneath her, and forced herself to stand. The pain intensified to the point where she thought she was going to pass out, but she managed to slap her hand to the control pad to the side of the bulkhead and open the door.

Neo-Xenos entered – three thralls and three runners, as they were easier to grow than slayers and ravagers due to their smaller size. A runner grabbed hold of her as her legs collapsed, lifted her into its arms, and cradled her like an infant. Hardly an army, but they would have to do. As she'd lain waiting for the Neo-Xenos to arrive, she'd located a memory in her host's mind. Before departing on their mission to Penumbra, Jena had given the team a tour of the *Kestrel*, and next to the engine room was an auxiliary bridge. It wasn't as grand as the name implied, simply a small room with a single console that permitted a crewmember to control the ship in the event that the actual bridge was damaged or for some reason inaccessible. The console permitted control of only basic ship functions – caravels weren't designed to be military craft, after all – but with luck, it might be enough to allow her to stop the *Osprey* from crashing.

If the Summoner had gained full mastery of Sidney's shapeshifting abilities, it could've healed her broken legs, but as it was, it would take time and concentration to do so. The Summoner would have to settle for being carried.

"Take me back the way you came," Sidney said.

The runner holding her turned and loped back through the open bulkhead door, and the rest of the Neo-Xenos followed.

"There's only one place she can go," Aisha said.

Luis nodded. "The auxiliary bridge."

They ran down the ship's main corridor, the boots of their EVA suits pounding on the plasteel floor. Ship's gravity was set to Earth normal, and although Aisha had only been on Penumbra a short time, her body felt heavy and ponderous after the planet's lighter gravity. It didn't take them long to draw near the auxiliary bridge. Caravels were relatively small craft, and nothing was far. Aisha wondered where in its death flight the *Osprey* was. Was it still flying upward or had it turned and started downward? With the inertial dampeners set so high, it was impossible to know. Hopefully, the ship would crash before Sidney – or rather the creature that now inhabited her body – could alter its course. But Aisha knew they couldn't take that chance. They had to proceed as if Sidney would succeed.

Neo-Xenos exited the auxiliary bridge and came running toward them. She gritted her teeth and fired her SMG, aiming for their heads, and Luis did the same with his machine gun.

There weren't that many Neo-Xenos – only five, a mix of thralls and runners – but they came so swiftly that Aisha and Luis killed a couple before the remaining three were on them. A runner slashed at Aisha, but its claws skittered across the front of her EVA suit without doing any real damage. She jammed the barrel of her SMG into one of the creature's compound eyes and pulled the trigger. Blue ichor splattered the wall behind the runner. A thrall tried to jam its claws into Luis' face, but he tilted his head right then left to avoid the blows, and he shoved the barrel of his machine gun into the Neo-Xeno's mouth and fired. The back of its head exploded, and the monster joined its siblings in death.

That left one Neo-Xeno remaining, a runner. This one was more cautious than the others, and it held back, swaying from side to side, as it was trying to make itself a harder target to hit.

"Go!" Luis said. "I've got this one!"

Before Aisha could respond, he ran toward the Neo-Xeno, firing his machine gun. The creature ducked to protect its eyes and mouth and then ran to meet him. When the Neo-Xeno was almost on top of Luis, he stopped firing and smashed the butt of the gun against the monster's head. The impact knocked the runner into the wall, and she heard its skull carapace crack.

"*Go!*" Luis repeated, and Aisha ran past him and the runner. She didn't look back.

Sidney's attention focused on the console screen. She was dimly aware of pounding footfalls approaching, of the Neo-Xenos racing out of the room – with the exception of the one serving as her legs – and of the blast of gunfire that followed. None of those things mattered, though. Finding a way to stop the *Osprey* from crashing was of the utmost importance.

She searched frantically through the console's system, looking for something, anything that would do the job. And then she found it – an option called CONTROL OVERRIDE. Smiling, she began to activate it.

She detected movement from the corner of her eye, and she turned her head in time to see Aisha enter the room. *You're too late, soldier!* Sidney thought with glee. She needed only a few more seconds to initiate the override, but as she started moving her hands across the console, they suddenly froze before she could complete the sequence. She tried to force them to work, but they refused to obey her. From deep within her mind, the remnant of her original personality – the *true* Sidney – laughed. She had chosen her moment to strike, and she had chosen it well.

Aisha raised her machine gun and fired. Rounds cut

through Sidney's head as if it were paper and did the same to the runner. Blue blood sprayed the air, and as she and the Neo-Xeno went down together, the fragment of the Summoner within Sidney realized, for the first time, that it might actually fail.

When Sidney and the Neo-Xeno were dead, Aisha hurried to the console monitor. Sidney had been about to activate the control override, but she hadn't been successful. Nothing could stop the *Osprey*'s destruction now.

Aisha ran out of the room and saw Luis straddling the runner, which he'd somehow managed to knock to the floor. He blasted the thing's head to gory mush, and then turned to her.

"It's finished," she said, nearly exultant. "The ship's going down."

He slumped against the wall in relief. She ran forward and grabbed his arm.

"That doesn't mean we have to, though. Where are the escape pods? You should know, right? This ship is the same as yours." She shook his arm to get his attention.

He looked at her blankly and, for a moment she thought he was too tired to go on. That he was going to give up, slump to the floor, and sit there until it was all over. But a look of grim determination came over his face.

"This way," he said and started running down the corridor, Aisha at his side.

She felt a tug at her consciousness then, as if something was trying to reach into her mind.

Don't leave me!

It was the Summoner, making one last-ditch effort to save its life.

Screw you, Aisha thought, and continued running.

THIRTY-NINE

Aisha and Luis stood side by side on the surface of Penumbra, looking at the plume of black smoke rising above the horizon. Behind them rested a white lozenge-shaped escape pod, hatch open. Neither of them had helmets when they'd gotten into the pod, but it contained a pair of EVA suits as well as survival supplies – MREs, water, extra oxygen containers – and they swapped out their old suits for the new ones before exiting the pod. These suits were basic ones, without any armor, and there had been no weapons. They still carried the guns they'd had aboard the *Osprey*, but the weapons were both almost out of ammo.

"So now what?" Luis asked. "We head back to the research station and wait for the Coalition to arrive?"

"If we can find it," Aisha said. "I have no idea where we are. Do you?"

"No."

"You know, we don't *have* to wait for the Coalition. We could try to repair the *Kestrel* ourselves and take off before they arrive."

He smiled. "That would make you a deserter."

She smiled back. "Like I give a shit at this point." Her eyes widened then. "Oh, I almost forgot. Hold on."

She went back into the escape pod, opened a container on the side of her old suit's belt, withdrew something, and returned. She held out a glowing blue rock.

"I saved this for you. So you can pay off your parents' debt."

He laughed. "Thank you." Taking the Neo-Xenium, he put it into his belt container.

"Pick a direction," he said, clapping her on the shoulder.

"How about that way?" Aisha pointed at random and together, they started walking.

Kilometers away from Aisha and Luis, the wreckage of the *Osprey* lay scattered across a barren yellow plain. Much of the debris was unrecognizable, but one piece resembled a human head with its facial features caved in. A large fissure in its artificial skull exposed organic brain tissue. Nearby lay a small clump of blue mold. Slowly, tortuously, the mold began to move toward the head, a centimeter at a time. It took a while, but eventually it reached the head, crawled up onto the brain, sank tendrils into its soft substance and began to grow. Sometime after that, a small purple creature resembling an Earth lizard – curious about the strange objects spread across the plain – crawled close by the head. The mold sensed the creature's presence, stretched its awareness toward the animal's primitive mind, and thought a single word.

Come.

ACKNOWLEDGMENTS

As always, thanks to my wonderful agent, Cherry Weiner. Very special thanks to my editor, Gwendolyn Nix. This is a far better book because of her efforts.

ABOUT THE AUTHOR

TIM WAGGONER is the Bram Stoker Award-winning author of over fifty novels and seven collections of short stories. He writes dark fantasy and horror, as well as media tie-ins. He's also a full-time tenured professor who teaches creative writing and composition at Sinclair College in Dayton, Ohio.

timwaggoner.com
twitter.com/timwaggoner

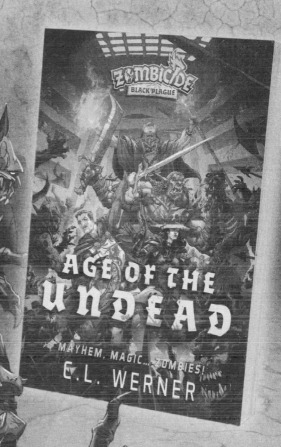

WORLD EXPANDING FICTION

Do you have them all?

ARKHAM HORROR

- ☐ *Wrath of N'kai* by Josh Reynolds
- ☐ *The Last Ritual* by S A Sidor
- ☐ *Mask of Silver* by Rosemary Jones
- ☐ *Litany of Dreams* by Ari Marmell
- ☐ *The Devourer Below* ed Charlotte Llewelyn-Wells
- ☐ *Dark Origins, The Collected Novellas Vol 1*
- ☐ *Cult of the Spider Queen* by S A Sidor
- ☐ *The Deadly Grimoire* by Rosemary Jones
- ☐ *Grim Investigations, The Collected Novellas Vol 2*
- ☐ *In the Coils of the Labyrinth* by David Annandale *(coming soon)*

DESCENT

- ☐ *The Doom of Fallowhearth* by Robbie MacNiven
- ☐ *The Shield of Daqan* by David Guymer
- ☐ *The Gates of Thelgrim* by Robbie MacNiven
- ☐ *Zachareth* by Robbie MacNiven
- ☐ *The Raiders of Bloodwood* by Davide Mana *(coming soon)*

KEYFORGE

- ☐ *Tales from the Crucible* ed Charlotte Llewelyn-Wells
- ☐ *The Qubit Zirconium* by M Darusha Wehm

LEGEND OF THE FIVE RINGS

- ☐ *Curse of Honor* by David Annandale
- ☐ *Poison River* by Josh Reynolds
- ☐ *The Night Parade of 100 Demons* by Marie Brennan
- ☐ *Death's Kiss* by Josh Reynolds
- ☐ *The Great Clans of Rokugan, The Collected Novellas Vol 1*
- ☐ *To Chart the Clouds* by Evan Dicken
- ☐ *The Great Clans of Rokugan, The Collected Novellas Vol 2* *(coming soon)*
- ☐ *The Flower Path* by Josh Reynolds *(coming soon)*

PANDEMIC

- ☐ *Patient Zero* by Amanda Bridgeman

TERRAFORMING MARS

- ☐ *In the Shadow of Deimos* by Jane Killick
- ☐ *Edge of Catastrophe* by Jane Killick *(coming soon)*

TWILIGHT IMPERIUM

- ☐ *The Fractured Void* by Tim Pratt
- ☐ *The Necropolis Empire* by Tim Pratt
- ☐ *The Veiled Masters* by Tim Pratt *(coming soon)*

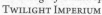

ZOMBICIDE

- ☐ *Last Resort* by Josh Reynolds
- ☑ *Planet Havoc* by Tim Waggoner
- ☐ *Age of the Undead* by C L Werner *(coming soon)*